YOU CAN'T HIDE

YOU CAN'T HIDE

A Nut Cracker Investigation

Katherine Ramsland

First published by Level Best Books 2025

Copyright © 2025 by Katherine Ramsland

This novel is entirely a work of fiction. The names, characters and incidents portrayed in it are the work of the author's imagination. Any resemblance to actual persons, living or dead, events or localities is entirely coincidental.

Katherine Ramsland asserts the moral right to be identified as the author of this work.

Author Photo Credit: Noelle Means

First edition

ISBN: 978-1-68512-999-6

Cover art by Level Best Designs

This book was professionally typeset on Reedsy.
Find out more at reedsy.com

Praise

For *Dead-Handed*

"A creepy old mansion, a wealthy dying man, a mysterious enclave, and a tenacious investigator all add up to form an intriguing mystery. Katherine Ramsland's *Dead-handed* is a well-plotted, devilishly twisted tale of murder and mayhem."—Bruce Robert Coffin, international bestselling coauthor of *The Turner and Mosley Files*

For *In the Damage Path*

"No one understands the criminal mind like Katherine Ramsland, and *In the Damage Path*, starring her determined and brilliant Annie Hunter, is another winner. Sinister, captivating, and propulsive—I could not turn the pages fast enough! Not for the faint of heart, but Ramsland, a talented storyteller, does not flinch at reality—and the authenticity of this gripping novel will haunt you long after its final pages. Ramsland is a force of nature—passionate, brave, and relentless. True crime fans will be riveted, and no reader will ever look at the psychology of crime and the science of investigation in the same way. Do not miss this!"—Hank Phillippi Ryan, *USA Today* bestselling author

For *I Scream Man*

"I was intrigued by the first sentence. All true crime fans will be fascinated, then hooked immediately as they immerse in the culmination of the lead character working crimes that haunt her. Annie Hunter is the perfect mix of brilliance and successful field application, much like Ramsland herself. No one conveys the kind of intellect and mystery in a book like Katherine Ramsland."—Laura Pettler, forensic criminologist, author of

Crime Scene Staging Dynamics in Homicide Cases, and owner of Laura Pettler and Associates

For *You Can't Hide*

"Intellectual gymnastics, bravado in the face of danger and a protagonist you want to bring home with you—*You Can't Hide* has it, along with all the suspects you could ever want. A roller coaster book well worth the ride."—Diane Fanning, crime writer, author of *Lizzie*

I

YOU CAN'T HIDE

Chapter One

It seemed like a simple request. Find a packet in the attic.

It wasn't simple.

And it wasn't safe.

I gathered a crew and scheduled the search for Thanksgiving week so I could wrap it up with a grand feast. Now that this oceanfront house on North Carolina's Outer Banks finally felt like home, I wanted to celebrate it with friends.

Kip Hawkins had the longest drive—six hundred fifty miles—but he'd insisted on helping. His father and mine had been joint caretakers of a dodgy property called Dacretown near Concord, Massachusetts. Kip's dad, Gregory, had been murdered for his trouble. Mine, Lang Hunter, had contracted a neurological debility. Just before these blows, they'd discussed that place in *this* house. Then Dad had vanished, leaving his house to me.

I'd pieced this all together when I'd finally located him. However, our reunion was brief. Before Dad left to work on a cure for his Dacretown blight, he'd asked me to look for a 6x9-inch white envelope. He thought it was in the attic. "It has a wax seal," he'd said. "It's private. Please don't open it. Just tell me when you find it."

I'd concurred…but I hadn't promised.

I knew Dad might be dying. He'd grown ill from experiments he'd tried to stop. His "vanishment," as he calls people gone missing, had robbed me of five years with him. Growing up, he'd been my anchor in a home full of shifting winds. He'd left my mother when I was a teen, but his advice from a distance had kept me on track. I could grant him this small favor. At least,

I thought I could. To be fair, he hadn't adequately warned me.

I'd already seen the multiple boxes, notebooks, and stacks of papers from Dad's years of vanishment research. Locating a single envelope, I knew, would be like finding a one-eyed ghost crab on our beach. Doable but not quick.

Recently, Kip had pushed to complete this task, so I'd scheduled the quest. In Concord, he and I had started on the wrong foot, but a common mission involving my dad had pulled us together. It made sense to include him.

Two days before Thanksgiving, I stood at my picture window watching the wind push white caps toward the beach. Layers of cobalt and azure clouds hinted that rain was on the way. I hoped Kip would beat it. I expected him within the hour.

Natra Gawoni, my case manager, strode in. She tugged on the long brown ponytail that draped over her shoulder and gestured for her Doberdor, Mika, to come. The dog padded over to me for an ear rub.

"Coffee's fresh," Natra said. "The unit's ready."

"He'll like it. Gives him privacy but also access to us when he wants it."

We'd prepared the largest of my two rental studios on the ground floor. Off season, they weren't used. My personal living space was on the second floor, adjacent to my great room conference area in the center of the house. Natra's apartment was on the other side. My two-car garage sat below us, between the rentals.

A chime sound. A car had entered the driveway.

I gestured toward Natra's unit. "Can you put Mika in her room? Let's let Kip get settled."

Natra took the dog out.

Kip knew this house. He'd been here with his dad two months before Gregory died. I thought it might be rough for him to return. Just sixteen then, Kip hadn't said what he'd witnessed, but he believed he knew what we were looking for.

I opened the sliding glass door to the balcony. A cold gust blew past me to ruffle papers inside. Kip stood below, next to the white Range Rover my father had gifted him, a long wool coat protecting his slender frame. A breeze jumped the backyard dune to ruffle his dark wavy hair. He looked up and waved. That afternoon, under a darkening November sky, I couldn't have guessed at the perilous burden this young man bore…and brought to my door.

Chapter Two

Kip gestured toward the back of his SUV. "Got a full car. More files from Kate."

He meant from Kate Gardiner, the lawyer handling my late grandfather's complicated estate. I pointed to my right. "Pull in over there. We'll get that stuff later. You've had a long drive."

At twenty-one, Kip was the oldest of three brothers. His legal name was John Kinney Hawkins, named for an outlaw killed by Billy the Kid. He'd adopted 'Kip' on his own. It fit him. Tall and lanky with brown eyes and a headful of dark curls, his demeanor suggested a burdened soul. He'd protected his brothers while solving his father's murder. He now worked for his cousin in a home restoration business, carving marble and restoring woodwork. He was quite the craftsman. I'd hired him to work on Dad's Concord properties. In a convoluted way, Kip was family.

When he came level with me on the balcony, I hugged him. At just over six feet, he was taller than me by at least six inches. I ushered him into my living/dining/conference area, which has the best views in the house. From the large window facing the ocean, we watch sunrises and storms, dolphins and pelicans.

"Coffee?" I asked. He accepted. I gestured toward a wraparound leather couch. "Please, have a seat."

He snorted. "I remember that couch. Fell asleep on it a few times."

"Dad had good taste. I kept the furniture."

"All of it?"

I nodded. "Pretty much. I made this room a conference area and installed more tech, but till last month I always thought he'd come back. Most of Dad's things are still how he left them." Kip's face showed a flash of relief. That seemed odd. "You stayed in Philadelphia last night?"

"South of there. Saw a friend. Helped break up the trip."

Natra came in. "Hi, Kip. Nice to see you in person."

They'd talked thus far only by video. He shook her hand. "Thought you had a dog."

"I do. You like dogs?"

He nodded.

"I'll get her later. She made a big fuss over not greeting you."

"Let 'er loose."

I brought over the coffee pot. Kip accepted a mug and sat down. "Is your daughter here?"

"My ex has her this weekend. Kamryn's in South Carolina."

I sat opposite Kip while Natra took a seat on the other side of the couch. She's the observer. I count on her for a second opinion.

Kip looked around. "Seems like you've settled in."

I picked up my mug. "It wasn't easy, despite the impressive location. I didn't move in right away. Each time I came, I just felt empty and sad."

He nodded. "I get that."

"It took almost a year, but I finally saw an advantage in the extra space. That's when I started our PI consulting." I gestured toward Natra. "I brought in Natra after we worked a case together. She named us the Nut Cracker Investigations."

"Annie likes complicated cases," Natra explained. "Nuts that are hard to crack."

Kip raised an eyebrow. "I noticed."

Natra flipped her hand. "The name's unique, so people remember it. In just three years, we've gained a solid reputation. Not many investigators are also psychologists."

I smiled. "Ayden was next." Kip had met him in Concord. "He tricked me into hiring him as my PI. He used a case I couldn't resist and proved his talent. Plus, he's an artist and, as you know, he does carpentry on houses around here. Then there's our part-time digital examiner, Joe Lochren. He's been increasingly valuable, although he has a demanding career in cybersecurity. He helped me set up my podcast, *Psi Apps*, and I've developed a network of forensic consultants. Jackson Raines—you'll meet him on Thursday—has become our go-to legal counsel. My executor's fee from my grandfather's passing last month helps with the bills."

Natra pointed at me. "We need that, cuz she's drawn to cases that don't pay."

"Spoken like a business manager." I leaned toward Kip. "Have you made plans for joining Lang in Scotland?"

Kip shrugged. "He's been ill. Bedridden. Hasn't communicated in a week."

I felt a stab of jealousy. I wished I didn't, but there it was. My dad had taken to Kip like a son he'd never had. During the five years Dad was "missing," he'd secretly worked with Kip and his brothers in Concord. They'd been privy to his darkest secrets, partners in his work, the recipients of his attention. Kip had been his main point of contact. For me, that left an aching gap. I'd had only a few days with Dad in October before he left again. He'd urged me to give Kip some maternal guidance. I wasn't old enough to be his mother, but I could offer a sensitive ear.

"I'm so glad you came," I said. "When I first got this house, I couldn't go through Dad's things. I made a start but always stalled. Dad wasn't organized, and there's a lot to go through."

Kip nodded like he knew Lang's habits. He'd probably spent more time in the attic than I had. More to the point, he'd been a witness to multiple important transactions that bound our families.

"We've got you set up in the studio suite downstairs," Natra told him. "Same one you had before but nicely updated."

Kip smiled. "Good thing. I remember the shower not working."

As he talked, his left hand, scarred from stonework, rubbed the side of the mug, perhaps the way he caressed a piece of marble to evaluate its challenges for carving. A heavy insignia ring adorned a finger on his right hand.

Kip turned to me. "I'll help with whatever you need, but I have a reason for coming. I'm looking for something myself. Dad brought several things here I'd like to retrieve. Lang didn't want them. They argued when they thought I was outside. It was pretty intense."

I leaned toward him. "What things?"

"First, that envelope Lang asked you to find."

I shook my head. "No, that's something Dad—"

"I know which envelope he means. It's white. Stamped with a wax seal. I told Lang my dad left it here. That made him angry. He meant to come back to get it."

Natra cocked her head. "What's in it?"

"A communication Dad got from someone they both knew. I think it's a threat. Dad wanted Lang's help. I remember Lang saying, 'You can't do this. It's too risky.' But Dad left it here, anyway. I saw him take it up to the attic and come down without it. Besides that, there's a package, a couple inches thick. That's in the attic, too. I think it holds a binder that has some records. On the way home, I asked Dad about it, but he wouldn't tell me. He said he had to protect us, me and my brothers."

I squinted. "You saw this binder?"

"Yes. It's a leatherbound, three-ring binder with lined note pages, like an accounting ledger. It has transparent sleeves for maps and pictures. I saw it at home when I was ten or eleven. I tried to look through it, but Dad grabbed it. He told me to never touch it. After he died, I looked for it but couldn't find it. I think it might be in that packet."

"Sounds like we're on a scavenger hunt."

"Sort of. The binder's distinct. Shouldn't be hard to spot."

I cleared my throat. "So, you're not here to help me get this envelope for Lang."

Kip shook his head.

"Does he know?"

"No."

I narrowed my eyes. "Is this a secret you want me to keep?"

Kip clutched the handle of his mug. "I hope you won't have to. I didn't tell him I was coming this week. Only my brothers and Kate and Mark Gardiner know I'm here. She's your Concord attorney, and Mark's my boss. Lang wants to burn this stuff, but it belonged to *my* dad. I have the right to decide its fate." He lifted his chin.

I drew in a breath. "What if he asks if you're here? What do you expect me to say?"

"He's ill, Annie. He hasn't communicated since last week. He won't like what I'm doing, but…" He glanced over his shoulder toward the window. "Whatever disturbed our dads, it's still out there."

Chapter Three

We got Kip moved in and introduced to a very excited Mika before Natra went to set up for dinner. We take turns, but she's the better cook. Part Cherokee, she has a wealth of unique recipes. Eight years older than me, she lost her teenage daughter to a drug overdose, and she deals with her grief by taking care of others. I'm happy to be a recipient. She watches my back.

The delicious fragrance of baking cornbread followed Kip and I up a narrow set of wooden steps to the third floor. I stopped and tapped the second step from the top, pulling the tread outward. "Careful on this one. It comes loose. It covers a hollow spot, one of Lang's secret safes." I slid it open to show him. "I've found a couple, but he either didn't use this one or he cleaned it out. If Gregory put something here, it's gone." I opened a door at the top. "This is the hurricane room, a safe spot should the area flood from a surge."

We entered the 15x25-foot space. Kip hugged himself and looked around. "Been up here a few times."

"It's cold, I know. I'll bring up a space heater." I tapped a wall register. "Gotta get this fixed. Remind me to tell Ayden. He's my handyman." I pointed across the room. "The other one works, but it doesn't cover the whole space."

"Maybe I can fix it." Kip walked over to peer at the faulty register.

"I've tried to unscrew it, but the screw heads are stuck."

"Got tools?" he asked.

"Ayden does. He'll fix it. We have other things to do."

Kip looked at the ceiling. "An overhead trap door? I didn't notice that before."

"I put that in last year. It goes to the roof, in case there's serious flooding." I picked up the remote control. "I can open it from here and close it from up there. Goes to a platform where search helicopters can see me."

"Impressive. What if you lose electricity?"

"There's a pull-down rope I can grab with a hook. Look, it's overcautious, but the last thing I want is to be trapped in here. I'm terrified of drowning. I even had them customize these stairs so we could get Mika out. Cost a bundle, but I feel safer."

Kip snorted. "This room's pretty high up."

"Phobias. What can I say?"

"So, envisioning the worst makes you feel safer."

"Welcome to my life." I gestured around the cluttered room. "This is Dad's mind in a nutshell." All around us lay piles of papers, books, and boxes. Some stacks ran floor to ceiling, and a set of bookshelves on one wall held faded tomes that smelled of mildew.

Kip crossed his arms. "It's worse than I remember. I should've packed for a month."

"You can stay as long as you want. And I'd like to suggest that since we've got two dads involved in our search, let's use their first names to discuss them."

"Good idea."

I pointed at a table on my right. "I made a start. Over there are the files for Dad's—I mean, Lang's—missing-persons cases. I'm going through them for possible investigations for my team."

Kip went over and picked up a file. "These are missing people? *All* these files?"

"Lang collected information for hundreds of incidents from around the world, but only certain types appealed to him. He was interested in vanishments—his word for them—that seemed inexplicable or happened in locations where several unrelated people disappeared at different times."

Kip glanced at me. "Like a Bermuda Triangle."

"Like that, yes. He thought these cases would reveal portals to a liminal space, maybe an alternate reality."

Kip made his way to a pile of banker's boxes and tapped one. It sounded full. "That portal stuff, that was Dacretown's appeal to him."

Dacretown's the piece of property near Concord that several generations of my family had owned. Residents of a nineteenth-century settlement there were reportedly plagued with deaths and mental aberrations before the place was finally abandoned. Merrick Hunter had acquired the land for its supposed paranormal powers. Kip's grandfather and mine had used it for unethical experiments. I'd inherited Dacretown but had no interest in being its guardian. Kip did, so I'd transferred the deed to him.

"Not on board with Lang's mystical notions?" I asked.

He raised an eyebrow. "Are you?"

I shrugged. "Some of his cluster vanishment cases are odd. They end up in books about weird things we can't explain. But… you know, I wasn't much of a receptor for his spirit writing research. If I had been, he might've told me more."

Kip crossed over to the bookshelf and rubbed a hand over the top. "Cheap wood. You should replace this before it goes brittle." He tapped a pile of papers on the middle shelf. "My dad—Gregory—wouldn't want me doing this. He thought he was protecting me. Then he died."

"So, coming here to see Lang didn't save him."

"Maybe it would've if Lang had…" He put his hands in his jeans pockets.

"Well, look around, Kip. Take whatever you think is his. I only ask that you show me what you find. I can give you a laptop to—"

"I have one. Just bought it. I tried to pay attention back then, but sometimes they talked late into the night, and I couldn't stay awake." His frown deepened.

I peered at him. "What makes this so urgent?"

Kip turned toward me. He looked distressed. "You know, it's been a while. I thought it might be resolved, but recently—"

Heavy footsteps sounded on the stairs. Had to be Ayden Scott, my intrepid PI. I went to the stairs to greet him.

He came up to the landing and waved at Kip. He'd lost his tan, given the season, but his shaggy blond hair still pegged him as a beach boy. They'd met in Concord under urgent circumstances. Since then, they'd talked by video about their mutual interest in home renovations.

Ayden looked around. "Wow, boss. Didn't know you were such a packrat."

"This is Lang's stuff. *He* was a packrat. And you get to help us organize it." I pointed to the table. "Those cases will fascinate you. They're all missing people. And I have a fix-it project for you as well, if there's time." I pointed. "I need that register checked, maybe the duct replaced. Might be a bigger job than it looks."

Ayden went to the table and picked up a folder. "How many?"

"Dozens. I tried looking through them, but I couldn't decipher Lang's categories. Some were investigated, but some weren't followed up at all. Maybe you can figure it out."

He cocked his head. "We takin' 'em downstairs?"

I looked around. "We'll start up here, try to organize things, and take the files that interest us to the conference room."

"Copy, boss." He opened a file to skim it.

Kip walked deeper into the room. "How long did you say it was between when Lang left and you moved in?"

I crossed my arms. "Hmm. I don't know the precise day he left, but I can pinpoint it to the week."

"Just generally, how long did this house sit empty?"

"A few months, maybe six. I checked it every two or three weeks, especially when I thought he'd be back. I asked neighbors to tell me if they saw him. But I was still working in South Carolina. It took time to reorganize my life, since I was freshly divorced and had a child."

"Did anyone else have access?"

I watched him. He kept rubbing his hand over his shirt. "What's on your mind, Kip? Do you think someone came in?"

"Maybe."

Ayden looked up. "What's going on?"

"Kip's looking for something related to when he was here with Gregory."

"You did have that break-in," Ayden reminded me.

I nodded. "I did. Seemed like an ordinary incident, though." To Kip, I said, "People look for houses closed for the winter, sometimes to rob, sometimes to camp out, because so many are vacation homes or rentals. At the time, I didn't know about the Dacretown experiments. I thought Lang was just a reclusive nut who believed in fairy portals."

Kip smiled but still seemed tense.

I held up my hands. "Someone got in, I'll admit, but I had no inventory, so I couldn't tell cops if anything was taken. I hired a caretaker to check on the place, and I installed an alarm."

Kip put his hands on his hips. "Well, you know someone ransacked our house in Massachusetts."

"That man's no longer a threat." That man, we both knew, was dead.

"Unless it wasn't him. We never knew. We just assumed."

Goosebumps prickled my arms. "Let's search this mess before we conclude anything. We'll talk to Lang when he's better. Maybe he knows more."

"I asked him already. Won't talk. Just wants to burn it all."

I took a breath. "I still don't see a cause to worry."

He shrugged.

Ayden sorted through the folders. "I'll research these for updates. Maybe we can check some off the list."

Kip looked alarmed. "Can I read them first?"

Ayden and I turned toward him.

Natra called to get us down for dinner. Ayden raised an eyebrow at me.

I peered at Kip. "What's going on? Why are you really here?"

"I'll tell you. Then you'll see why *my* plan is better than Lang's."

Chapter Four

Natra had set out a cold seafood platter with warm cornbread and a romaine salad. I'd added an Italian wine with a *Welcome, Friends* label to honor our guest. Now, I wasn't so sure. His mission positioned me against Dad. The last thing I wanted was to lose Dad *again*, especially from someone else's act.

I closed the curtains against gusts that chilled the windows—or maybe the gust that chilled *me*. I heard the ocean but saw only an expanse of darkness past the dune. We were on the cusp of a North Carolina winter. I turned on the backyard lights.

As we served ourselves, Ayden described to Kip his renovations at an investment property just north of Duck, on the Currituck Sound. I'd loaned him funds for a down payment. Staying there when he worked for me shortened his commute versus driving from his home in Rodanthe, especially during the tourist season.

"Lots of OBX houses have names like Pelican's Perch or Lollygaggers," he told Kip. "We need one, but for now, we just call it the Duck House. Has a sunset view, a dock, four bedrooms, and a huge great room. I'm adding a bathroom to make a third ensuite and updating the kitchen. Hoping to put more stonework in."

"Not bad." Kip gave him some tips and offered to assess the place if there was time.

But small talk didn't lessen the tension. I needed answers. I set down my wine glass and looked at Kip. "So, what's the mission? What's at stake with your visit?"

He poked his fork into his salad before he looked around the table. "Do you know who Ketch Ryder is?"

I nodded. "I do. We have a local crime attached to him, a double homicide."

"Wait," said Ayden. "I need a refresher. I know the name. It was Nags Head or Kitty Hawk, right?"

"Nags Head," I said. "Ryder was caught making a fraudulent bank transaction, maybe six or so years ago. On his laptop, police found news items related to two cases of missing couples. He had notes, too, with some cryptic details and a victim's credit card. Dad looked into it. We talked about it. I think a local author wrote a book about it."

Natra passed the cornbread. "Didn't Ryder lead cops to the bodies?"

I leaned back. "Not exactly. He gamed them, trying to cut a deal. Made it sound like he'd offer more victims if they played by his rules. He was caught in Virginia, as I recall, but he'd traveled to other states."

"Including New Hampshire," Kip added.

"Right. That was the other couple on his computer. Lovello or Lovato was the local couple's name, I think. Ryder eventually copped to it. He described it in detail, and some items from victims were recovered, but not the bodies. What he did…" I hesitated. "Maybe not so great for dinner fare."

Ayden gave me a chiding look. "It's us, boss."

"We have a guest."

Kip smiled. "I can take it. I know the story, though, and you have a couple things wrong. He said he entered a town where he'd never been, so no one would connect him." Kip gestured with his right hand. "Nags Head, south of here. He said he cased homes with layouts he could guess and easy points of entry. He'd built his own house, so he knew what to look for. He picked a house at random and waited for lights out."

"How do you know this?" I asked.

"His interrogations are public. Easy to find online. I watched them." He sipped some wine before he continued. "He made sure there was no sign of a dog. He entered the Lovatos' home through the window of an attached garage. The door into the house was unlocked, so he didn't make any noise. He went in and woke the couple, using a gun to keep them under control.

He'd already staked out an empty house, and he forced them to drive him there. I think he hid his own car somewhere, a rental he'd gotten with a fake ID. He told cops he wanted to torture them where he wouldn't be interrupted."

"I want the link to that," Ayden said. He looked at me. "If that's one of your dad's cases—"

"It's not," Kip said. "It won't be in that pile, not this case. He looked into it, as Annie said, but it won't be with his other cases. This one...it meant something."

I stared at him. Kip glanced at me. I tried to seem open. In Concord, we'd had each other's backs: he'd saved my life, I'd saved his ass. Where was he going with this?

"What details did Ryder give?" Natra asked.

Kip continued. "He bound them both and made the man watch what he did to the woman. He made her strip, and he put duct tape over her mouth and eyes. He let her stumble around the room, blind, while he beat her and burned her. When she fell, he raped her, then made her crawl across the room. He said the point was to make the man feel powerless. Finally, he strangled her before he beat up the man and killed 'im."

"Didn't he say he untied the man so they could have a fist fight?" I asked. "There was something about him wanting to get brutal."

Kip nodded, now animated, his brown eyes alight. "Right. And the man bested him and nearly got away, but Ryder used a rope to choke him. He said he left the bodies in the basement and moved their car. Dumped it in a swamp. He figured they'd be found, but he didn't live in the area, so he knew they wouldn't link it to him. He wore a hoodie so surveillance cameras in town wouldn't have caught him, and he'd shifted a license plate on his rental car."

Natra crossed her arms. "Wow. Careful."

I added more. "No search turned up the missing couple. They'd already located the car, and it was where he said, partially submerged in a swamp, but they got no helpful evidence from it. By the time the police heard the confession two years after the abduction and went to the crime location, the building was demolished and the debris hauled away. A search at the dump turned up nothing. Ryder said he had a map where he'd marked locations, but they didn't find that, either."

Kip nodded, but he let me continue.

"Essentially, he was convicted for the Lovatos' abduction based on his guilty plea, the few found items he knew about, and the fact that the couple seemed to have vanished."

"Yes," Kip said. "There were some victim-related items in a communal hunting cabin he had access to, but the only solid thing they had was what he told them." He set his jaw before he added, "So, he could've been making it up."

We all looked at him. Natra snorted. "Making it up? That's pretty elaborate."

Kip's shoulders hunched slightly, and the left side of his mouth tightened.

I hovered between calling him out and rescuing him. I chose the latter. "We know about serial killers who fabricate their numbers, often for notoriety." I cocked my head. "I hadn't heard that anyone believed Ryder was lying. Sounds like you know something."

"That's what my dad thought. He said Ryder was a fraud. He thought Ryder put the news items on his computer so he could claim them as his own murders, and he copied another killer's descriptions for his narrative." He peered at me. "Doesn't it sound familiar to you?"

I dug into my memory of such offenders and nodded. "It does. But that proves nothing."

"Look up Israel Keyes. Except for the car, Ryder tells the same story."

I glanced at Natra. "Keyes should be in my files. He was a unique suicide case." She typed a note to herself on her phone.

Ayden looked skeptical. "If Ryder wanted credit, why didn't he turn himself in?"

Kip waved a finger. "First, why was Gregory Hawkins looking into this? Because he thought there was another guy doing these things, a guy he and Lang both knew."

I sat up. "Another guy? So, Ryder's covering?"

He frowned. "Not exactly."

I leaned forward. "What was Gregory concerned about?"

"At first, he believed Ryder and thought Ryder had committed other murders." Kip gave me a serious look, his dark eyes widening. "That's what launched his investigation. He wanted evidence that the bad things happening to graduates from his Dacretown experiments were, you know, not because of being in the program. Ryder seemed like a good suspect."

"Why?" I asked. "Nothing about Ryder's cases linked him to the Dacretown deaths."

"Getting there. Dad made a…what do you call it?…a case analysis? A chart. He even consulted a psychologist. He found stuff the cops didn't know. That's when he decided that Ryder had lied about the Lovatos and that someone else was the killer. He showed it all to Lang right here in this house."

I shifted in my seat. "Did he buy it?"

"Lang pointed out flaws. They argued, but Lang could see…" Kip struggled for words.

"Had perspective?" I asked.

Kip nodded. "What Lang said made sense. But I had the impression they were scared. Lang said something like, 'I won't contact him under any circumstances.' I didn't catch a name."

My skin felt prickly. "Let me get it straight. Based on Gregory's research, you think Ketch Ryder confessed to murders he didn't commit. You think someone else killed those people, and you think our dads knew this person."

"Yes." Kip pointed upward, toward the hurricane room. "That's the envelope we're looking for. It contains a letter to my dad from *that* guy."

Chapter Five

yden scooped more crab from the platter. No matter what we discuss, his appetite never ebbs. "Any idea who it is?" he asked.

Kip pressed his lips together. "I don't. After Dad died…sorry, it's hard for me to call him Gregory. I'll try. The important thing is that he found inconsistencies and errors in Ryder's statements. He also thought Ryder described stuff he'd read in other accounts." Kip looked at me. "And this letter was in Gregory's file. I thought that's what he said—that when he started asking questions about Ryder, the killer sent him a warning."

I frowned. "He didn't take it to the police?"

"I don't know. If he did, nothing happened. He showed the note to Lang, but he wouldn't let me see it. Lang told him to burn it."

I looked at Natra.

"Should I take notes?" she asked.

"Not yet. Let's consider this. Ryder played games. He played the cops, the FBI, the prison guards, anyone he could. He kept switching his story and was caught in several lies. And they never did find the bodies of the couple he directed them to. There was another missing couple mentioned in news items on his laptop. He said he'd provide directions to that grave only if they met certain conditions."

Natra nodded. "Then he killed himself, didn't he?"

"He tried, but he survived. He got ahold of a sharpened piece of metal. He used it on himself to draw blood for his suicide note." I looked at Kip. "That's what Israel Keyes did, as I recall, except he'd been issued a razor. I think you're right. Ryder used other stories to embellish his own."

Ayden tapped his fork. "Was there any corroboration with Ryder's movements?"

I squinted. "The suicide note was odd. He made some drawings, but no one figured them out. Once he recovered, he stopped talking about the crimes." I turned back to Kip. "Do you think Ryder knew the real killer?"

"Maybe. I mean, he had victim stuff, like trophies."

Ayden wiped his mouth. He'd been processing through his own investigative frame. "Back to my question. Why didn't Ryder turn himself in?"

"I don't think he wanted to be caught, but once caught, he used Keyes' description to seem more credible."

Ayden glanced at me, then Kip. "Suppose we find Gregory's analysis. What will you do?"

He shrugged. "Depends on what it says."

"Planning a solo investigation?"

Kip shook his head. "If I thought I could, I wouldn't have said anything." He made a sweeping gesture. "Not to *this* group."

"So, you want our help."

Kip's face flushed. "Maybe it will interest you."

Ayden leaned against the edge of the table. "It matters to you. Why?"

Kip eyed his plate. I exchanged glances with Natra before he sat up straight and looked at each one of us. "For the same reason my dad wanted Lang involved, and for the same reason Lang left this case out of his vanishment files. The missing couple in the clips on Ryder's computer, the woman. She's related to us. Ella Steadman. She was a Hawkins before she married Clark Steadman. I think she was in the Gray Hollow Group."

This news astonished me. The Gray Hollow Group was a land trust conservancy that had protected Dacretown. My grandfather had founded it with Kip's grandfather, Mathew Hawkins, but they'd dropped the ball. Years later, their sons, Gregory and Lang, had taken it over. The membership was secret. We'd investigated it every which way but found no official list.

I cocked my head. "Why didn't you say this before?"

He grabbed the back of his neck. "I'm still trying to figure it out."

"How do you even know this?"

"My mother told me. She knew Ella. Said she'd had a tough life with an abusive, controlling husband. She stayed with him only a couple years. Then she met Steadman. I tried asking her about their abduction, but she told me to stop prying. Mom hated the whole Gray Hollow thing. She didn't want Dad bringing me here or getting me involved. She said his work was toxic."

"She was kind of right about that. So, you hope to use Gregory's analysis, which is somewhere in the attic, to find this couple? Is that your mission? It's for family?"

Kip blinked. I sensed he didn't know what to say. "It's more than that. The Lovatos went missing from here, Nags Head. Ryder drew a horse head in his suicide note. I found it online. So, I think that's about..."

I gripped my napkin. "*My* dad?"

"Lang wouldn't talk about it. But he's, like, a common factor."

Blood drained from my face. "You think he's hiding something? Or *involved* in something?"

"Look how he reacts. Burn the note, don't read it. As if that will erase it all. But it won't because..."

"Because?"

"Other people know things. And I think Gregory had proof. He wanted Lang's support, but Lang said no. Lang knew Ella Steadman. They talked about her. I think he also knew the Lovatos. That would be in my dad's analysis. And Lang wouldn't want anyone to see that."

This made no sense. I leaned toward him. "Kip, are you saying that the Gray Hollow Group has some association with these missing couples? With Ketch Ryder?"

He shook his head. "Not Ryder. Whoever the killer is...*that's* who our dads knew." He pointed back and forth from me to him. "And that name is probably on some document in this house."

I sat back. "So, you want to reopen a case Lang wants closed, destroyed even. Don't you realize what he'll do if you cross him? He'll take back everything he just gave you. Your car, all those renovation projects in Concord, maybe even Dacretown."

"I know, Annie, and I risk your support, too. You don't have to help me.

I'll just take Dad's stuff if we find it and go." His gaze remained steady, as if he knew I wouldn't just give this up.

He was right. I felt torn between rising anger and the need to know more. Multiple questions suddenly attached to my father. This was shaping up to be a conflict I didn't want. My relationship with Dad was already tenuous. In some ways, Kip was my link to him, and Kip now threatened to clip this.

Ayden held up his hand. "I have an idea. Let's look at the videos of Ryder's interrogation. See what we think. Annie, you're good with body language. So's Natra. If there's something there, one of us will see it."

I breathed out. Tension had curdled the mood. I wanted to assure Kip that Lang wouldn't cover up something criminal. Yet how often had I told the relatives of a killer that he had a dark side they'd been too close to see? I'd already discovered some of Dad's secrets, terrible ones. I couldn't say for sure Kip was wrong.

Kip gave me a puppy dog look. "If we figure it out fast, he doesn't have to know."

He'd invited me to collude. My stomach lurched. I glanced at my team. Natra opened her hands in a gesture that said *it's up to you*. Ayden, I knew, wanted to keep going. He always does.

I frowned at Kip for cornering me. But I gestured to the computer area and said, "Let's look at the videos."

Chapter Six

My computer was set up to project onto my large retractable screen. We could use the rolling whiteboard next to it for notes. While Ayden and Natra cleared the table and set up the room for viewing, Kip helped me locate the series of interrogation videos. He'd watched them a dozen times, he admitted. He picked one that would prove his point. "He's confessing in this one. Day two. He talks about the Lovatos, the stuff I told you at dinner."

I still felt uneasy. I envisioned Dad's disappointment in me for pursuing what he'd asked me to leave alone. I was half-tempted to shut this whole thing down, but I had to see how those Gray Hollow guardians figured into this. If my father was involved, it could come back on me. The house now felt less homey.

Ayden and Natra took a seat. Kip started. "I should tell you about the interrogators. It's a tag-team. One is a sheriff, the other an FBI agent. He's out of North Carolina, and he's trained as a profiler. That's Reid Broward. He's the one to watch, because he *owns* this case, if you know what I mean. He's featured in a book and a documentary as the one who got Ryder to confess. Does a lot of speaking on it."

"I know about him," I said. "I did a podcast about his method in another case. It wasn't really profiling. He never completed the training, but no one had called him out. I did, though. He's on a lot of media as a consultant. Gets a hefty fee."

"Yeah, he didn't much care for your episode," Ayden said. "He wrote on your chat board."

I nodded. "He had this catchphrase, said it summarized his success. Something about his skill at observation." I looked at Natra. "What was it?"

"Watch…hmmm…."

"Watch and catch," Ayden said. "Observe carefully and you'll *catch* the small details that solve the case."

"Ha!" I nodded. "That's a *catch* phrase, all right. Had a dramatic pause, as I recall. Watch…and catch. Did I mention that in the podcast?"

"You did," Natra said. "Described it as a play on words. Catch the clues, catch the perps. You called it clever."

"It's even better with a perp named Ketch, isn't it?"

Natra handed us pads of paper and pens. "For notes."

Kip waved it away. "Don't need one."

"Each of us should form separate impressions," I said to my team. "Then we'll discuss what we see."

I pressed the *play* button. The first thing I spotted was a common interrogation error. They'd put Ryder at a table across from them, his back to a bare gray wall. Tables are barriers. They let suspects feel protected. On this table were papers and photos. Research has shown that photos provide cues about what interrogators hope to hear.

Ryder leaned forward as if eager to engage. Bags under his bulging dark eyes, a sheen of sweat on his sallow face, and his unkempt dark hair and mustache suggested he was unwell. I could almost smell the stench from his stained brown prison shirt.

I looked at Kip. "How long have they been at it by this point?"

He stared intently at the screen. "'bout three hours. Second day."

The camera showed the small room from a corner view. The uniformed balding sheriff, Ed Gibson, clasped his hands over his protruding stomach. Broward sat to his right, slightly behind him. Even if I'd never seen this man before, I'd have spotted the FBI in him a mile away. A white shirt with a patterned red and blue tie. Perfectly barbered brown hair. Authoritative posture, trim physique, dark gray suit. I recognized the interrogation style. Never let the suspect doubt, deny, or retreat. Work him till he cracks open the door, then push in for the kill. Effective but prone to eliciting false confessions. Cops deny this. The data affirms it.

Ryder wiped his face with his sleeve again and again. Frazzled nerves. Without watching these tapes from the start, I couldn't calculate from his baseline behavior his deviations during specific subjects. However, certain types of signals would alert me to possible deception.

Gibson pushed some papers toward him. "We've got your computer records here." He tapped. "Your news searches, your stash."

Ryder rolled his eyes. "It's not even eighty, and you could go out to see the rooster. He wants his camera. Then send him to the moon."

"Cut the act!"

Ryder raised his chin. "Want…my…candy." His voice sounded thick, and his words came slowly.

I paused the tape. To Kip, I said, "I recall a psychiatric evaluation. Is Ryder on meds here?"

"Maybe, but I'm not an expert."

"I'll check." I pressed *play* again.

Broward tossed a *Snickers* bar toward the prisoner. Ryder tore off the wrapping and ate it slowly while the other two watched.

"Keyes did that, too," I observed, "although he didn't talk nonsense. Just wouldn't cooperate unless he got his cigar or whatever."

Ayden wrote something on his pad. Or he was drawing. He tends to sketch out his perceptions.

"I's just curious," Ryder finally responded. "Told ya that a'ready."

"You told us someone else used your computer to search."

Ryder shrugged, shifted his eyes, and shook his head.

I saw evidence from his shaking left arm of a psychogenic tremor. Under the table, his leg or foot was moving. That part of the body often delivers a more honest reaction. A tremor releases pent-up stress, but the table blocked their view, so they wouldn't see this…unless Broward was in his Watch and Catch mode.

The sheriff hammered Ryder about the deal they'd apparently made, candy for a clue. The impasse lasted several minutes as Ryder showed his chocolate-smeared teeth and savored his treat. Then he drew himself up, slapped the wrapper down, and said, "I took 'em. There's yer clue."

Broward sat up straight. Here was the moment. "Tell us," he said. "Tell us what you did. You know you want to get it off your chest. Had a thing for the woman, right?"

Ryder's face squinched up. His eyes shifted, and he rubbed his cheek. "Sure, yeah." But a micro hand-shrug contradicted him. He *wasn't* sure. He'd let Broward frame the narrative. I wanted to shout *leading*, as if I were yelling at an attorney. To my surprise, Broward continued to suggest things, a signal he had a theory he wanted corroborated. He used the photographs to point to specific items at the abduction site, like apparent pry marks on the door. I felt Kip look at me, but I didn't acknowledge it. I made a note. So did Natra.

Ryder launched into his account of abducting, raping, torturing, and killing the Lovatos. Some details were like Keyes, some were not. Broward had to know this. He kept up a stream of encouragement and incentives. More important to me was Ryder's behavior...and what was missing. He shook his head "no" six times during his account, as well as blocking his mouth with his hand and closing his eyes. He also gave irrelevant details. He kept looking at the photos in front of him. At one point, he moved back from the table as if to distance himself from the case. When he was finished, he blinked fast and looked down at his hands. His shirt showed sweat rings.

They took a break. Broward handed Ryder a bottle of water and got up. The tape cut off.

Chapter Seven

I felt drained. If what Ryder said was true, the Lovatos had truly suffered. Ryder sure sounded like he'd done it. Maybe he'd copied Keyes in the act, not just in the description. He'd been animated, as if reliving it. Yet, something had seemed off. I put the screen saver on and turned to my team. "What did you see?"

Natra urged Ayden to go first. He looked at his notes. "Table barrier present, like you always tell us, and hand over mouth five times after significant disclosures. Twitch under his right eye when he described the fight. Curling his lips inward. Arms tight against his body when he described the empty house where he took them but otherwise loose. Hesitant phrases. Sometimes, I thought he either didn't believe what he said or wasn't sure. Tone of voice—that upward lilt—seemed to ask if he was right."

"Good list," I said. "You caught some I didn't see. Anything missing that should be there?"

"Didn't say how he got their car to where it was found or how he retrieved his own, which was some distance away."

I nodded. "Yes. Suggests someone else involved, which they didn't pick up on."

"They do later," Kip told us. "But only after he'd stopped confessing. Those later tapes are just him sitting there saying nothing, looking at the ceiling or closing his eyes. Another thing you'd see only if you watch several tapes is him saying idiotic stuff when he doesn't get what he wants."

"I spotted some of the same behavior," Natra said. "I also saw stress signals, like movement and sweating. Poor eye contact. Like you, Annie, I thought he was on meds. And Broward was *so* leading him. You'd think he'd know better. Ryder also used the photos to populate his narrative. He seemed hesitant about the crime scene location, as if he hadn't actually been there. What's missing for me is consistency. He described the interior of the Lovato home with a precision that's lacking for the abandoned property. Seems like the crime scene would be more vivid in his memory. Maybe he saw them get abducted but not the rest."

"Maybe so." I told them my list. "Those times he shakes his head 'no' are crucial. He seems to contradict himself. And I agree about the descriptive thinness of the crime scene and crime activity. He's able to describe things he sees, but the most important scene was deficient. He's animated about it but not like he's reliving the details."

Kip seemed pleased. He held out his hands. "So, you believe me? Is it worth pursuing?"

I took a breath. "We need to see more, watch the interrogation from the start, but you're right about the red flags. They're strongly suggestive. And Broward does use questionable methods. He's been called on it by several journalists."

Kip pointed to the computer. "Look at the suicide note. He draws things. I think it's important."

Natra got on the computer to search. She brought it up on the large screen. The scrawled message was brief. *Thanx 4 the ryde. Ill tell um ur looking. She shouldve dun wat I aksed. Wont find um now.* The blood used to write it had turned a reddish brown. Included was a row of smeared images: a horse head, a hunched four-legged stick figure, an arrowhead, and a wavy line. Below this was an image that looked like a symbol.

Kip pointed to the horse head. "That's what I think referred to Nags Head. Maybe these other images show other locations. One looks like an arrowhead, so maybe a Native American burial place?"

"Is he this illiterate?" I asked Kip. "I know he lived in some kind of insular community."

"I've seen some of his letters. He doesn't write well, and he's not that bright. I think his IQ's like 80."

Ayden pointed at the screen. "Look at how he spelled 'ride.' Like his name."

I got up and went to the screen. I leaned in to peer at an intricate image at the bottom of the page. "This looks familiar."

Kip's eyes widened. "Then you've seen it."

I looked at him. "Seen what?"

"The white envelope. That's what Dad stamped on it." He pointed. "It's hard to see on the note because it's drawn in blood, but can you make out the GH initials kinda hidden in it? That's for Gray Hollow." Kip held up his right hand, backside outward, to show us his ring. I'd noticed it earlier. It resembled those that royalty had once used to stamp hot wax. "Dad used this for sealing documents. It has that design. It's for Gray Hollow Group business. They all had one."

He took it off and passed it to Ayden. He compared it to the image and nodded. "Looks close." He gave it to Natra. She concurred.

After I looked at it, I returned to the table and asked, "Why would he know about this design? I thought you said Ryder's not associated with this group."

Kip shook his head. "I don't know, Annie, except his wife knew Ella Steadman. I think they met at a fundraiser for domestic abuse victims. Ella wanted to help her. That's what she told my mother."

I watched Kip closely. How had he not told us *this*? "Ryder's wife was an abuse victim?"

He nodded. "She was trying to get away from 'im. He beat her up and kept her captive, sometimes tied up the kids. She managed to leave, finally."

"With her kids?"

"I think she took one, the youngest."

"Hmmm. Maybe she's the woman he's referring to. 'Should've done what I asked.'"

Ayden cocked his head. "Or maybe he retaliated. He targeted Ella for interfering. That supports his guilt, though. Acquainted with her and angry at her. People do get killed for assisting abuse victims."

Kip's mouth formed a firm line. "Then why would he take her husband?"

Natra nudged me with her foot under the table. I tapped my little finger to acknowledge it. The way Kip doled out information told me we were getting bread crumbs from a sizable loaf we couldn't yet see.

"Good question," I said. "But Ryder's description of the murders suggests he liked punishing people by making those who love them watch."

Kip's nostrils briefly flared. Whatever he was holding back wanted out. I had to keep the pressure on without scaring him away.

I held up a hand, a signal to my team that I wanted to organize our thoughts. "Okay, we're just spit-balling here, which might lead us down the wrong path. Setting aside the question of Ryder's guilt, we've got things to look into. Somehow, this all crosses through this house, and I need to find out why. Lang's reaction, according to Kip, tells me *he* knows. I'll see if he'll respond to an email. We'll search the attic tomorrow. At the very least, if Ryder's note designates the victims from Nags Head *and* he knows about the Gray Hollow Group, we should learn more about Ella Steadman. A full victimology. I suggest we table this until we're better prepared." I looked at Kip. "And if there's anything *else* we need to know, it would be nice to know it sooner than later."

What I *didn't* say was that I worried about my dad as a common factor in two abductions that might be double homicides. That he might also know the killer—and sought to cover it up—just made it worse.

Chapter Eight

I was up just before dawn. I hadn't slept much. Before bed, I'd composed an email to Dad about the GHG membership. I'd pretended that I'd found some papers about it and was curious. I'd once broached the subject with him, but he'd been curt, saying that the Hunter and Hawkins families had cofounded the GHG before he was born. He'd been involved, but after he left Concord when I was nine, he'd put it behind him. Nothing more to say.

But there was more, maybe a *lot* more. I'd learned that he'd returned to Concord several times to deal with GHG issues.

I prepared for the day, then went to my computer to check for Dad's response. Nothing. But I saw an email from Shona Teagan, a woman who worked with him. Her message was brief. *Lang is ill. He said to tell you this: Six members. You know four. The GHG ended with Gregory's death.*

I hit the desktop in frustration. "Not true, Shona! You and I both know it was still active after that. They filed a lawsuit just last year."

She was deflecting. I had to find my answer elsewhere. I knew about Dad, Gregory, and two members who'd been ejected. Kip had revealed a fifth member, Ella. The sixth one had persisted past Gregory's death. *Someone* knew who it was, and *that* person might know more about Ella.

I went to make coffee. While it dripped, I moved the curtain to peek outside. I couldn't see the ocean yet, but my outside light illuminated a single set of footprints heading up the dune toward the beach. Had to be Kip, because Natra's tracks would show Mika's beside her. I'd sensed last night that Kip had seemed troubled about more than just his missing relative. I'd spent enough time with him in Concord to spot his tendency to reserve information. He kept things close, probably a survival tactic for bearing burdens beyond his age. Something heavy was on his mind, but I hadn't pressed. The evening had ended soon after my decision to pull back. Kip had gone to bed, and Ayden had taken some of Dad's files with him to the Duck House.

Once Kip was out of earshot, Natra had confirmed my impression. "He's got a load. Something's up."

His revelations brought urgency to our search. Someone was out there, perhaps someone dangerous. Natra would go right to work on the Ryder information and find whatever was available on the Lovatos. Ryder might have made a false confession, but I wanted to know why he'd chosen *these* victims. I believed he'd been at the abduction site, but I knew of false confessors who'd visit such places later.

The morning temperature hovered at forty degrees, with a brisk wind coming from the west. I spotted a lean figure hunched against it—a metaphor of his life. Kip, the oldest of three boys, had endured a broken home. He'd tried and failed to be his father's right-hand man. Despite this, when Gregory was killed, Kip had defied the official determination of an accidental death to prove the murder. Our team had helped. He'd been grateful but not fully trusting. I understood. But I wouldn't give him my time and resources for something he kept secret. Why did he even care about Ketch Ryder? Ayden had asked, but Kip had deflected.

Natra came in with Mika. She caught sight of Kip. "I think he was in the attic already. The light's on."

"Not surprised. He's determined to find his dad's stuff."

"He's got us figured out, too." She filled the dog's bowl. "He knows we tackle tough cases. He planted seeds—hooks. You know Ayden's already looking."

"Copy that. The hook for me is Dad. If Kip's telling the truth, Dad's behavior is so odd. Scary, even. I hope he's not involved in all this. It would make living here feel creepy."

"Did he respond to your email?"

"He sent a message through Shona, but he said almost nothing."

"Almost?"

"There were six GHG members when Dad first left. Two were eventually removed. That leaves Gregory and two others. One was Ella. But Dad wants me to believe it all ended five years ago when Gregory died. It didn't. Someone kept it alive, and Dad was secretly part of that."

Natra gave Mika fresh water. "Sounds complicated."

"Yes, and I need to keep perspective. Kip's behavior signals a hidden agenda, an urgent one, that risks his relationship with Lang and its considerable benefits. He and his cousin are getting a ton of work in Concord from Dad's inheritance, not to mention Dacretown and his Range Rover. I mean, why bother with Ryder? How could it matter that much?"

The sound of Ayden's truck interrupted us. I cocked my head. "Let's get Kip back in here. I need to really press him."

"I'll set up."

I returned to the window and glanced outside. I saw Kip to my right, but his back was to me. He stood on a neighbor's wooden platform over the dune, talking on his phone. The sky beyond him had brightened to show several large boats on the ocean. I looked north, then froze. About thirty yards away, a slender figure in a hoodie stood on the dune. He seemed to be watching Kip.

Chapter Nine

"Natra!" I called. "Come and look."

She came to the window, but the figure had vanished. I told her what I'd seen.

"Kip didn't notice?" she asked.

"The guy was behind him."

"Maybe just a beach walker. I see them sometimes before dawn."

"This time of year?"

She shrugged. "If they live here."

I didn't feel reassured. Kip's hints about a killer "out there" were getting to me.

Ayden entered with a box of fresh bagels. In moments, Kip came through the sliding door, as if drawn by the yeasty aroma. Ayden opened the box, Kip peeked in, and I noted a growing camaraderie. It gave me an idea.

Ayden followed me into the kitchen. "Expecting someone?"

I shook my head. "Not today. Why?"

"Saw a guy parked just off the road nearby, lights on. Almost on the bike path. Thought he was looking at your house. I slowed down near him, and when I passed, he turned around and took off."

"How far away?"

"Two houses north. No one's home at either of them. They're summer people."

"Right. So, he wasn't there for them. What kind of car?"

"Audi Q6, medium blue. Picked it up on the dash cam if you wanna see it."

"Make me a clip. And I just saw a guy on a dune up that way. Seemed to be watching Kip on the beach. Let's hope someone hasn't tracked him here."

Ayden leaned on the counter. "Want me to take 'im aside, hang out, see what he might tell me? He offered to look at my Duck House renovation."

"You read my mind, Ayden. That's a good idea, but let's get organized first. Look for an opening, make it natural, maybe during lunch."

"Copy, boss."

I placed the platter of bagels on the table. Kip stood at the window, looking out.

I went over to open the curtains. "Saw you on the beach."

He turned to me. "Yeah, I liked going out in the mornings here."

"D'you happen to notice anyone else?"

He shook his head.

"Just…I thought I saw someone else. A guy. Maybe it's nothing."

Kip's eyes widened. "Where?"

"On the dune, north of you." I pointed. "He took off."

"Watching me?"

"That's what it looked like. Maybe he was just curious, but it struck me as odd."

"Guess I should keep my eyes open. Thought I was alone."

I went to the table, sat down, and looked straight at him. "There's something else. When we met, you said your Skeleton Crew had taken over the care of Dacretown. Did you know much about the Gray Hollow Group?"

Kip grabbed a salt bagel before he sat. "Not really. Not 'til after Dad was gone. He didn't tell me about it. Mom did. Mark Gardiner and I started the Skeleton Crew just kind of to honor Dad."

"So, you didn't know the group was still in operation?"

Ayden pulled out a chair and sat down to listen.

Kip pressed his lips together. "I didn't. Mark probably did, though. He wanted to disband the Crew. Was kind of insistent about it. My brothers and I kept it going, but we only worked on the property. I mean, we didn't own it, but no one chased us off."

"Someone was paying taxes and blocking developers. I read an article about it, and they specifically named the Gray Hollow Group as the trust managers. Did Lang ever tell you who the members were?"

Kip put down his bagel and sat back. "I guess that's what I'm investigating. I didn't know about Ella 'til recently. You had to be in the family to be a member, I know that, and *your* family started it."

"Yes, my grandfather, Judson Hunter, but he started it with Matthew Hawkins. Then Gregory and Lang took over. Did your mother say anything more about Ella? Victimology is our first step."

"Well, she knew her. I think they all hung out together before my parents split. Mom showed me a picture. Ella was pretty, probably around Mom's age. Thin and elegant. There was some kind of falling out, so Mom doesn't talk about her. Maybe Dad had a fling with her. He did that kind of thing." Kip made a dismissive gesture. "I met other people who knew her. She did a lot of volunteer work. She was an anthropologist. So was her husband. A news article said that the last time they were seen, they were at a dinner party. They said they were planning a trip overseas, so no one looked for them for a while, maybe a week."

"And the trail was cold," Ayden commented.

Kip nodded.

"Maybe there's a police record of who was at the dinner," Ayden said. "Maybe someone spotted an opportunity, knew no one would look for them for a while."

Kip raised his butter knife. "I think that might be in Gregory's analysis. There were police reports. If we find his file, that'll answer a lot of questions."

I rubbed my face. "Let's get organized. First, we'll go over what we know. Develop a chronology. That'll show us our holes and what type of information we need."

Kip retrieved his laptop. Natra had already sent the file she'd created to me and Ayden. She got on the computer and sent it to Kip, who responded with some media files from his.

We drank coffee and perused the Ketch Ryder case. Natra had located a documentary that featured Reid Broward discussing Ryder's confession, so we watched it together. His direct gaze at the interviewer showed confidence and authority.

"I think he really believes it," Ayden commented. "He comes across well in this."

I had to agree. "He probably sees what he wants to see, though. Lots of interrogators do that. And if it *feels* right to them, it *is* right."

The documentary also offered background on the Lovatos. Natra added notes to what we already knew on the whiteboard. The couple had been in real estate. They'd lived in OBX before Dad came. I wondered if they'd sold him this house. I made a note to look for his records. News articles provided more about the Steadmans, but not enough to name suspects.

Ella Steadman's link to Kip gave me a different sense of that incident. Dad had known her. He had a part in this. I wanted badly to renew my past sense of him and love him unconditionally, but he'd once knowingly put people at risk. My whole family legacy had been built on fraud and secrecy, through multiple generations.

By late morning, we'd filled in several charts. I thought it was time for a group discussion. "I'll start. On the surface, the facts are these. The cases of missing people related to Ketch Ryder seem to have started nine years ago, although we can't be sure about the first one, or even if it's the first one. He hinted at it. That's all we have. Then two years passed before another one—the Lovatos—then one year passed before the Steadmans. So, the third and last incident before he was arrested was six years ago. Ryder wasn't a suspect for any of them, but when he was caught with a stolen credit card a month after the Steadman incident, he had news clippings on his laptop about them and the Lovatos. After a task force team interrogated Ryder, he confessed and claimed to have murdered both couples and indicated there was a third."

"From where?" Ayden asked,

Kip filled in the blank from his own research. "Richmond Hill, Georgia, south of Savannah. Ralph and Sharon Pryor. That's what they deduced, given the things he said. They're missing."

"That's still unclear," Natra added. "Law enforcement hasn't said anything official about a link."

Ayden held up his pen. "I see a possible theme, though. All upscale communities."

I glanced at Kip before I continued. "Ryder provided details for two investigations, so we focus on those. No physical evidence, like fingerprints or DNA, linked him, so they relied on his confession. His *multiple* confessions, which don't all match. For the Lovatos, Ryder gave body locations, but they weren't found. He gave only hints for the Steadmans' location, but then he clammed up. He ended up in prison here in North Carolina because it was the strongest case they could make." I looked at Natra. "I assume this is where you discovered inconsistencies."

"The most obvious ones, yes," she said.

Kip moved in his seat, alert. "Like what?"

"Basic things, like the wrong name of a street, incorrect about the weather at the time, and a faulty description of the scenes. He said the Lovatos were home all evening, but they weren't. If you're the killer stalking them, that's a significant detail to get wrong. He changed his story only after he was told they'd been abducted on their way into their house. The killer didn't get inside the house, but Ryder says *he* did. He offers a detailed description, too. Then he said he went back afterward, so that's how he knew the layout."

Kip held up a finger. "Did you notice this? He got the description of the Lovatos wrong. So did reporters, and he seemed to repeat what they'd said, like he prepped his confession off the news reports."

"Not the first false confessor to do that," Ayden remarked. "And I looked at the Israel Keyes confessions last night. Ryder lifted plenty of details. Who knows if he revealed *anything* about what he did? But then, why not just make it up entirely? Why pirate someone else's murder method?"

Natra turned to another page. "The photos show that the Lovatos were of Mexican descent, but reporters said Italian, maybe because the initial police report got this wrong."

"And Ryder changed his statement after the detective showed him the photos." Kip looked around the table. "In the video, he seemed surprised."

"I watched some of those interrogation videos last night, too," Ayden said. "Ryder seemed uninformed about what cops can do for him. He suggested deals they can't make, and he played pointless games." He turned our attention to a news article. "Found this interview with Reid Broward. Lots of praise for his skill at getting killers talkin', like in the documentary. He seems like one of those 'aw shucks' kind who still wants you to know his achievements. He describes how he got Ryder talkin' with candy and compliments. But honestly, I think Ryder wanted to talk. It wasn't Broward's skill that made it happen."

I asked Natra to make a note. Ayden looked pleased.

"There's one odd thing," Natra said. "Media. Ryder didn't want this in the press, so he wasn't seeking attention."

I held up a finger. "Actually, it wasn't so much about attention. And this might be why he was drawn to the Keyes case, because Keyes made the same demand. I'd say Ryder studied the Keyes case and used whatever might work for him. Like Keyes, Ryder wanted to keep it from his daughter. She was thirteen, I think, when he was arrested."

"Almost fourteen," Kip said. I glanced at him. His jaw muscles looked tight when he added, "Vaughn Ryder was in this co-op sort of community, off the grid. Ryder thought she wouldn't see the news, anyway, but he wanted to be sure the cops didn't approach her."

Ayden watched him. "D'you know her?"

Kip glanced down before he said, "She's not isolated anymore. She's made comments on social media. I dug it up, because I thought I'd find some answers."

I leaned in. "And....?"

"Not really. She defends her dad, says he's innocent."

"Do you know how to contact her?"

His cheeks reddened. "I could, I guess."

"Let's keep that in mind, then. She could be a resource. Maybe no one's asked her the right questions."

"Okay." Kip made a note. His face remained flushed. Ayden raised an eyebrow at me. I nodded. *Look for an opening.*

Chapter Ten

Natra had scoured the Internet for items associated with Ryder. I'd mentioned the book a local author had written, and she'd looked at summaries and reviews. We learned that Ryder had collected an extensive network of correspondents, from collectors of murderabilia to groupies to haters. Some had posted notes from him on their social media accounts. We pay attention to such information. We'd once investigated a case where a correspondent had gathered enough information from a killer's coded letters for us to locate a buried victim.

Natra offered multiple clips from Ryder's posted letters. Most were to females. She handed the sheets to each of us and gave us time to look them over before she asked, "Notice something?"

"I thought his thing was couples," Ayden commented.

"Exactly. That's missing. I've read through a bunch of these, but he doesn't seem to get anyone talking about their significant other. You'd think he'd fish for that. We should note this, especially if we're looking for *his* pattern vs. the couples killer's pattern."

Kip grew animated. "That's what I thought!" He narrowed his eyes. "So, you look at patterns?"

"That's part of it." Natra tapped the table. "You build a sense of them from what they say, what they don't say, the way they say things, what they focus on, when they deviate from their normal behavior, things like that. Then you can better spot when they're hedging, hiding, or lying. And you can anticipate certain expected behaviors."

"Like when he flirts with one girl but is rude to another?"

"Yes, that's important. You'd want to see which behavior he does most often and with whom. We make lists and then build a chart for reference."

I shifted gears. "He talks a lot about himself. A narcissist. He's not interested in his fans except for what they can do for him. He doesn't ask questions. Just doesn't care."

Ayden tapped his pen. "He keeps referring to the *Eyes,* with a capital E."

"That's in a lot of the correspondence," Natra stated. "It seems to be a paranoid idea that he's always under observation, so anyone who contacts him will be, too."

I rubbed the table near my laptop. "There was little time between the interrogations and the suicide attempt. He accepted a plea deal on the murders to which he confessed, so he didn't go through the typical evaluations for court. He had a public defender who seemed to just roll over, but maybe there's a competency evaluation. Natra, do you have much sense of him from what you've researched?"

"Crime journalists have looked into him, as have crime media junkies. His background isn't well documented because he was raised by survivalists who lived off the grid—another similarity with Keyes. Primitive conditions, sometimes solitary, sometimes with other like-minded people. He's the oldest of five kids. His father went to prison when Ketch was ten for planning an attack on a federal building." She looked up. "So, we know he was raised around conspiracy theorists. His paranoia makes sense."

"Ryder has a juvenile record," I added.

"Right. He was caught for property crimes as a teen, like arson, and was charged once for animal cruelty. At the juvenile facility, he met other kids from families with similar beliefs. He formed his own network, which continued when he got out. Two members were caught smuggling illegal arms. Another is suspected in a serious hate crime. Around this time, Ryder moved to New Hampshire with a common-law wife, Ivy. She adopted his last name. They had two kids, a boy and a girl."

Kip poured another cup of coffee. "Ella knew Ivy. She helped her get away from him. Ivy took the boy, the youngest, but left her daughter behind."

Natra raised a finger. "Right. And Ryder's mother lived close, so after his arrest, she took over the girl's care."

This surprised me. "Ivy didn't come back for her?"

"Apparently not."

"Ivy went to Virginia," Kip offered, "to another branch of that community."

"Did they question her after Ryder confessed?"

Natra looked through her notes. "They did. She said he was violent, but she didn't know anything they could use. Or she wouldn't say."

Ayden turned toward Kip. "I looked up more about the Steadmans. They vanished from their home during the night, like the other couples, but I saw some differences. Their house was vandalized, and things were missing. We have to keep that in mind for the linkage analysis. Also, their car wasn't taken."

I stood to clear the plates. "Let's look for Gregory's analysis, and that letter. Kip recalls him taking both to the attic. If we find the letter, we can compare Ryder's suicide note against it. If the handwriting matches, Ryder remains a viable suspect. If not, there's someone else."

I brought a space heater into the attic. We partitioned the room so we could work systematically. For me, delving into Dad's work now that I'd reconnected with him felt like I'd just met someone I wanted to more deeply explore. He'd left my mother when I was fifteen, so I'd seen him only sporadically until I was old enough to visit on my own. When he'd purchased this house, I was in grad school. I'd married and moved to South Carolina, but after five years, my marriage fell apart. Soon thereafter, Dad had vanished. I hadn't wanted his house. Then I *had* wanted it. Now I didn't know.

I put aside several documents Lang had written to read later. The others had their own file organization categories. Ayden and Natra would both know to hold back things I'd want.

Worked commenced for a couple hours. No one found Gregory's items. I gave Ayden a look. It was lunchtime. I wanted him to make his move. He nodded like he already had it in hand. Another ten minutes went by. His phone rang. He went down the steps to take it. Then he came back.

"Hey, Kip, I need to go over to the Duck House to check something before everything closes early for the holiday. I could use your expertise." He looked at me. "Can you handle this part without him? We'll get lunch out."

"Just when the going gets tough," I said. "Yes, we can handle it." To Kip, I said, "I know what we're looking for. Go ahead."

He hesitated, but Ayden gestured for him to follow and went down the steps.

Kip glanced around, seemed to realize there could be hours of sorting left, and asked, "You're sure? I came here to help."

"Absolutely. If we find the analysis, we can get it up on the board." I pointed to Natra. "We have a system. I'll text you when we find it. You won't be far away."

Kip still looked reluctant, but he followed Ayden down the steps.

When we heard the truck engine, Natra said, "I smell a set-up."

"Yup. Those two get along. Ayden will get Kip talking."

"Hope so. Did you notice him when we talked about Ryder's daughter?"

I cocked my head. "Notice what?"

"He seemed tense. He flushed a little. I don't think he's lying, exactly, but he's holding back."

"Seems to be his MO. We'll get it out of him. If he *really* didn't want to talk, he wouldn't be here."

My text tone sounded. It was from Ayden. *Audi's back.*

Chapter Eleven

We went to Natra's apartment on the north side to look. She took a north-facing window, I took the west onto the main drag. Mika whined and paced between us. We stayed back to prevent anyone outside from spotting us.

"I see it." I pointed. "He's just up the street, driving slow. No one's behind 'im."

Natra joined me in time to see the Audi pull into a driveway, turn around, and head north. I texted Ayden. *Just left. Maybe following you. Check your truck.*

"Who could it be?" Natra asked.

"If he's focused on us, it could be about Kip. Ayden saw him this morning and thought he was watching the house. And there was that guy on the dune."

I went to the northeast window to scan the dunes. I saw no one. "Let's check the doors."

Once we secured the house, I looked for the Audi again. It seemed to have left. I pulled up Ayden's clip, but mud obscured the license plate number. "Looks like a custom plate, maybe Virginia or Georgia."

After our adrenaline spike, it was tough to settle down to the drudge work of sorting, but we had limited time. I hoped to locate Gregory's analysis before Kip got back. I didn't think he'd just take it, but I was invested now.

We ate a quick lunch and kept looking. By midafternoon, we'd searched more than half the attic. I opened a lidded brown banker's box. The contents looked like more of what we'd already seen—Dad's labeling. I sighed and lifted a handful of items off the top and set them aside. More of the same. But halfway in, I spotted a thick brown envelope. I pulled it out. A broken wax seal on the flap showed the impression we'd seen on Kip's ring. I held it up. "Got something."

Natra came over to look. "Let's take it downstairs."

"I wanna see this *now*."

She put a hand on my arm. "What if there's stuff about Lang? Stuff you won't like. Let's do this where we can lay it out methodically."

I yielded. "I'll check if there's more in here first."

I searched through the box for the white envelope but didn't find it. "Gregory must've distributed things in different places. We'll have to keep searching, but let's look at this package before Kip gets back."

We took it down to the conference area. I removed the contents and placed the pages one at a time in two rows. "There's no binder like what Kip described, but this looks like a pretty full case analysis."

Natra opened her laptop to prepare. "I see victim names, police reports, photos, a map, maybe a timeline."

"Let's dig in."

We sorted through Gregory's items and supplemented them with online research. His case file was fascinating. We gained a clear sense of Gregory's concern about Ketch Ryder. Kip's father had been a meticulous researcher, so much so it was hard to distinguish minutiae from substance. He'd made some comparisons, offering a list of pros and cons, and had scribbled several alternative chronologies. Natra crystalized pertinent items and transferred them to our charts on the whiteboard. She chose five different colors to distinguish the different investigative strands. She also made a list on paper for items to further research. We had to move some things around, but we were getting somewhere.

To my relief, I found nothing that implicated Dad in a crime, but Gregory hadn't even mentioned the Gray Hollow Group. We'd noted some codes, so it seemed possible he'd shielded some information, aware that Lang could decipher it. Gregory *had* included Dad's connection to two of the missing couples. Hovering over all of this were references to the man he thought had killed them.

"Looks like Gregory was right to fear for his family," I observed. "I can't say I'm happy about how he tried to pull in my dad. Still, the Lovatos were forced out of their home just seventeen miles from here, *and* they knew Dad. Gregory's visit happened *after* that. He's giving us the connections."

I looked out the window. Fog had rolled in along with misty rain. Ayden texted that they were on their way back. He'd stop at the local wine store.

I called him and told him to put me on his truck's speakerphone so Kip could hear. When he did, I said, "We've got stuff."

"The letter?" Kip asked.

"No, sorry, and not the binder, but we found Gregory's case analysis. It's comprehensive. We've got it all laid out, ready. We can get right to work once you're back."

I ended the call and gave our chart a once-through, out loud. "Two double homicides in known locations. One that Ryder vaguely described in an unknown location, with at least three candidate incidents from Gregory's research. He includes the Pryors from Georgia, whom Kip mentioned. One couple was connected to the Hawkins family and Gray Hollow Group. We don't have the letter sent to Gregory, but we know who wrote it." I pointed to the items Natra had penned with the black marker. "Our bad guy seems to have had a surveillance system, based on places Gregory crossed paths with him—including this house." I felt a chill. Was this guy watching now? Kip thought he was "still out there."

"I wonder if he drives a blue Audi," Natra said.

"Don't even say it. But I see one more connection to Keyes, maybe the one that explains why Ryder knows so much about the guy's crimes."

"Yup. Lock and key."

Ayden's truck pulled in. I looked at Natra. "Shall we work up to it or just tell them?"

She gestured toward the whiteboard. "Kind of hard to hide that."

I felt proud of our work. I could hardly wait for Kip to see it.

They came up the outside steps to the deck. I opened the sliding door to let them in. A cold wind off the ocean accompanied them. They removed their wet shoes, and Ayden handed over a bottle of wine. He noticed the whiteboard and stopped to squint at it.

I gestured for them to take a seat. "We've got some things to tell you. It might spoil our holiday, but this is urgent." I pointed to the whiteboard. "We have a name. Jordan Christopher Locke. He was Gregory's chief suspect. We can't find the letter, but Gregory says it's from Locke, and he describes threats he received by phone. Apparently, Gregory talked with some of Locke's relatives and colleagues, and Locke didn't like it."

Kip put his hands on his hips and shook his head. "No, no! You're wrong. It's not him."

I looked at Natra. We hadn't expected this.

"We're not wrong, Kip." I gestured toward the papers on the table. "You can read the notes yourself. This is your dad's work."

His eyes lit up, and his jaw tightened. "Then Dad was wrong! It's *not* him. Jordan's a friend! He's a good man."

Ayden looked at me in alarm. I realized that Kip had just taken a blow. He was blocking it. He turned as if to walk back out the door.

I strode over and grabbed his arm. "Kip, stay here. We need to hear what you know. Maybe Gregory *is* wrong."

His nostrils flared. "Of course, he's wrong. He's definitely wrong."

I turned him and pointed at the board. "Look at the list. Do you know that Locke was Ella Steadman's first husband, the abusive one?"

Kip frowned. "No. No, he wasn't."

"He was. We have a copy of the legal record, the marriage certificate. He had another wife before her, too, who disappeared. He has an arrest for assault from that relationship."

Kip stared at our list. He curled his fingers into fists.

"And also," I added, "he knows Ketch Ryder."

Kip shook his head. "I don't…he doesn't…he didn't say any of that to me."

I got him to sit down at the table. He stared at the board, blinking hard. Without meaning to, I'd just forced him to choose between his father and a friend. But Locke, I knew, was unlikely to be a true friend. I suspected Kip had been set up.

Chapter Twelve

I sat next to him and put my hand on his arm. "Take your time. This is hard."

Kip's jaw remained tense. In a conflict between facts and feelings, feelings fight hard to win. I gestured for Natra to bring him something to drink. When Kip's shoulders dropped, I made my approach. "How do you know this guy? Gregory seemed to think he was quite dangerous. So did Lang. That's all in the notes."

Kip clasped his hands together on the table. "He's just Jordan. He's a nice guy. He can't be…"

"When did you meet him?"

Kip sat still. Natra placed a mug of coffee in front of him. When he took a sip, his hand shook. He closed his eyes and breathed out, rubbing his GHG ring, before he shook his head and looked at us. "After Dad died, Jordan came by the house a few times to check on us, see how we were. Mom knew him. She wouldn't tell me much, and I heard her ask him to stop coming around. I thought she just didn't want us—my brothers and me—to be reminded. But when I went to college, my cousin, Mark, brought Jordan to meet me. Took me to dinner. He said he knew my dad, they'd been good friends, and offered help if I needed it." He took another sip. "He seemed okay. He's a lawyer, a real sense of justice type. I mean, you couldn't *not* admire him for how passionate he was about righting wrongs. Made you wanna help him. He had some business transactions with Dad, and my cousin liked him. Jordan said he and Dad had a contract, and he just wanted to look at his records, get things in order."

"Did you let him?"

"No. I'd given what I had to Lang, and we had no access to Lang except when he just showed up. I had no copies because Lang said it was better not to. I couldn't tell Jordan how to reach him, and Dad's lawyer had no record of anything like that. Jordan said it was off the books."

"Did you tell Lang about him?"

Kip shook his head.

"So, you gave Locke nothing?"

"I told him what I could remember. And my cousin knew stuff, too."

I'd met his cousin, Mark Gardiner. He was married to the attorney, Kate Gardiner, that I used there, and he worked on my father's properties. Seemed like a salt-of-the-earth type of businessman, hardworking and conscientious.

Kip looked at me. "Should I warn Mark?"

I held up a hand. "Let's work through this first. Apparently, Gregory didn't tell anyone but Lang what he suspected about Locke."

"Jordan only came around after Dad died. I'd never seen him before that. He never said anything about Ella. And he didn't stop coming, even after I had nothing to give him. He was kind. And smart. He listened to me. He even paid for my tuition my final semester so I wouldn't have to work."

I knew that move—leveraging with gifts. Kip would figure that out himself when he had time to process. "Was Jordan involved with the Gray Hollow Group?"

Kip looked confused. "I don't think so. But I guess I don't really know 'im."

"So, what's up?" Ayden asked. "Who is this guy?"

I looked at Natra but kept a comforting hand on Kip's arm. "Give us the gist."

She went to the whiteboard. Mika jumped up, excited. Natra urged the dog to lie back down. She glanced at Kip before pointing at our first column. "These are the known victims, the Lovatos and the Steadmans. We know what Ryder said about them, and Gregory added more. He and Lang knew both couples." She stepped back. "This second column lists five incidents Gregory identified as potentially related. They're all good candidates, especially the Pryors in Georgia, so we'll do a more detailed linkage analysis."

Kip leaned forward. "Five missing couples? *Five?*"

"Yes, although two were found, or at least partially. In one case, only the male was found. And one thing we noticed is that the found victims were left in wooded or swampy areas, places difficult to access. Hunters came across them. One missing pair was a team of cops. They were checking out a complaint and ended up gone. Some were missing—"

I shook my head. She didn't have to say out loud that some had been beheaded.

"…parts," she finished.

Ayden took a photo of the board and scribbled notes on a pad.

"In the third column," Natra continued, "in two parts, we placed items that might either implicate or exonerate Ketch Ryder. In the fourth column, we have items that implicate Locke, including his association with Ella and his arrest for assault."

Kip flinched.

Ayden scanned the list. "Locke and Ryder overlap. Ryder's wife knew Ella, and Locke was once married to her." He looked at me. "Could this be an accomplice situation? We had a case where the accomplice accepted responsibility because the main killer threatened him."

I nodded. "I thought of that. It's possible. And Locke and Ryder both lived in New England."

"No," Kip said. "Locke's from Georgia. Has a law practice there. He comes to Boston for business and has a cabin in Vermont, because he's part of a hunting club."

Natra added this to the chart.

Kip went stiff. "Wait! My dad would've known that. Why isn't that in his notes?"

"We do have his Vermont location," Natra said. "Just not the Georgia connection, aside from one couple missing from there. We haven't read everything in the packet yet. Maybe he included it on another page."

I applied gentle pressure to Kip's arm. "Anything else?"

He seemed to concentrate. "He had that cabin. He invited me and my brothers to go hunting, like he wanted to be a substitute dad. Mark went a couple times. Jordan said Dad was at the cabin a lot."

"Gregory was a hunter?"

"He taught me and my brothers. Sometimes, he hosted hunts at Dacretown." Kip blinked. "I almost went with this guy. What would he have done?"

"Probably nothing," I assured him. "He wants to figure out what you know. You're more valuable alive."

Kip went still, as if thinking of something. Then he looked at me. "You said someone broke in before you moved here. Locke could've been here, could've taken stuff."

Natra gestured toward the papers on the table. "But wouldn't he have taken *this* stuff?"

"Yes, likely," I said. "So, he either didn't break in or didn't know where to look. It was pretty deep in one of Lang's boxes."

Kip tapped the table. "My dad came here with stuff about Jordan, talked to Lang, and then Jordan came to me looking for that stuff?"

"Sounds like it," I said. "He used your cousin Mark as a go-between, maybe because your mother deflected him."

"But why would he keep coming when I said I didn't have it?"

"That's a good question."

"And you think he's the killer?"

"I don't know, Kip, but if Ryder's lying as you say, and Locke's concerned about information Gregory gathered on him—information that you might also know, then…."

"Then I'm a threat to him."

"Possibly. We're trying to figure that out." I looked at Ayden. "Did that car follow you?"

"Didn't see it. No tracker on the truck."

Kip looked from me to Ayden. "What car?"

"A blue Audi. Looks like Virginia or Georgia plates."

Kip swallowed.

"Know something about it?" I asked.

"Just…I saw a car like that where I…. when I stayed at my friend's place on the way here."

"You trust this friend?"

The left corner of Kip's mouth turned down. "I…don't…I thought so. I don't know who to trust." He looked alarmed. "Did I do this? Did I bring someone dangerous here?" He stood up. "I should leave!"

I grabbed his hand. "Please sit down, Kip. We don't know who it is or what he wants, or whether it has anything to do with you. Even if it does, leaving now could be dangerous."

He didn't sit. He hugged himself. "What does he want?"

"Who did you stay with?" Ayden asked.

"Just…I mean…I don't know what she has to do with this."

Again, I urged him, "Kip, sit, please." He did so, but I sensed from his flushed face that he'd jump up at any second. "Tell us about this friend."

His eyes darted around the room. "I need to warn her."

I gestured. "Call her. We'll wait."

Kip got up and strode from the room.

"I blocked his car," Ayden said. "He can't leave."

I crossed my arms. "This is distressing. He's in the thick of something. Let's check *his* car for a tracker. Got any intel?"

"I think this friend is someone he likes. He didn't tell me much, but he asked a lot of questions that made me think he's exploring a relationship. She's in Delaware. I think he met her on social media, but he wasn't sharing many details. I tried. I didn't push too much, or it would've been obvious."

When Kip returned, he asked to see the documents. Ayden pushed some toward him that he'd already skimmed. Kip sat down but seemed restless. His eyes kept darting toward the door.

"This house is secure, Kip," I assured him. "Even if Locke or someone he hired is out there, he hasn't made a move. We have a dog that will alert us if someone tries to break in, we have an alarm system on the doors, and we all have weapons."

He nodded. His mouth remained tight.

"You can come back to the Duck House with me," Ayden offered. "Plenty of room."

Kip shook his head. "I'm fine. I'm just...I can't believe I was so stupid. I should've realized."

"He's likely a clever manipulator," I said. "And we don't know if he's connected to the car."

"I tried my cousin but got voicemail. Maybe he knows something."

Natra leaned toward Kip. "What does Jordan Locke look like? That'll help."

Kip considered this. "He's stocky, maybe six foot two. Big, strong hands, like a wrestler. Completely bald, but with thick dark eyebrows. A mustache that kind of runs down his face." He placed his fingers near his chin.

This man sounded vaguely familiar. I searched my memory. "Eye color?"

"Blue. Dark blue. Walks kind of stiff."

"Anything that would make him instantly recognizable?"

"Mmm...maybe the gold loop in his right ear. Looks like a pirate. That's what I thought when I first met him. Oh, and rings. He wore several big rings on both hands."

I nodded. "Yeah, I think I met 'im. I remember that bald head and earring. He came up to Dad in a restaurant in Boston when I was visiting. You're right. Imposing but charming. Great voice. I'd just gotten engaged, and he congratulated me. Lang definitely knew him. Didn't seem pleased to see 'im, though. I think Locke was there to remind Lang of something. Maybe a meeting. I'll try to remember."

I gestured toward the five piles I'd made of Gregory's papers. "I've arranged these to align with our chart. If you're ready, we should go through them to figure out where we need more research and what we can put aside. We have a key suspect, and Gregory had a lot of information about him. Kip, if you're up to it, I want you to focus on what your father learned. Ayden, I have several missing persons files for a linkage analysis. Look at the five cases Gregory had and the two I added from Lang's pile. Natra will develop fuller victimologies, and I'll add more to our bio of Ketch Ryder. He's the center of this."

Kip looked at me. "Why don't you go interview him? You do that, don't you?"

I stared at him. "Why would I? Your dad already gathered information."

"Not since…not from the past five years. Maybe he'd talk to you. You'd see if he was lying. You could confront him, get him to tell you why he's doing this. The prison's just a few hours from here."

"It's more complicated than you think. I can't just walk into a prison and see someone. I need his attorney to invite me or to be added to his visitor's list, which can take a while, and why would he do that, anyway? He's not talking."

He leaned over the table. "Vaughn can take you in. She has an attorney."

I blinked. "Vaughn? His daughter?"

"Yes."

Some pieces fell into place. "Is Vaughn the girl you just called?"

Kip hesitated. His cheeks reddened. Finally, he nodded. "Yes."

Chapter Thirteen

This changed things. We had a connection, a close one.

Kip crossed his arms. "I'm helping her because it…because my dad would've. So, you can talk to Ryder. She can take you to see 'im." He gestured across the papers. "That's better than all this 'maybe this, maybe that,' isn't it?"

I looked at my team. Ayden leaned back and crossed his arms, a bemused expression on his face. Natra lifted her chin.

I had to admit, I was intrigued. As a suicidologist, I'd initially followed the case. I had a file on suicide among serial killers. It's a rare event but often fascinating. Israel Keyes was among them, notorious for the mocking, bloodstained note he left that suggested many more undiscovered victims. Ryder seemed to have mimicked this, too. I know of no other similar behavior.

But I needed more information. "How long have you known her?"

"Not that long. Couple months. Really, mostly these past couple weeks, once I knew I was coming here. At first, I noticed her on a social media page. I followed her to see what she was posting. She's been bold about her relationship to Ketch Ryder, so she's attracted a lot of trolls."

Natra glanced at me. I understood her look, so I stopped him. "Start over. Your interest in her doesn't seem that random. From what we've pieced together, your parents divorced just before Ella disappeared. Ryder was caught a month later. Gregory was aware of him then, so six years ago. You were fifteen."

Kip nodded. "Right. But I didn't live with Dad then. I barely saw him. He didn't talk about Ryder in front of me, not until we came here, when I was sixteen. So, he'd done his research on Ryder by then. Still, he wasn't sure. That's why he wanted to talk to Lang. I never heard him mention Jordan Locke. I only knew he thought the guy who'd confessed didn't do it."

Ayden moved in his seat. "Vaughn was around fourteen, right?"

"Almost, but Dad never mentioned her, either. After he died, I looked up Ryder, but the name of his daughter in the news reports was *Fawn*. She changed it to Vaughn, to protect herself, because she did know what Ketch had done. After he corresponded with her last year, she started a web page and owned her association with him. The name, Ryder, caught my interest. She posted articles about the Steadmans. To be honest, she kind of annoyed me. She made claims, but it seemed like she had no evidence. I wrote her a note, and she responded."

I glanced at the whiteboard, then returned to Kip. "She didn't talk about Jordan Locke?"

Kip shook his head. "No. We talked about losing our dads, mostly. I didn't want her to know my relation to Ella, in case she thought I was setting her up. But she does know Locke. I just asked her, and she said yes." He looked around. "I like her. She's…vibrant. Passionate. But she doesn't have what she needs to exonerate Ketch. I thought I might find it in the files here."

"What did she say about Locke?" I asked.

"She wouldn't tell me on the phone. I think she's scared of 'im."

"There might be evidence," I said. "We didn't find his letter, but we have Gregory's description of receiving it. Said it was a threat. Locke sent him something of Ella's, to prove he'd taken her and would do the same to others he knew if he didn't back off."

Kip squinted. "Something of Ella's? Did he say what?"

"Something she wore. So, if Gregory brought it here and it was carefully handled, there might be usable DNA."

Kip frowned. I waited. He shrugged. "Dad didn't show it to me."

"Did you see anything in his hand? You saw the white envelope and the other packet. Anything else?"

"Not that I remember."

"All right," I said. "This really *is* a scavenger hunt. Let's look at Vaughn's website and go through these files. I want to be very clear about what we have here, especially if Lang's involved."

Kip sat up as if to argue, but I stopped him. "Evidence. If Vaughn has a good attorney, that's what he'll expect."

We got to work on the papers. By the time we were ready for the crab soup simmering in a crockpot, we had a full chart and a good sense of the principals involved. The Steadmans had known the Lovatos. They'd also socialized with Gregory Hawkins and his wife until that marriage went south. Ella knew Lang from the GHG, and they'd done some investigations together. The Lovatos had found Lang the house I now lived in. Jordan Locke had been married to Ella, who'd then helped Ivy Ryder, so there was a tentative link between Locke and Ryder, although Ella's help had come after she left Locke. This man also knew Gregory and Lang, but we rejected him as the mystery GHG member. He'd lived primarily in Georgia and wasn't related by blood to any Hawkins or Hunter, not to mention the likely hurdle of a restraining order from Ella.

I proposed that we watch another interrogation video. Kip excused himself to go talk with Vaughn.

"Is she alone for the holiday?" I asked. "Would she want to drive down here? She's welcome."

"Actually, she's close," he said. "She's near Norfolk, so she can visit Ketch on Friday."

"Then, please invite her."

Kip went down to the studio.

"That'll be interesting," Natra said to me. "What she won't say over the phone she might say in person."

"I hope so, but she doesn't know us, and we'll have Jax here. An attorney could intimidate her."

We watched two more interrogations. Many of the same behaviors were present. On a second screen, Ayden pulled up Vaughn's website and scrolled through it. He stopped and pointed. "See that image?"

"The arrowhead?" Natra asked.

Ayden sorted through Gregory's papers and pulled out a map of Vermont, placed in a three-hole plastic sleeve. He turned it so we could see it and tapped what looked like a red arrow near a body of water.

"I see a lake," I said.

"Look at the name."

"Arrowhead Mountain Lake. Hmm."

"There was an arrowhead on Ryder's suicide note." He pulled out his phone and did a quick calculation. "This lake is about four hours from Concord, even less from Nashua, where the Steadmans lived. And Locke had a hunting cabin in Vermont."

Natra pulled up the image of the note we'd viewed the night before. Ryder had placed an arrowhead next to the horse head.

I stared at it. "If these images designate victim locations, maybe Vaughn can fill in some holes. But why didn't Broward figure this out? A confession is never sufficient, and they haven't actually located the bodies."

"Any idea what these other drawings are?" Ayden asked. "A weird stick animal that looks like it's puking, and a wavy line. Maybe the ocean?"

I rubbed my jaw. "You got me. Maybe I *should* interview Ryder."

Kip returned and told us Vaughn had accepted the invitation. We were about to meet the serial killer's daughter.

Chapter Fourteen

A noise woke me in the night. It came from the room across from mine…a room I kept locked. Dad's former office. I drew in my breath and remained still. I heard nothing more. Had to be a dream. I slowly exhaled.

Then *mmrrrr…thunk…*a wooden drawer slid closed.

I sat up. My heart raced. I considered texting Natra, but Mika could frighten the intruder away. I wanted to see who it was. Had I set the alarm? I thought so, but Ayden had gone in and out a couple times before leaving. Maybe I'd overlooked it.

I reviewed the situation. A man in an Audi seemed to be watching us. Dad had once been targeted in this house. Jordan Locke seemed to want something in here, and Dad had secrets, some that had shocked me. That's why I'd locked that room. Until I could go through his things in private, I wanted no one in there.

But *someone* was in there now.

I drew back the covers and brought my legs over the side of the bed. It creaked. I stopped, then moved more slowly. A gust of wind rattled the house, which provided cover that let me get free of the bed. My heart thumped so hard I could barely breathe.

Across the hall, a door closed softly. I almost didn't hear it. *Metal on metal.* A key in a lock. How was that possible?

I should've changed that lock, made it digital with bio-ID. I put on my robe and retrieved my Glock, loaded and ready, from my nightstand drawer.

Most of Dad's files were in the attic, but some remained in his office. I'd left it just as he'd done when he'd abandoned the place.

Barefoot, I strode to the door, opened it, and flicked on the hallway light. The blinding flash made me blink.

The hallway was empty. I tested the office doorknob. Locked.

Glock ready, I went down the hall to the great room. I had enough light to see that no one was there. Despite my bare feet, I went out to the deck. A frigid November breeze pushed back, but I leaned over the railing as far as I could. That didn't work. I pulled my robe closer and went down the icy wooden steps until I could see the studio window on the ground floor. The curtains were closed, but a faint glow behind them said Kip was awake. I'd granted him easy access to the house. I'd trusted him. I now regretted this.

But I didn't *know* it was him. Maybe his light was on for his own security.

Shivering, my toes curling, I went back inside. I sensed a residual presence, the way people describe a haunting. *Someone* had been in here. I walked around to look behind furniture and in the kitchen. In a few hours, we'd fill this room with warmth and the fragrance of food for our Thanksgiving feast. But this violation had spoiled it. Somehow, the person who'd crept into the office had a key.

Kip was the most likely culprit. After all I'd done for him since we'd met, I wouldn't have expected this rude trespass. I recalled his expression of relief when I said I hadn't changed much in the house. He'd been planning this.

I returned to my room to put on slippers and fetch my own key. My feet were so numb I couldn't feel the fur inside. I didn't have to be quiet. This was *my* house. My heart still raced, but more from anger. I'd been shut out. Again. I went to Dad's office, unlocked the door, and turned on the overhead light. Before I crossed the threshold, I looked for signs of a disturbance.

I hadn't dusted in here in a year, but a month ago I'd cleaned the floor. I doubted I'd find shoeprints, but I crouched to look, anyway. At first, I noticed nothing. Then I saw near the massive desk the faint impression of a footpad and toeprints—someone wearing just socks. I returned to my room to fetch an evidence ruler and an alternate light source from my kit. Slanting the ALS near the floor illuminated more of the print. It was longer and broader than my foot. I got down and measured it. Pulling out my phone, I looked up the translation of inches to size. A men's size ten and a half. A guy around six feet, give or take. I stood and looked around.

I hadn't exactly memorized how things were arranged, but I thought that a stack of four hardcover books placed on the desk had been on the chair seat. Still, I might've moved those books and just forgotten.

I breathed in. The room smelled musty. I'd opened it up a couple times when I'd first moved in but had postponed an inventory. I pulled on the handle of a file cabinet drawer that remained firmly closed. I opened a desk drawer and thought this was the noise I'd heard, but what might be missing I couldn't calculate. I moved the contents around. Some old pens, a sketch pad, an envelope filled with stamps, and even a zipped leather packet. I opened it and saw a few small bills. He wasn't after money.

A 3x5-inch red spiral notebook at the back of the drawer caught my eye. I removed it and thumbed through the dozen or so lined pages. It looked unused until I opened the back cover and saw a set of numbers and dashes. A code, perhaps for a combination lock.

I looked around, unsure where this lock could be. Then I froze. On the wall, a primitive rendition of a storm-tossed ship in a carved wooden frame looked slightly askew. This painting had occupied that spot ever since Dad had first acquired the place. I went over to it and ran the alternate light source over the frame. On both sides in the dust were clear areas the size of hands. Someone had gripped this painting. *Recently.* Avoiding those areas, I tried to lift the painting off its hook. The frame made it heavy. I braced myself and tried again. Finally, it came clear of the wall. I set it aside and stared.

My father had a wall safe.

I wondered if something from it was now in Kip's hands. He'd said he wanted to find something. He'd searched alongside us but had looked in here on his own.

I hesitated to confront him. I hadn't caught him red-handed. Still, if he took something, I wanted to know what it was, and why.

I used the code from the desk drawer to unlock the safe. Inside, I found envelopes and some boxes. I removed them, closed the safe, and rehung the painting. I spent another uneasy night as I pondered my next move.

Chapter Fifteen

atra had the dinner prep under control. She'd started early. I absorbed the smell of roasting turkey and melting butter. I helped where I could, but my mind was elsewhere. I'd been vigilant all night for the sound of Kip's car. I'd half expected him to take off, though that would obliterate our relationship. Something was way off.

Kip had a quick breakfast, barely conversing with me, then excused himself to read Gregory's files. He'd been jumpy and evasive. I'd hoped he'd volunteer to reveal what he'd done, but he hadn't. Still, his behavior confirmed my suspicions. I waited until Natra took a coffee break and asked her to come with me to Dad's office.

"Someone was in here last night," I said. "I think it was Kip."

Her mouth dropped open. "He broke in?"

"Seems to have had a key."

"He didn't ask?"

"No."

She crossed her arms. "I can't believe it. Why would he do that? Are you sure?"

I held up my hand. "No alarms went off, and Mika didn't bark. That means someone already in the house who wouldn't alert her and who knew to be quiet. And not wearing shoes."

"What?"

"I found a footprint in stocking feet. Male."

"But you didn't call him out."

"Because I thought about it. He had a key, and he knew what was in here.

Maybe Dad directed him."

Natra walked deeper into the room. "Even so… Did you ask Lang?"

"Tried. He still doesn't respond."

"Then ask Kip. I don't like him sneaking around."

"I want to see if he'll offer something first. I don't want to spoil the day, and I need him on the ground in Concord."

"He needs you more than you need him."

"True, but if I confront him, he'll leave. I'm sure he heard me get out of bed, but he was gone before I opened my door. I might not've even realized what he was doing if I hadn't searched. Everything looked in order, and the door was locked."

"Mika got up in the night. She heard him. She didn't bark, but I looked out the window. Didn't see the car and didn't hear anything, so I settled her down, but she was restless."

I gestured. "Let me show you what I discovered."

I went over to the ship painting and lifted it off the wall. Natra's eyes widened. "A safe!"

"Yes. I didn't know about it. Never even thought to look. I'm sure Dad kept his passport and bank accounts in here, which he took, but he left other stuff behind. I found the combination and opened it last night." I pointed to items on the desk. "That's what was in it."

I went over and picked up a zippered pouch. "There's money in here, over a thousand dollars, plus foreign cash. Our intruder didn't take it." I put it down and picked up a spiral-bound notebook. "Dad kept some notes in here. I haven't read them." I used my finger to stir through a box of keys. "Five keys in here. I don't know what these are to, although one is the spare key to Dad's car, which he left behind. There's an expired insurance policy, his divorce decree, and this." I pointed to an unloaded Ruger .357 revolver.

"Nothing unusual."

"I suspect that whatever might be unusual is now in Kip's hands."

"How did he get the key?"

"Off the key rack. It's gone, so he didn't have time to put it back. He'll probably try when he thinks it's safe. But that's why I think Dad's part of this. How would Kip know which key went to this door?"

Natra shrugged. "Maybe he saw your dad use it. Did you shift anything, like change the key holder?"

"Hmm. I didn't. And Kip looked relieved when I mentioned leaving things the way Dad had them."

Natra put her hands on her hips and gave me a stern look. "You have to talk to him."

"I will. I'm sure he took *something*. I just don't know what."

Mika came looking for us. She sat and whined. She wanted to go out. "I'll take her," I said. "It'll give me a chance to look for that Audi."

"And get you out of helping in the kitchen."

"That, too, although my stuff is made. I need to consider what to do. Kip's behavior really disappoints me. I hope he has a good reason."

I found Mika's leash and took her down the outside steps. The morning sun made the sand shimmer, but a dark patch south of us said a storm might be on its way. While I walked the dog, I looked around for the Audi. No sign of it. Maybe our spy took holidays off.

Then I called Jax. He'd soon be on his way here.

Jackson Raines had assisted with several of our recent cases. I'd invited him for Thanksgiving, partly because I wanted him to meet Kip but mostly because I missed him. He lives in Georgia. I'd met him during a tough case involving sex trafficking in a juvenile detention network. Then he'd helped me on a more personal case in South Carolina. We'd grown close, despite his tendency to play devil's advocate. My daughter adores him. Even my ex, Wayne, respects him. Best of all, he has connections everywhere. He's one of those adoptable types for whom people do favors or overlook rules. It's a gift.

Jax had worked on a case in North Carolina this week, so he was about three hours away. He picked up my call. "Annie?" I love his resonant voice. I could imagine him right there with me, his dark eyes reassuring me. "Everything okay?"

"Dinner's still on, same time, but there's been a development."

I'd already told Jax about Kip's ideas about Ryder. Now I filled him in on

Locke and Kip's association with this potential killer. Finally, I described the incident in the night. As a juvenile advocate, Jax has more tolerance than I do for youthful misconduct. Kip was a young adult, but trauma and a lack of support had scarred his adolescence. Jax would get that.

"Sounds like you need some context," he said. "He obviously knows about the safe, so that's probably from Lang. Would he have something in there he'd want Kip to have?"

"Maybe, but I can't really say."

"He waited until his second night there. Did something happen to trigger it?"

"The first night, he could've been tired. Or he wanted to see how things played out. But yesterday, he got quite a shock regarding Jordan Locke. He thought the guy was his friend. And then he called Ryder's daughter. Oh, and about that—"

Mika jerked her head up from the crab hole she was nosing. She stiffened. I heard it, too. A car engine.

"Call you back." I ended the call and ran up and over the dune, arriving in time to step in front of the Range Rover as Kip swung around. I put my hands on the hood. So much for strategy. It was confrontation time. Natra came out on the deck. She saw me and called for Mika.

Kip rolled down the window. "I'll be back."

I came over and leaned in. "Where're ya going?"

"To pick up Vaughn."

"You and I need to talk, Kip. Now."

His jaw set. He didn't get out. "She's waiting, Annie. I'll be back."

I saw an oblong black box, around five inches long, on the seat next to him. I pointed. "Is that from Dad's office?"

Kip looked at it and back at me.

"Kill the engine, Kip."

He did so, his cheeks coloring.

I reminded myself to stay calm. "Mind explaining?"

Kip breathed out.

I crossed my arms. "I know you were in Dad's office last night. You left a footprint. You opened the safe. Let me remind you, this house is mine, not Lang's."

Kip looked up at me. "He doesn't want you pulled into this."

I felt blood rush to my face. "Was this violation *his* idea?"

"It's *my* dad's stuff. Lang told me to get this box."

"When?"

"Last month, in Concord. He forgot to take it when he left."

"And you didn't think you should tell me? What's in it?"

Kip held up his left hand and pointed at his GHG ring. "Ella's ring."

"Ella's?"

"It's distinct." He gestured toward the box. "It has diamonds and emeralds. This is what came to my dad as proof she'd been abducted. It's evidence."

I was floored. "You heard me say that Locke sent something of Ella's to Gregory that could contain her DNA. You knew about this ring, and you didn't say a thing."

"I didn't know till I opened it last night. Lang told me not to look inside."

"But you did, anyway. And now you're just going to take it?"

Kip gave me an enigmatic look.

"Ahhh. You're getting Lang out of what Gregory thrust him into."

"No."

"Then what?"

"I'm taking it to Vaughn. As soon as I saw it, I knew she could use it. If there's DNA, she can support her case."

I leaned in. "I'm not pleased about this, Kip. Lang told you to do something in *my* house, behind my back, that upset me. It scared me. I have a gun. I might've shot you."

Kip nodded. "I'm sorry, Annie. If you want me—"

"Here's what I want you to do." I held out my hand. "You're going to give me the box, and you're going to go get Vaughn and bring her here."

"Lang doesn't—"

"Let me deal with him. Like you said, he's not communicating. Maybe we can resolve this before he does."

"But she can *use* this!"

"Let me be clear. Someone's watching us, and my own father might be assisting a cover-up. I can't side with him on that. You go get this girl and bring her back. We've already sorted through Gregory's records. I want to hear what she has to say. Then we'll figure something out...*together.*"

Kip frowned. But he grabbed the box and gave it to me.

I saw relief on his face before he drove away, as if he'd handed off a ticking bomb.

Chapter Sixteen

atra thought I'd been too easy on him. I shrugged. "He's walking a tightrope. Dad wants him to protect his secrets, but that risks Kip's relationship with me. He's still a kid. Doesn't think very far into the future. Little by little, he's revealing things."

"If you say so." She eyed the box. "Gonna open it?"

"With gloves. It's possible there's evidence on it. I don't want to mess that up, although the provenance already has serious issues. If Gregory's the only one who's had it and he didn't touch it, there's a chance. But Dad might've handled it, too."

I fetched a pair of evidence gloves from my kit and joined Natra at the conference table. She'd made room and positioned a sterile sheet of white paper under a lamp. I put on the gloves before I moved the black box into position. I shook it slightly. It felt light. Natra took pictures, and I measured it. Three inches wide by four and a half long and two inches high.

I opened it. Brown paper wrapped the contents. I peeled it back with care until I saw a plastic baggie resting on a silk-covered cardboard inlay. "Good," I said. "We can see it without touching it." I pulled out the bag and placed it on the sterile paper. The ageing plastic had filmed over, but when I pressed on it with a pencil tip, we could see a gold ring with tiny diamonds and emeralds that formed the GHG insignia.

Natra leaned in. "Wow! Much more elaborate than Kip's ring."

I straightened a fold in the plastic to make the ring more visible. "This is what Ella's kidnapper supposedly sent to Gregory Hawkins as proof of possession. Possibly his DNA is on it. Maybe he demanded a ransom payment. We need that letter."

Natra stepped back. "I wonder why it's not with the ring."

"More to the point, why would Gregory hide the letter but give Dad the ring? Makes no sense. I'll see if Kip knows more about it when he gets back with Vaughn."

"Think she's more than an acquaintance?"

I nodded. "Seems likely. Kip gravitates to troubled girls. Her mother abandoned her to escape Ryder's abuse. What might he have done to this girl? Vaughn was probably home-schooled, but she ended up in a college in Delaware. She's nineteen now, so probably a sophomore."

"Studying neuropsych. That's impressive."

"Right. And in the past year, she's been speaking up for Ryder. I found some of her interviews with reporters. They dismissed her as deluded, and I've certainly met the children of killers who are. We'll see for ourselves."

I wrapped the ring and placed it in the box, then hid it in my room before we went to the kitchen to finish the meal prep.

Natra mixed mushrooms into a bowl of stuffing. "D'you think Vaughn's the reason Kip's willing to work against Lang?"

"I hope not. That would be stupid."

"There's a lot of potential for bias. Vaughn's invested in her dad, and Kip apparently in her."

I sliced apples for a fruit salad. "Nothing I've seen so far exonerates Ryder, but he wasn't necessarily a lone wolf. That's my concern. If we have someone else walking free who might be dangerous to us, we should learn everything we can."

"Call Shona. Insist that she tell you why Lang won't talk to you."

"Tried that, too." I looked at her. "Went to voicemail. And I'd think Dad would call *me*, or at least text, since it's a holiday. I'm worried he's really that ill."

When we were done, I called Ayden to relate what had happened, then returned to Dad's office. Just a ten-by-ten-foot space, it wouldn't take long to go through the desk drawers and file cabinet. First, I sent Dad an email, then texted him to check for it. I avoided mentioning Kip but made it clear

I was worried that he wasn't responding. Shona would see all this. She wasn't a gatekeeper, exactly, but she was the closest he had to a caretaker. I considered flying to Scotland myself after the holiday. I hated this silence.

Finally, I started my search in the office. It absorbed me until Jax texted that he'd arrived.

I stepped out to the deck. A brisk wind cooled the sixtyish temps. Jax got out of his red Wrangler and looked up. I pulled my sweater close and waved. He smiled. We hadn't talked about a future together, so I never knew what to expect. Neither of us was ready for a serious commitment. Still, seeing him excited me. His black hair and Creek heritage gave his features a fiercely handsome poise, but I engaged more with his stability. Even when we'd been in the worst circumstances—a hurricane, an abduction, a gun stuck in his face—he'd remained steady. Nevertheless, I sensed the thunder under the surface that had inspired his tribal name, Tenetke.

I zipped down the steps as Jax strode toward me and swept me into a tight hug. Though I'd seen him just last week, it felt far longer. I hugged him back and received his eager kiss. I relaxed. We were still connected. Then he pulled away. "We should go in. I saw that Audi. It's parked at a house up the road, maybe at a rental." He retrieved his bag and followed me up the steps. The odors of apple pie and baking bread made the place feel extra welcoming.

Natra came into the great room with a stack of plates. Mika ran in to greet Jax. A dog lover, he knew how to handle her enthusiasm. He pulled a treat for her from his pocket.

"That Audi's still here," I told Natra. "He didn't follow Kip."

She welcomed Jax and said, "At least we're fortified now."

Jax produced a bottle of wine. He knows we pick labels relevant to a given situation. This one said *The Prisoner*. Jax winked. I shook my head. "I haven't decided."

"I know you, Annie. This case has all the marks of a Nut Cracker puzzle. Poor investigation, clandestine schemes, missing people."

Natra snorted. "Got that right. A nut cracker in a nutshell." She accepted the bottle and called for Mika. I took Jax's coat and helped him put his things in my area. We kissed again.

Ayden's truck rumbled outside. Mika barked three times. Then she went into a frenzy.

Chapter Seventeen

I tracked the barking to Natra's area, with Jax behind me. By the time we got there, they were both gone. Natra shouted from outside. I thought the Audi guy must have made his move. We rushed down the steps.

Ayden stood in my parking lot, looking north. "What's up?" he asked. "Natra just took off."

"I don't know. Mika started barking and—"

I heard a distant *pop*. Then another. Gunshots. I made a move in that direction, but Jax grabbed my arm.

"Careful!" he said. "Are you armed?"

"No. Are you?"

"Yes. Stay behind me."

Mika yelped. My heart stopped. "She must be hurt."

"I'll head up the beach," Ayden said. He patted his coat where he kept his gun. "I'm set."

"Stay close to cover," I warned. To Jax, I said, "I'll get the first-aid kit."

"Got one. Let's go." He pulled me toward his Wrangler. I took the front passenger seat. Jax sped out to the street and turned north.

I could hardly breathe. I rolled down the window to listen for Natra's call or Mika's bark, even just a whine. She had to be okay. I gripped the seat and watched between houses for activity. They couldn't have gotten far. Then I heard a familiar bark. "Mika! Let me out, Jax. I need to get her."

"We're in a Jeep, Annie. Hang on."

"You have to air down."

"I'll stay at the edge. We're good."

He turned off the main road and cut down a lane.

I pointed ahead. "There's a maintenance entrance up there." I directed him, and we came out on the beach. This wasn't exactly permitted, but it was an emergency. I sat forward. "There!"

Natra knelt on the sand beside her dog. I jumped out and ran to them. I saw blood on Mika's fur and dark spots in the sand. "Oh my God! We need to get her in the Jeep!"

Mika tried to lift her head, but Natra held her still.

Ayden ran up. Natra directed him to follow the tracks of the person she'd been chasing.

Jax knelt beside Mika with a first-aid kit. He has a ranch full of animals with various medical needs, so he's always prepared.

Natra pointed. "It's her left front leg. Bullet grazed her."

"Okay, hold her. Keep her quiet."

I scanned the dunes. "I heard two shots."

"I think just one hit," Natra said, her voice shaking. "She'd caught up to him. He was shooting while running, not really looking."

I went to Mika's head while Natra held her side. Mika panted. I caressed and reassured her. "Good girl. So brave."

She whined and tried to get up. Natra spoke in Cherokee, "*E-hlo-we-hi.*" The dog went still but continued to pant.

I gripped Natra's wrist. "We should get her to a vet."

Jax focused on the wound. "You might not find one today. I think I can take care of this. It's not deep. I'll wrap it here, and we can get a better look at the house. Doesn't look broken. Might just need cleaning and stitches."

A tear rolled down Natra's cheek. She wiped it away.

"What happened?" I asked.

"Someone was downstairs, a guy. Inside! Mika heard him. I tried to hold her back, but she got away from me. He ran out and headed to the beach. She ran after him. He shot at her. She still tried to run but couldn't keep up. I caught 'er here."

"That suggests she's not too badly hurt," Jax commented. "Nothing broken. That's good news."

Jax took a syringe from his kit. "This will calm her. I use it on Digger to get him to the vet. It won't hurt her." He administered it. Mika yipped but remained still. Jax wrapped her wounded leg with a clean bandage.

"This guy," Natra said. "He was just a kid. Don't know what he was doin'."

"He was in the house?"

"Yes. The studio."

It sounded like the person I'd seen watching Kip. I looked for Ayden but didn't see him.

Jax made room to get Mika into the Wrangler. He carried her over and placed her in the back. She whined a little. I got in the front passenger seat while Natra sat with Mika. When we arrived at the house, I jumped out.

"Can you handle this?" I asked Jax. "I need to find Ayden."

"I got it."

I went to grab my car fob and my Glock. Mika was in good hands, with both Natra and Jax trained for search-and-rescue operations. Natra had plenty of medical supplies. I hated to leave, but my PI was out there chasing a guy with a gun.

I got in my Jeep Liberty and took off, driving as fast as I dared while scanning the area. Many of the homes were investment properties, rented out during the summer but closed during the off-season, with only occasional owner visits. I saw a few cars in driveways, but none was the blue Audi Jax had spotted. Several narrow lanes turned off the main road. Ayden could be on any of them. I rolled down my driver side window to listen for sounds to guide me, but my heart thumped too loud to hear much. I took a breath. *Get it together, Annie.*

A grey Subaru Baha going south passed me with a lone male driver. He glanced at me, causing a chill. I watched in the review mirror to note the license plate. New Jersey. I pulled over onto a sandy area and texted Jax and Natra. *Audi gone. Lock doors. Stay vigilant.*

A knock on the passenger side window startled me. It was Ayden. I unlocked it and he got in.

"How's Mika?" he asked.

"Hurt, but Jax thinks she'll be okay. I was looking for you."

"He got away. Cut between some properties. Maybe got in a car. I lost his track. But I called a buddy, Sidney Karro, who's on patrol today. I know 'im from my auxiliary work. He's driving around, looking."

"Good, because we'll bring charges if they catch someone. The Audi was here and now it's gone, so he might've gotten in that. Natra said he was in the house, outside the studio where Kip's staying. When I rushed out, I saw the door standing open."

"Was Kip there?"

"No." I turned around while I explained about our run-in this morning.

Ayden squinted. "He went in your dad's office?"

"Yes. Says Dad told him to."

"I don't like this, Annie. I really thought he was a good guy."

"We don't know anything yet."

"Seems like this is all about him being here."

"I agree. Let's hope he comes back."

"Think he won't?"

"Let's see what we find in the studio. I think that person on the dune yesterday *was* watching him. Natra described a kid. That's what I saw, too."

We arrived. Mika was on her dog bed near the fireplace, bandaged and sedated.

"She'll recover," Jax said. "The bullet grazed her. I stitched her up and applied some antibiotic."

I hugged him. "Thank you."

Natra was in the kitchen trying to finish the meal prep. The rolls and dressing had burned. She dumped the rolls in the trash. She looked wiped out.

"I'll do this," I told her. "I don't think there's gonna be any peaceful holiday meal today. Whatever's burned, they'll understand."

She hugged herself and nodded.

"I'll eat that." Ayden pointed to the stuffing. "Don't toss it. I love crusty stuffing." To me, he said, "Sid's on his way here. You should look at Kip's room before he gets here."

Jax came with me.

"I'm so sorry," I said. "I didn't mean to expose you to any risk."

He gave me a sidelong look. "That's our theme, Annie. We'll deal with it together."

The door to the studio apartment stood open. Without touching the doorknob, Jax examined it. "Looks picked, not forced. A bad job, but fixable. He's not a pro."

"Clearly not. He didn't know we had a dog in the house. And it's the middle of the day. He must've seen Kip leave and just acted. I think it's a kid."

I pushed the door with care to avoid messing up possible prints, then entered. Jax stayed just inside the door. I looked around. The bed was made and there was no evidence of ransacking. "Maybe he didn't get in before Mika was on him. Kip's laptop is gone, but he probably took that with him."

I checked the bathroom. "Looks like he left things here." I opened the closet. "I see his suitcase."

Two piles of manila folders on the table drew my attention. They looked undisturbed. I picked one up and opened it. "These are from Concord. Stuff from the attorney. He brought them for me. And some are files from here that I gave Kip to read."

I heard a car drive in—the cop. I texted Ayden to bring him in.

Jax carefully backed out of the room. "I'll watch the dog so Natra can come down and tell him what she saw."

Alone, I looked around. I didn't want to invade Kip's privacy, but he'd seemingly brought danger to this house. Maybe he knew it, maybe he didn't, but *someone* had tried to get in here to look for something. I checked the small galley kitchen and looked under the bed. Nothing there. Three books sat on the nightstand, undisturbed.

I returned to the pile of folders and files. I'd inventoried those I'd assigned to Kip, and they were all here. Still, if something had been removed from a folder, I wouldn't know.

Natra's voice outside confirmed they'd be in here shortly.

I walked to the bed. Something dark stuck out from under the pillow. I moved it and froze. I heard Ayden outside the door, so I pushed the pillow back in place and went out. I hoped my flushed face wouldn't betray me. I'd wanted the cop here. Now I wanted him gone.

Ayden introduced Sidney Karro, a Black patrol officer from the local police department. I shook his hand and pointed at the doorknob. "Looks like our dog heard this and scared him away before he gained full access."

Karro cocked his head. "You're sure?"

"Our guest is away, so I don't yet know if something's missing, but besides the doorknob being jimmied, there's no sign of a disturbance."

"Mind if I have a look?"

I ushered him in. He looked around and took some pictures with his phone. "You're right. Looks undisturbed. We get problems with break-ins around this time of year, usually for unoccupied homes. It's odd happening here, though. You got a lot of cars around."

"Actually, two came in just as he was being chased out, so only two were here, and they were in the garage. Still, the guy was armed. He shot at the dog."

Karro made a note and said, "I've got the pictures and saw the tracks. I'll check the area again for the bullet."

I explained that we had a guest who'd come two days earlier.

"Anyone else know about him?"

"He's from Massachusetts. I'm sure he'll give you a statement when he's back. He's picking up a friend."

"Got some place else he can stay? Can't process this till tomorrow."

"Of course. We'll figure it out."

Karro asked more questions, gave me a card with his number, and finally left. I put the card in my back pocket. Ayden went out to see him off.

I strode over to the bed and grabbed the item under the pillow. It was a zippered leather binder with three intertwined letters embossed on the front—GHG. I unzipped it and saw several transparent plastic loose-leaf pages on three rings—like the one in Gregory's stash that held the map of Vermont. No time to look at them. I took the binder upstairs and hid it. Kip had some explaining to do.

Chapter Eighteen

We set up the meal as a buffet. I'd dropped my plan for a pleasant sit-down at the table. Everyone pitched in while Mika snoozed on her dog bed. When I was alone with Natra, she told me what she'd reported to Officer Karro. "Mika went alert. I saw Jax drive in, so I thought that's what caught her attention. She kept pacing and whining, so I took her to my area, but she ran down the steps and barked so furiously I knew something was wrong. Downstairs, she scratched at the door to get out. I opened it and saw a guy running over the dune. Mika tore after him. So did I. When she gained on him, he turned and shot her." She blinked away fresh tears.

I touched her shoulder. "She'll be okay. We'll take care of her. What did he look like?"

"Short and thin, like a kid. Black sweats, a hoodie. White, I think, but I focused on the gun. He shot and then ran up the beach. He cut over to a house. Did he take anything?"

"We won't know till we talk to Kip, but I think Mika interrupted the guy. He picked the lock. I don't know if he got in very far. Nothing seems out of place, but we'll have to move Kip. If that guy's looking for something, he's not giving up."

"Unless he *got* what he was looking for."

Ayden entered the kitchen. "Kip's back."

I lifted a platter of veggies and dip to take out to the table. "I'll go tell him before he sees the damage. I need to see his reaction."

"Boss?"

I raised an eyebrow. He knew that signal: I had my reasons.

"That guy's full of riddles," Natra said. "We should watch 'im."

"Copy that."

I beckoned for Ayden to follow me, grabbed a coat, and told Jax I'd be right back. I went outside. It felt much colder under the clouds, with sunset just two hours away. I usually like the darkening afternoons of autumn, but on this day it felt ominous. The ocean sounded like it wanted rain.

Kip and a young woman stood outside the Range Rover as he unloaded a bag. She saw me, strode toward me with a warm smile, and held out her hand.

I saw what had caught Kip's interest. Vaughn Ryder's dark eyes were bold and direct, even sassy, despite a petite stature that might suggest timidity. A serious confidence radiated from her. Thick brown hair that formed loose curls around her head and past her shoulders framed a round, defiant face. I sensed she'd persist until she got what she wanted. Under an open denim jacket, her teal silk blouse with a pair of dark slacks softened the impression, but an undercurrent of pushing her way through life stamped her posture.

"Dr. Hunter," she said in a throaty voice, "Vaughn Ryder. Thank you for inviting me into your home. I'm so pleased to meet you." She had only a slight New England accent, as if she'd worked to purge it. A hint of floral perfume confirmed her attention to detail.

I shook her hand. "You're welcome here." I glanced at Kip. Head back, he looked as if he were ready to get back in his car and drive away.

To Vaughn, I said, "This is no way to welcome you, but something has happened that I need to tell Kip." I introduced her to Ayden. "If you don't mind, he'll escort you upstairs to meet the others, and we'll be up soon."

Vaughn looked at Kip in a way that suggested they'd expected something like this but went with Ayden. Kip waited with a wary expression.

"We had a break-in," I told him. "Your room."

His eyes widened. "A break-in?"

"Did you take your laptop with you?"

"I did. It's in the car."

"Good. I was afraid he got that." I gestured for him to accompany me.

Kip locked the Range Rover and fell into step with me. "I locked the door. Was he after the…but how would anyone know?"

"If you mean the ring, I don't know. Maybe someone's monitoring your communications with Dad. I have a burner phone you can use for now. Let's look around, see if anything else was taken, but we've had a cop here. We can't touch anything. They need to process it."

"Why would someone break in?"

"I don't know, Kip, but the guy was armed, and when Mika chased him off, he shot at her."

He stopped. "Oh no! Is she all right?"

"Wounded and stitched up, but we've had quite a day. Whoever this is, he's dangerous. And he must know about you. He knew you were gone."

I pointed to the broken lock before we entered the apartment. Kip stood still and looked around. Then he walked through the room. I watched him, waiting. I thought he'd go straight to the bed, but instead he sorted through the files on the desk. "I think they're all here. I have an inventory. We can check." He opened the closet with a pencil. "Nothing out of place here." He entered the bathroom and came out. "It all looks the same, Annie, just how I left it. Did he actually get in?"

"We don't know. That's why I want you to check."

Kip stood in the middle of the room and shrugged. "I didn't bring much. If he got in, maybe he didn't see what he thought was here. I'm so sorry, Annie. I don't know who did this, but I don't want to cause trouble. I'll leave after dinner."

I crossed my arms. "Forget that, Kip. I need your help. This might be about what our fathers did here, so we'll tackle this together. Ayden will check your car for trackers, and we'll have you stay at the Duck House. Tell me again, why did Lang want you to take the ring out of here?"

"He said it would sever the rest of us from—as he put it—this mess."

"What mess?"

"Whatever my dad—Gregory—brought here."

"Did you tell Vaughn about the ring?"

"Of course. She wants to see it. If there's DNA, it really could help her."

"Did you take anything else from the safe?"

He shook his head. "No."

"You didn't see that binder?"

Kip blinked. He looked confused.

"The one you're looking for. It has the Gray Hollow Group insignia on the cover."

His eyes widened. "You found it! So, it's here!"

"Yes. I found it."

"Where?"

"What do you mean?"

"Was it in the attic?"

I peered at him. "Kip, it was under your pillow." I pointed to the bed. "Right there."

He looked at the bed, astonished. "*My* pillow? Here?"

"You didn't put it there?"

"No."

My heart thumped as I realized what this meant. We stared at each other before I said, "That guy…he didn't come here to *take* something."

Kip finished my thought. "He *brought* something. For me."

Chapter Nineteen

We returned to the great room. Kip went over to sit with Vaughn. She handed him a plate of food she'd prepared for him. He sat so his leg touched hers. She grabbed his arm and said something in a low voice. He shook his head. These two, I surmised, were more than friends.

Kip had wanted to see the ledger, but I'd said, no, we'd look at it together later, when things were quiet. He'd resisted but had no real choice. The mystery vexed me. Someone had gotten into private GHG records. The members of the Gray Hollow Group I knew about were dead or inaccessible. Getting Dad to talk was now pressing.

Natra motioned that she'd made a plate for me as well. She'd also covered our charts on the whiteboard and closed the curtains, a wise move, considering how visible we'd be on a darkening afternoon to anyone outside. The ocean view would soon be obscured, anyway. Rain tapped on the window. I sat next to Jax on the couch. He gave my back a reassuring rub. We'd arranged the seats around the fireplace. Despite my unease with the day's events, this moment felt cozy.

"Great mushroom stuffing," Ayden said. "And the turkey's just right."

He'd taken the burnt part of the stuffing to leave the rest for others. I can always count on him to lighten a mood.

"Thanks," I said. "Looks like we salvaged the important stuff."

The others chimed in with compliments before I cleared my throat to get their attention. "I have things to say about what's happened here today, but let's enjoy a few minutes of peace first. I'm so pleased to have you all here as my guests."

Ayden nodded. Jax nudged me. Natra remained withdrawn. Someone had hurt her dog because Kip was here. She wasn't going to forget that. He'd apologized to her, but she still simmered.

Despite my request, our attempt at small talk felt strained. Things had to get sorted. We'd been spied on and violated. We didn't know why or what might come next. But I watched Vaughn. She had solid social skills. She sat across from me and Jax, and she liked to talk. She seemed to know something about each of us, as if Kip had coached her, yet she engaged us with a smooth, natural manner. Jax and Ayden seemed charmed.

Vaughn asked Jax about his law practice. He offered a brief rundown of his specialty in juvenile justice.

"Could've used you when I was a kid," she commented. "You work in this state?"

"My practice is in Georgia, but I have some cases here."

Vaughn sat straighter. "I worked with an attorney in Raleigh. Roy Nozer. Heard of him?"

Jax nodded. "I had a case with him once. He was effective. Smart. Has a good reputation."

"Maybe, but he just backed out on me. I think a cop got to him. Scared 'im off. He was all on board with our case, had all kinds of ideas, then last week he said he got too busy."

"Pro bono?"

"Nope. I said I could pay his fee. I paid some already. He gave it back."

Jax frowned. "That's unusual."

Vaughn seemed to be angling toward something. Ayden glanced at me. He'd caught it, too. I moved my foot against Jax's in warning. *Don't get involved.*

He ignored me. "What makes you think he was scared off?"

"Because that same guy approached me. Warned me to steer clear. Said I didn't know what I was doing."

"Which agency?"

"FBI. It's a multi-state case." Vaughn looked around. "I'm sure everyone here knows who my father is. I'm trying to prove he's innocent." She returned her gaze to Jax. "This agent's been featured in a book as a super profiler. He doesn't want anyone to see the holes. I need an attorney who can stand up to him. Are you interested? I have a FundMe site. I can pay."

She had to mean Broward. I opened my mouth to interrupt this. Jax beat me. "I appreciate that, Vaughn, but I have a full caseload. I can offer suggestions."

Vaughn wasn't deterred. "Maybe you can take it just long enough to—"

"Vaughn!" Kip nudged her and shook his head.

"I just—"

"Not now."

She looked at me. They'd discussed me. They had a plan.

Vaughn drew up her shoulders but seemed to know she'd overstepped. I put my plate on the coffee table and said, "Looks like it's time to wrangle the elephant in the room."

For a moment, I heard only Mika's quiet snoring and the crackling fire. Jax's slightly amused expression seemed to say *I brought the right wine.*

"I'm glad we're all here together," I said. "I'd originally planned just a nice holiday dinner with friends, but a lot has happened, some of it pressing." I looked at Kip and Vaughn. She watched me as if waiting for her cue. "It seems that someone's been watching the house since Kip arrived, and today an armed man broke in. He hurt Mika. We don't know if he'll be back or if there might be others."

Kip raised his chin. Natra dropped her right hand to Mika's head.

I continued. "I invited Kip here to help me locate something for my father, Lang. With Gregory Hawkins, Kip's father, Lang managed a secret trust, the Gray Hollow Group. One member, Ella Hawkins, disappeared with her husband. They were likely abducted and murdered. Gregory apparently linked this abduction with other missing or murdered couples in various places, including here—close to Lang. This all started nine years ago."

Vaughn sat up straight. She put down her plate. I gestured toward her. "Your father was arrested around six years ago and confessed. I'm aware of the agent you're talking about, Reid Broward. He claimed Ketch Ryder fit his profile, and he consulted on the interrogation, so he's got something to lose if you prove him wrong. You, Vaughn, think Ketch made a false confession, and we have some evidence from Gregory's records that this could be true."

She nodded and clasped her hands together as if to keep herself quiet.

I glanced around. "Gregory came here five years ago to persuade Lang, who'd left the Gray Hollow Group, to help him." I nodded toward Kip. "Kip was here, then. He heard some of their discussions, which sent him on his own research path and led him to Vaughn. The reason I've invited Vaughn here is, well, it's Thanksgiving, but also to hear her part. Ordinarily, we'd take our time with an investigation like this, but we need to act quickly. If Ketch Ryder isn't the killer, then that person is still out there. Maybe close. If he guesses what we're up to, he'll try to stop us."

Vaughn couldn't contain herself. "I should say something. I have much to tell you about my father, things you should know."

Chapter Twenty

I hadn't finished, but I nodded for her to speak. Kip watched me, probably wondering why I'd said nothing about the binder or ring.

Vaughn pulled her arms together and took a deep breath. She looked first at Kip. "You helped a lot." To the rest of us, she said, "Kip told me Ella Hawkins helped my mother, Ivy, escape my father, Ketch—we called them by their first names. All we knew was that Ivy ran off and took my brother, Clay, but left me with Ketch. His mother took me in, and that's where I was when he was arrested. We lived in an intentional community, they called it. Survivalists with a mission. We lived off the grid, raised our own food, all that. You know who Jordan Locke is. He was part of our community, a traveler. He came and went, visiting different branches of our group along the East Coast to keep us all connected. Ketch admired him, wanted to be like him. It's important you know this, because I think that's why Ketch confessed."

I blinked. "Sorry. You think your dad's trying to please him?"

"Not to please. To *be* him. Jordan's the killer. Ketch knew it. That's why the cops found the news items on his laptop about the missing couples. Ketch studied Jordan's moves. He even stole some of the victims' items and offered false information to throw cops off Jordan's trail."

Ayden waved his fork. "Or maybe he was planning one himself."

Vaughn shook her head. "Don't think so. When you meet him—" She swung toward me. "You're going to meet him, right? You'll see. He can't plan. He can't think straight. I'll show you his letters. I kept them. They're all scrambled. He can barely think a day ahead."

I tried to interrupt. "I hadn't—"

"The way I see it, Ketch doesn't have…he's not all there. Never was. You can't tell from one minute to the next what he'll be like, whether he'll make you a cake or wallop you. I've got scars. He got worse when Clay came along. That's why Ivy took him away. Ketch beat her up a lot, too."

"Why wouldn't they have found him incompetent to confess?" I asked.

"His confession sounded good. It was only a judge who decided. They didn't use any experts."

I nodded. Some judges adopt this role. And some make poor decisions about a defendant's mental state or ability to proceed.

"I'll show you everything," Vaughn continued. "If I can just get Ketch tested, I'd have proof he's got brain damage. They've been blocking me."

I cocked my head. "Vaughn, how do you know Locke's the killer?"

"Got proof. Ketch described what he saw and what Locke wanted. I have a recording."

"From a prison call?"

"Before they got 'im. I didn't know what he was talkin' about till later. It just sounded crazy, but I figured it out."

I feared this wasn't actual proof. "Was he delusional?"

"No. Had a head injury, a bad one. It scrambles him up sometimes. He got shot. Bullet's still in there. I want his brain scanned. That's what I'm studying."

"Do you have this recording?"

"Of course, yeah."

"And he'd verify this? He'd admit saying these things?"

Vaughn made a face. "Can't say for sure. Broward's trying to stop me. He visits Ketch an' talks 'im out of it. Ketch caves pretty fast under pressure. But I'll try."

I noticed that Natra had her phone out. She was recording this. I sat back. "Okay. Keep going."

Vaughn glanced at Kip. "Sorry I couldn't tell you this over the phone, but I have to be careful. They watch me. I didn't know you, not really, till this week."

He made a dismissive gesture. "Of course."

Vaughn continued. "There was a group, three or four who'd go off together with Locke on hunting trips. They called 'em soul journeys."

Ayden leaned forward. "A group. Are these others involved in the murders?"

"They might be. They had secret meetings. They'd come back with weird ideas, like believing we all had to fast for a week, or the kids had to be chained up. Ketch followed orders, but he'd always take it too far tryin' to prove himself. He's a weak man. Ivy must've said something to someone because he got arrested for child neglect and domestic abuse. She wouldn't press charges, but she went to a shelter. She came back but only to pack up Clay's things and take 'im away."

"Is this Jordan Locke still around?" I asked.

"He is. Keeps tryin' to find out what I know."

I looked at Kip. His mouth formed a tight line. I turned back to Vaughn. "When did you last see him?"

"Yesterday. He approached me in Norfolk." She looked at Kip. "In fact, he asked about Kip. I didn't know they'd met."

So, he was close. This alarmed me.

"I didn't see him there," Kip said. "Vaughn told me, though. Seems like we need to do something. When you go see Ketch—"

"Kip, I haven't said I'd do that."

"I thought you'd want to figure it out. It helps you, too."

"Me? How?"

"It…um…kind of…maybe it could clear Lang. Show he's not part of this. That's why—"

Kip's car alarm blasted. Everyone froze. Then Vaughn jumped up. "The recording! We left it in the car!"

Chapter Twenty-One

Vaughn ran to the sliding door with Kip behind her. Ayden grabbed his coat, drew his gun, and followed them. I strode to the window, but Jax pulled me away. "Don't make yourself a target."

He went out, letting rain blow in. I stepped onto the deck and closed the door behind me. Below, Ayden tried to get Vaughn and Kip away from the noisy car. A back door was open, and Kip was yelling, but the ocean's noise blocked the words.

Natra opened the door to hand me a jacket. I accepted it and walked to the north side of the balcony. I didn't need to be on the ground. I had more perspective on the second floor. I scanned the beach as far as I could make out and thought I saw a figure. I held my hand up to focus my eyes. Kip finally silenced the alarm.

Ayden looked up at me. "See anything?"

I pointed north. "Out there. I think someone's moving away."

Jax had his Wrangler in motion, and Ayden jumped in. They took off.

Natra came out. "I called Karro. He'll come by."

Kip was still in the back seat. Vaughn stood nearby.

"She's getting drenched," I said. "I'll get her inside."

"I'll find something she can wear."

I went down the slippery steps and approached Vaughn. "Come inside. We have a cop on his way."

"They got it," she said. "Kip's laptop. We copied the recording onto it."

"But you have the original."

"Yes, but now he'll know what we have. He'll make Ketch recant it."

Kip came out of the Range Rover. "They broke a window. I should've brought the laptop inside."

I gestured. "Let's get out of the rain."

Headlights caught my attention. Officer Karro arrived. I sent Kip and Vaughn up the steps and invited Karro inside to take a statement.

Natra offered him some coffee and pie, which he accepted. I gave him an uncut pie to take back to the station for everyone else on holiday duty.

Kip told him what happened. "When we got back, I went to look at the break-in damage downstairs in my room. I left my laptop in the back seat."

"Anything taken from your room?"

Kip glanced at me. "Not that I could see."

"You lock your car?"

"Yes. They broke a window. The alarm went off."

"Was the laptop visible?"

Kip nodded. "I meant to take it out. Forgot."

"Any idea who might do this? Someone you know?"

Kip shook his head.

"Know its value?"

"It's new. Just got it." He told him how much he'd paid.

Karro wrote it down before he asked, "Was there something on it that could help us figure this out?"

I saw Vaughn, behind Karro, subtly shake her head.

Kip shrugged. "I'm just visiting. I don't know anyone around here." It was a safe response. He'd told the truth without giving anything away. "There's a sticker, though, right on top. A skull that says Skeleton Crew. It's distinct."

Karro asked a few more questions and made a comment about off-season break-ins before he went out to take photos. I went with him.

"Doesn't make much sense, Dr. Hunter," he said. "With all these houses sitting empty, and people clearly in yours, and they come at yours twice in one day? Maybe your young visitor knows more than he's saying. Strikes me that way."

"I don't think he knows who did it. He was surprised about the earlier incident. And no one wants to lose a laptop or get an expensive car damaged like this."

"You have any surveillance video set up here?"

"What I have for the apartment I use only during tourist season. In fact, it got corroded from salt this summer, and I haven't replaced it. The other camera's set up for the front, but maybe we got something. Ayden can look through it. Here he is now."

Ayden and Jax drove in. Ayden got out while Jax parked. I let Ayden talk to Karro. Out here in the rain and wind, with the ocean roar, was no place to offer ideas about our situation. We'd need a police report for Kip's insurance, but this officer couldn't do much if Jordan Christopher Locke and his crew were targeting us.

Jax and I went up. Natra and Kip were on a computer.

Vaughn, standing nearby, looked at me. "His laptop's protected. They're trying to remotely wipe it."

"Is the original recording in a safe place?"

She nodded. "In a bank deposit box, and a copy in my hotel room. But we put my documents about Ketch on Kip's laptop so we could show you. If they get into the contents, they'll know my strategy."

Kip looked at me. "Not to mention some legal records for you from Concord. I should've grabbed it."

"It's no one's fault," I said. "I distracted you with the break-in. And that wasn't about theft like we thought, it was about leaving something here."

I felt everyone's eyes on me.

"I'll get it."

By the time I was back, Ayden had come in. "He's gonna notify a detective. Said we should leave the outside spotlights on tonight and use every videocam we have." To Kip, he said, "I patched your broken window with cardboard and tape. It'll keep the rain out."

I tapped the binder against my left hand. "All right, everyone. Here's what our earlier visitor left behind." I held it up. Natra and Kip stopped their work. "This is a record from the Gray Hollow Group, the binder from Gregory Hawkins."

Vaughn gasped. "How did you get that?"

I looked at her. "What d'you mean?"
"Ivy…she took it when she left."

Chapter Twenty-Two

Vaughn held out her hand. "Let me see it."

"I'll hold it," I told her. "I have gloves. No one else should handle this if it's relevant to a crime."

Vaughn stuck out her chin. "I've already handled it. I'll tell you what's on the first page. There's an elaborate design in black ink of a gate. It's by someone named Merlin."

Kip's eyes widened. "That's Ella Steadman's nickname. I heard my dad say it. It's about her Hawkins name. A Merlin hawk. Can I see it?"

I waved the binder. "This is a record for the Gray Hollow Group, so it's evidence of Ella's abduction."

Vaughn shook her head. "No, you're wrong. It was in our house. Ivy took it when she left. I remember Ketch being mad it was gone. He cussed her out. Then he cussed *me* out for letting her take it. As if I had any control."

Ayden looked at me. "Maybe that's how she got Ella's help. She took it to Ella."

Kip crossed his arms. "Then who put it in my room?"

Vaughn shook her head. "Not Jordan, that's for sure. He wouldn't break in. He'd just give it to you. Nope. You said it was a guy? Has to be my brother, Clay."

I frowned at her. "Your brother?"

"He doesn't want me doin' this, helpin' Ketch." She pointed to the binder. "Last time I saw it, Clay had it. He was tryin' to prove I was wrong about Ketch."

Natra stood. "Your brother shot my dog?"

"He might've. Not meaning to, but I can't say he didn't. He's sixteen 'n' sometimes stupid."

"Does he drive a blue Audi?" Ayden said.

She shrugged. "Think he has a truck."

"What's his build?" I asked.

"Scrawny. Maybe five-seven or eight."

"That fits, but why would he leave it here?"

Vaughn took a breath. "I wanted his help with Ketch, but he just got mad. He knows Jordan. In fact, Jordan paid off Ketch's old truck so Clay could have it. Clay said I shouldn't try to get Ketch out." She looked at Kip. "So, if he gave you these records, he wants you to stop helpin'. Ketch circled and marked things that make 'im look guilty." To me, she said, "Put it on the table. I'll show you something."

I looked at Jax, the attorney in the room. He seemed fascinated with her tale. "It's been through so many hands it's likely useless as physical evidence," he said. "Any claim in court could be challenged. What matters is Vaughn as a witness and the recording she has."

"Let's be careful, anyway," Natra said. "I'll get gloves."

I placed the binder on the table, unzipped it, and opened it to the gate drawing in ink, signed by "Merlin." The name seemed vaguely familiar to me. The gate looked like cast iron. A design in the center drew my attention. "This is the GHG emblem."

Kip leaned in. "That gate's at the north entrance to Dacretown, but it's all corroded now."

Vaughn bent over the binder. "I've touched all these pages, so it doesn't matter. I'll be careful." She flipped through several until she found a map of New England. She pointed. "See here? This area. Ketch circled it. The cabin's here. I've been in it. Ketch said he brought things here for people who were tied up."

"We made that connection," I said. "It's near Arrowhead Mountain Lake. Gregory had a Vermont map among his papers. It was in a plastic protector like these, so it was probably once in this binder. We think it's linked to the arrowhead drawing in Ketch's suicide note."

"I'd like to see the note," Jax said.

Natra dumped a pile of evidence gloves on the table and sat at the computer to pull up the note on the large screen. I pointed at the arrowhead.

"And I think the horse head is Nags Head," Kip added.

Jax studied it. "These might follow a pattern. Nags Head. Arrowhead. What other places have 'head' in the name? Hilton Head, Frozen Head, Bald Head Island."

"Marblehead," Kip offered.

Jax leaned in and pointed at one we hadn't figured out. "That image looks vaguely like Caesars Head. I helped on a search and recovery there last year."

"What's Caesar's Head?" Kip asked.

"A wooded area, noted for its view. It's on the border of North and South Carolina, so it fits geographically."

Natra found an image of the mountain and projected it. An overlook showed a distinct outline on a distant mountain.

"It kind of resembles a face," I said. "And it looks like the line he drew. Good catch. Nags Head. Arrowhead. Caesars Head. What can we—"

"Gotcha!" Ayden moved closer. "We look up unidentified remains found in these areas."

Jax nodded. "Exactly."

Natra's face lit up. She pointed at the stick figure. "I bet that's a bucking horse or cow. Buckhead. The couple from Richmond Hill lived in a development called Buckhead. Also, there's a Buckhead in Atlanta."

Ayden gestured to her. "Let's get on NamUs. Start with Arrowhead."

I felt the energy rise. We had a lead, maybe several. Ayden and Natra went to her private office to access our NamUs account on the computer there. The National Missing and Unidentified Persons System was a centralized database we'd used many times, especially for cases we'd picked up from Dad's files. Participating medical examiners and coroners provide info about their unidentified remains, sometimes a lot of info.

I turned to Kip. "What do you know? You came looking for this binder. Is this the one you saw as a kid?"

"I'm sure it's the same one. I remember the tooled cover. Dad took it from me before I could see much, but I saw that gate drawing. I didn't know then what it was."

"So, Gregory or someone else in the GHG knew about the cabin's location and thought it was significant enough to keep this map in the binder."

"Could be a shared ledger," Jax suggested. "It's for that group. Maybe they passed it around. It's loose-leaf, so pages can be added and removed." He pointed to the whiteboard, still covered. "Can we use that? We should establish a chronology."

"We started one," I said. "We can add to it."

I turned the rolling whiteboard around, revealing a clean board on the other side, and picked up a green marker. "Here's the gist. We have three missing couples, likely deceased, and four people who seem to know something: Ketch Ryder, Jordan Locke, Gregory Hawkins, and Lang Hunter. We have a suicide note with suggestive symbols, which we think identify victim abduction points or burial sites. We have Ryder's confession, possibly false, and we have a list of circumstances that implicate Locke" I gestured toward Vaughn and Kip. "We now know he's a traveler who might link these locations. And we know he wants these records." I tapped on our chart. "We also have a GHG binder that seems to have passed through different hands: Ella, Gregory, Ketch, Ivy, and now us."

"When did it all start?" Jax asked.

"Nine years ago, with a couple from Richmond Hill, Georgia—Ralph and Sharon Pryor. The Buckhead development adds support that this is the first abduction. Like a trailhead. Then, two years later, we have the Lovatos from here in Nags Head. Then a year after that, the Steadmans went missing from New Hampshire."

"No 'head' in the name of their town?"

"No, but maybe they ended up at Arrowhead. Just before their abduction happened, Ivy left Ketch. She took the GHG binder, but we don't know when or how Ketch acquired it."

"So, Jordan Locke is a common factor for the first and third incidents," Jax said.

Vaughn nodded. "Definitely!"

I continued. "Ketch and Ivy knew Locke. He's a member of the Ryders' community, although he's based in Georgia, which puts him close to the first missing couple. He's an attorney, by the way."

Jax folded his arms. "I'll look 'im up."

"Locke was Ella's first husband, and he knew Gregory and possibly Lang."

"And my dad was involved with Ella in some way," Kip added.

I glanced at him. "That could be important. Ivy left Ketch, and your dad moved out just before the Steadmans went missing. They had Ella in common."

I returned my focus to the chart. "A few months later, Ketch was arrested, and they linked him to the Lovatos' stolen credit card. He confessed to the abductions and murders of four, possibly six people, giving details for what happened to the Lovatos. He directed cops to a stash of items related to the victims. He also suggested a location for the Steadmans' bodies, but they weren't found. Neither were the Lovatos. He didn't name the third couple."

Vaughn touched the binder. "He marked maps, though. Arrowhead's near the location he described for the Steadman burial. If Ivy took the ledger before they disappeared, that location was pre-planned."

"Except they weren't there," I reminded her.

"Or the location was changed, and Ketch didn't know it. Look, he circled other things."

Kip nodded. "On the interrogation video, he seems puzzled about cops not finding them."

"That's interesting," I said. "If Ketch was trying to become Locke, he'd study him and imitate him. Locke might've realized what he was up to. There's no doubt Ketch is a loose cannon. He wants to stake a claim, but him sending cops to dump sites could inadvertently point to Locke, too."

Jax offered a suggestion. "Maybe Locke exploited Ryder's hero worship to set him up."

I looked at the map. Another circle designated an area near Concord. It was in the right place for Dacretown. I turned the page and saw a condensed map of the East Coast. Half a dozen circles marked areas that now concerned us. I pointed. "Here's one in the Lowcountry, possibly Hilton Head. We should look for cases of other couples missing since Ryder's arrest. Gregory made a list of five potentially linked incidents. Some might be on later dates." I looked at Kip. "Locke told you about a hunting club. He said your dad was in it. Do you know who else might've been?"

"It should be in his notes."

"I didn't see any mention of it in the pages we read."

"Maybe in here, then." Kip put on gloves and flipped back to an earlier page in the binder, then to another page. He paused, blinked, and stood back.

"What is it?" I asked. "What do you see?"

He pointed. "That name. G-Man. That's Mark Gardiner." He looked at me in alarm. "My cousin. My *boss*. That's what they call 'im. He introduced me to Jordan…and he knew I was coming here. He knew *why*. Is he part of this?"

Chapter Twenty-Three

I looked at the page. It seemed like an official addition, signed off by a member. "You didn't realize?"

Kip shook his head. "What does it mean?"

"I read that," Vaughn said. "G-Man must be an attorney. It's a copy of a legal document."

"He's married to an attorney," I told her. "I use her for my legal affairs in Concord."

Kip looked like he'd been blasted from all sides. "I don't know how this paper could be in here."

"Maybe your cousin's our mystery GHG member. Didn't he start your Skeleton Crew?"

Kip nodded. "Jordan must've gotten to 'im."

"Maybe. But Jordan obviously didn't get whatever he's looking for." I turned to Vaughn. "Can you contact your brother? Maybe he'll tell you why he brought this binder here."

"I can try. He's been elusive. Don't know what he's even doing here." She went over to her purse.

Natra and Ayden returned. "We have something," Natra said. She went to the conference area computer. "I'll show you."

Ayden gave us the gist. "One of the students in the forensic art course I went to last month is from western Vermont. He's a cop who can draw, so he works with the cold case team. I texted him. I know it's a holiday, but he responded. He gave me some info to help narrow our search of unidentified bodies for the time frame and location. He'll search as well when he gets a minute."

Natra pulled up a NamUs webpage and projected it to the screen. "You can see how we filtered the thousands of available cases by using demographics, circumstances, date range, race, et cetera. We weren't too restrictive, so we got a lot of results. From those, we zeroed in on locations between the abduction and potential dump sites. We found this. About a year after the Steadmans went missing, a kayaker came across a skull in some shallow water. It was sent to an anthropologist, who identified it as an adult male Caucasian. Most likely a murder victim, she said, based on a large hole in the skull. There's no record of more remains being found. They made an extensive search."

"Just the skull?" Jax asked.

"Yes," Ayden said. "The *head*."

"Probably scattered the parts."

"Could be. We'll see if the cold case team had a drawing or clay bust done. If not, I'll ask for photos and draw it myself."

"Great work, you two," I said. "It seems promising."

Vaughn came over to Kip and showed him her phone. "Clay wants me to meet 'im. He's not far away."

Kip got up. "Does he have my laptop?"

"He said he didn't come back here."

I frowned. "Is he with Jordan Locke?"

Vaughn shook her head. "Didn't say."

"Wouldn't Ivy have told him how dangerous Jordan is?"

"She left Ketch cuz he beat her. I don't know what she knew about Jordan."

"She knew Ella."

Vaughn's mouth formed a stubborn line. "Clay's my brother. You have stuff here he should see. It'll change his mind about Ketch. Then he'll help."

I peered at her. "Vaughn, does Ketch even want your help?"

She looked at Kip before she said, "It's not right, him bein' in there."

They were doing this without the inmate's cooperation. Just asking for trouble.

Vaughn said something I couldn't hear to Kip and put her hand out. He shook his head. She leaned in. "Please."

"I'll take you."

"Okay, but just drop me off." Vaughn looked at me. "Is there a bathroom I can use?"

I directed her down the hall past the kitchen. She grabbed her coat and purse.

When she was out of the room, I asked Kip, "Should we bring that kid here? He could probably answer some questions."

He scowled. "She wants to take my car. I said no. I'll get her to tell me where—"

The sound of a door slamming downstairs made us freeze. Kip went to the chair where he'd left his jacket and searched the pocket. "She got my key fob." He ran to the sliding door, opened it, and went out on the balcony. I followed him in time to see the Range Rover's taillights in the dark.

"She won't just take it," I said. "She'll bring it back."

"I don't know." He sounded deflated. "I hardly know her. Her dad's a liar. Maybe she is, too."

Jax came out, his coat on. He noted the empty parking spot. "Kip, got anything on your phone that links it to the car?"

"A tracker for the GPS."

"Let's go."

They descended the steps. Despite how cold it was, I followed. "Sit in the front," I told Kip. I got in back. Jax started the engine and turned on the heat. Kip tapped an app on his phone. "North, on 12, toward Duck. She's moving fast."

"There won't be much traffic," I said. "We can catch up."

Kip watched his phone, shaking his head. I patted him on the back. I knew he felt duped…again.

"Looks like she's turning right, toward the beach."

Jax sped up. On the main road, we saw a few cars coming toward us. No one was in front.

Kip kept his focus on his phone. "Now she's going left."

"Some of these side roads just circle back to the main road," I said. "The only reason she'd go down one is to look for a specific house."

"Or to lose us," Jax said. "Let's try to anticipate her." He slowed down.

Kip handed me the phone. "You know this area. What's she doing?"

I looked at the moving object. I wasn't sure. "I think she's back on 12, close to the Scarborough Lane shops. They're all closed."

My phone rang. I handed Kip his and answered mine.

"Boss?" It was Ayden. "In my truck. Which way?"

"Stay where you are, in case she doubles back. We're tracking her."

"Copy."

Kip sat up. "Wait! Wait! She stopped." He looked up and pointed left.

Jax followed his direction. We found the white Range Rover in a parking lot off the main road on the left. Kip jumped out and ran to it. Jax and I got out as Kip opened the driver's door. He spread his hands, looked at us, and said, "She's gone. Left the key."

I went over to see for myself. The interior light showed an empty car. Kip grabbed the fob off the seat. I looked around. "The boardwalk's over there. If she went on it, she could get off at any number of spots and lose us."

Jax strode past the car, his eyes on the ground. "Here," he said. "There's a dry spot. Someone was waiting for her. She ditched this car and left in another one."

"And now we can't follow her," I said.

Kip got into the Range Rover. He opened the glove compartment and checked around the seats. He emerged with something in his hand. "She left her phone." He pressed it to light up the screen. "It's unlocked."

"Check the texts," Jax urged him. "Someone communicated with her."

I leaned in. "She must've left the car here, so we'd see it. She knew we'd come looking. It would've been easy to hide it, but she didn't."

Kip sat in the driver's seat to use the light. He shook his head. "There's only one text here. It's from her. She sent it to herself, so we'd see it." Kip held the phone up to me.

Sorry. Don't call cops. C in danger.

Chapter Twenty-Four

We arrived back at my place just after Ayden. He'd seen no one. Kip had insisted we call the police, but Jax nixed this. Vaughn might have gone willingly. He wanted to dig into her phone before we involved law enforcement.

I agreed. "She got texts from Clay. She must've deleted them, maybe to slow us down. We should be able to restore them."

We filled in Natra and Ayden before I handed Natra the phone for digital analysis. "We need the recently deleted texts, maybe from the past few days. See what you can do." Natra took it to her office.

Kip slumped into a chair. I sat near him. "Think about whether she told you anything that might give us an idea."

He gave a weak gesture of assent. I guessed he was processing the many jarring revelations he'd received, not to mention a lost laptop and damage to his car. If he'd gotten involved because he liked Vaughn, he probably realized the things he'd risked for someone who might've played him.

Ayden and Jax were at the table. Ayden gestured for me to join them. I went over to see two printouts of a skull, front and side, to which someone had begun to add soft tissue thickness markers. From the cranium to the chin and across the lower orbits, pencil erasers of different lengths had been glued. I thought it resembled a creepy Halloween mask, a skull with weirdly placed pimples.

Ayden tapped one. "Natra just got these off that cold case website. Looks like someone started it. Some markers are missing, but nothing crucial. There's enough here to let me work up a 2-D drawing."

"You can do that?" Jax asked.

"He can," I told him. "I just sent Ayden to an intensive workshop in Texas taught by the legendary forensic artist, Karen Taylor. Know of her?"

Jax nodded. "I've seen her textbook. Groundbreaking."

"The course was about producing identifiable images from decomposed or skeletal remains."

"Learned a lot," Ayden said. "Hopefully, I can apply it to this case."

I peered at the computer screen. "There's also a drawing by a police artist, but it's rough."

Ayden held up a hand. "No input. I'll do my own first. I'll get my kit."

When he left the room, I said to Jax, "I've taught him about cognitive distortions from prior knowledge and exposure. For this to work, he can't already know what the victim looks like or see anyone else's artistic interpretation."

"He's talented. Can't wait to see what he produces."

Mika whined. Jax went to check on her. "She probably needs to go out," he said. "I'll carry her down the steps to keep weight off that foot. Then we'll change the bandage."

Kip had wrapped his arms around himself. I brought him a glass of wine. "Any ideas?"

He raised his chin. "Just that she set me up."

"We don't know that. You're a good guy, Kip. You try to help. But you and I, we both have family legacies that made us targets. Let's remember what's at stake. Our dads dug us in. Yours is dead, mine is silent. But they knew this guy, Locke, and he seems to have a vendetta. We could both be in danger. You brought Vaughn here, so she hadn't planted a car somewhere, and I was the one who suggested she contact her brother. She didn't plan that."

His face softened. "How can we find her?"

"She'll have to contact us. For now, let's take it at face value. She was baited, maybe by Clay or maybe Locke. I think she knew who she was meeting, or she wouldn't have gone."

"What about my cousin? How's he part of this?"

"You'll have to ask him that. In fact, call 'im. It's Thanksgiving. He won't be surprised to hear from you. Then you can feel him out. Did he probe you about your trip here?"

"He knew I wanted Dad's papers. And he said he wants to see them when I get them, but he didn't pressure me."

"When was the last time you saw Jordan Locke?"

"He was in the shop recently, but I didn't see 'im. He had lunch with Mark."

"Then you need to be careful not to mention him when you talk with Mark. Maybe say we found some papers and see what he knows about the GHG."

Kip nodded.

Ayden brought in his sketch kit with two pieces of 12x18-inch Masonite board. He placed these side by side, used a T-square to position the front and side skull photos, and carefully taped them to the boards.

"Can I watch?" Kip asked.

Ayden nodded. "Yeah, sure. It's interesting."

Kip moved to a chair near the table but maintained a respectful distance. So did I. Jax came in with Mika. The dog went back to her bed near the fireplace. Jax stood over Ayden for a few minutes before he said he'd help Natra with the phone. I set out pieces of pie on a counter that separated the kitchen and dining area.

Ayden placed transparent sheets of vellum over each photo. I'd seen him do this before, but he'd said the workshop had given him greater precision. This was his first test. He taped the vellum at the top to hold it in place.

"When I'm done," he said, "I'll get this other guy from the class to check my work. I've already told him the context."

"Nice of him to work on a holiday," I commented.

"He thanked me for it. Said his house is full of his wife's family. He's happy for the break."

Part of the skull along the top right side was missing. The anthropologist had determined from a fracture pattern that this came from being hit rather than from animal activity. The accompanying report listed a few scenarios, with probable cause of death from a blunt instrument. It wasn't possible to identify what kind, but it was consistent with a blow from a hammer or rock. I winced.

Ayden drew some lines I could barely see—guidelines, I assumed—then placed a quarter inside the hollow right eye socket. With this, he traced a circle. He did the same with the left socket. From these, he sketched the eyes. "Can't tell the color from what we have," he said. "Karen told us to use ambiguity, and she likes to make irises look hazel so they're not too dark or too light. It's all about eliciting recognition from someone who knows the decedent, so you try to capture a feature peculiar to them." He made some measurements from the nasal orifice on both photos to calculate the nose length and width, using something from the side view to assist with its angle.

Dark hair strands had been found in a nest near the skull, which helped to show the decedent's hair length, texture, and color.

"Gotta guess on the style," Ayden said. "He's an older guy, according to the anthropologist. The teeth are worn, and the sutures fused, which makes him forty to fifty, give or take. You can figure out a possible hairstyle from that, as long as you're accurate on the time-since-death estimate."

As Ayden sketched, the features took shape. He shaded the sides, forehead, jaw, and cheekbones for a sense of dimension based on the skull. "His nose hooks to his right," Ayden commented. "And the ears are kind of low." As he drew, erased, and repaired his work, I saw Kip's eyes widen. He knew what Clark Steadman had looked like. I put a finger to my lips.

Finally, Ayden sat back. He has a knack for replication once he's seen someone, but this was free form, with some guessing. "I'll send what I have to this guy in Vermont. See what he thinks. He already has copies of the skulls." He took photos of his work and texted them.

Kip looked at me. I shook my head. Still, his expression told me we'd probably hit the mark.

I went to the back and checked on Jax and Natra. "Anything?"

Jax looked up. "That girl has a good eraser app, but we're piecing something together."

"Ayden's about done if you want to come and see this. I think we've got a case breaker."

"We'll be right there," Natra said. "Just want to extract the right stuff."

When I came back, I saw Kip on the floor near Mika, eating a slice of pumpkin pie. He looked up. "Can she have any?"

"Better ask Natra."

"I texted Mark. He hasn't responded."

"Where's Ayden?"

"Took stuff to his truck."

Natra, Jax, and Ayden entered the room at the same time. Ayden texted his photos to Natra. She went to the computer to project a full-frontal image to the large screen. "I have news reports about the Steadmans' disappearance with an image of Clark," she said.

Ayden held up his hands. "I didn't see it before, I promise."

Kip got to his feet. Jax came over and put an arm around me. I pressed his hand. I could hardly stand the suspense.

Natra projected Clark's photo and positioned it next to Ayden's drawing. Aside from the hair style being parted differently and darker irises, Ayden's rendering was strikingly close. Same long face, same crooked nose, same downward drift to the eyes, same ear placement. I felt a chill.

"It's him," Kip said. "That's amazing!" He looked at me. "But they didn't find Ella with him."

I gestured to Natra. "Send this sketch to the cold case team and encourage them to do some investigative genetic genealogy, with information about the potential ID. They should be able to confirm it, as well as to contact the decedent's family to get more information and possibly some direct DNA. Maybe they'll search the area again, though it's been a few years since the skull was found."

"Copy," she said.

Ayden got some pie and offered a slice to Jax.

I looked around. "Let's take a moment to absorb the enormity of this, not just for us but also for family members. Clark Steadman was abducted, possibly tortured, and certainly murdered. Maybe his wife was tortured or raped in front of him. Since she was Locke's wife, she might've received some harsh treatment. Ketch's suicide note and Vaughn's assistance sent us to the right area. The GHG symbol we see in the note likely came from the gate drawing in the binder. So, this confirms that Ketch's images are clues to locations."

"We have something as well," said Natra. She projected an image of the texts she and Jax had transcribed from Vaughn's phone. "We can't trace 'em till we get some help. We left out the texts between Vaughn and Kip." She glanced at him. "For privacy."

He blushed and nodded.

"These are the relevant texts from today, after she got here. The first three seem to be from her brother, after she asks him why he left the binder here. The next two are an unknown source."

Stop helping him.

[Vaughn]: *I'll do what I want.*

They'll hurt you.

[Vaughn]: *not scared.*

Get out of the house now.

New source:

We have your brother. Come to Duck alone with key or he gets hurt.

Get in his truck.

"What key?" I asked. "Any idea, Kip?"

He shrugged. "Her safe deposit box? Her hotel room? Maybe a key to your house."

"Well, she didn't get *that*."

Ayden turned to him. "What does Locke want?"

Kip threw up his hands. "I don't know. I wish I did. Maybe Ketch knows. Maybe he can tell us where they'd take her. Annie, can't you get me in? I could tell 'im my dad was trying to prove the stuff about Jordan. Maybe he'll talk to me."

"You can't just go in, Kip. You have to be on his visitors list."

"But *you* don't," Jax said to me.

I gave him a warning look. He pointed to the screen. "Annie. Vaughn's brother warned her to leave the house. *This* house. There's something here a killer wants. You need to find out what."

Chapter Twenty-Five

I prepared to see Ketch Ryder. We had no other viable options. I'd packed a folder with specific photos I thought would help. We'd spent a rough night armed and waiting for a possible home invasion, with everyone distributed in different rooms on the second floor. One surveillance camera worked, but the lens on the one I used in back was pitted from sandblasting. We'd seen a car driving slowly nearby, but nothing happened. We'd devised strategies for scenarios with and without Vaughn. She never called. Kip had wavered between fear for her life and fear for his own. He'd told her things, and she'd seen inside my place. She had intel, and we suspected she was now with Locke.

First thing in the morning, Jax had called Vaughn's former attorney, Roy Nozer, to convey her situation and our need to see Ryder. Nozer hadn't yet canceled his appointment for that day, so he said he'd arrange for Jax to be his co-counsel. Nozer had warned Jax that he'd backed off because Ryder was uncooperative and Vaughn naïve. He'd also revealed that Ryder had been diagnosed as schizotypal. With the head injury Vaughn mentioned, this made him fitful, hypervigilant, and prone to being manipulated. Nozer had suggested we bring a candy bar or two.

The local cops had come to check Kip's room. They weren't optimistic about solving it or tracking down his laptop. My digital guy, Joe, thought the remote work he'd done to secure it had likely fallen short if the thief had sophisticated extraction methods. This meant Locke might have that content. We had to do something quick.

Jax drove me to the prison, while Ayden and Kip continued to look for

Locke's letter. Natra wanted to deepen the victimologies. She'd located the cold case officer who'd led the Steadman investigation, Terri Frye, and alerted her to the developments. Kip had asked his brothers to go to the Dacretown property to document holes and caves.

This was not how I'd expected to spend the holiday, especially not with Jax.

"I'm so sorry about all this," I told him. "I'd hoped to just locate the stuff Kip wanted, introduce you to him, and relax. But you do look good in a suit."

He glanced at me. "It's fine, Annie. I'm glad I'm here. Whether or not Vaughn's posing, she's intriguing. I don't doubt she's been exposed to harm. She reminds me of kids in the system who pretend to have it together when they're really just scared. Lots of bravado. Kip, too. I think they're drawn to each other's trauma."

I touched his arm. "I see that. Kip's beginning to. He's taken some blows this weekend."

Jax said nothing for a minute. Then he breathed out in a way I'd learned to read as him preparing to broach a subject.

"What?" I asked.

"Just…I know you've been through a lot with Kip, but…have you considered he might be a plant? That this Jordan Locke sent him to get something, get right inside, use his connection to you?"

I sat back and watched the road.

"Annie?"

"I get it, Jax. He did go in Dad's office. Maybe he's pretending to be shocked about Jordan when he's only shocked that we discovered it. I've had those thoughts. So have Ayden and Natra. They've both warned me. But he didn't play it well if he's with Locke. And if he *is* working for the man, maybe it's because Locke threatened to hurt his brothers. I've thought of that, too. But then why bring in Vaughn? Even if he got involved with her, wouldn't he keep her away from the house?"

"They're in it together?"

"That would work against her mission. Unless she's lying about that. But he wouldn't need her to acquire from me whatever Locke's after. She's a complication."

"He got you out of the house."

"But he couldn't have anticipated that, and the house wasn't empty. You and I both said we weren't getting involved. He seemed surprised by our plan for today. He *wants* me to see Ryder. Locke wouldn't."

"Good points, but I say we watch him. Just stay flexible, Annie. Vigilant."

I leaned toward him. "That's why I'm lucky I have you to remind me."

Jax glanced at me. "You don't respond well to warnings from your team. You tend to *leave* rather than *lead*."

"Guilty. I know that. And it's the very trait I hate in Dad. I'm working on it."

"Keep that in mind when we see Ryder. Sit close, so I can warn you with my foot, and please take it seriously when I do. We're on tenuous ground, since I'm not his attorney."

"Copy that, counselor."

I had a color reproduction of Ryder's suicide note with me that showed the blood he'd used. I banked on this guy caring about his daughter. He'd made a deal on her behalf, but schizotypal tendencies include social withdrawal.

We got through the paperwork without delay. Only a bare bones staff was there. Since this was a legal visit, which allowed privacy, we were given a small psychiatric testing room with a long, narrow table and four metal folding chairs. A locked glass cabinet appeared to hold testing supplies, and someone had decorated the otherwise bland mint walls with a few landscape prints. They looked dusty. I used a paper towel to wipe off the tabletop before placing my folder on it. "I dislike buffers," I told Jax, "but in this case, we'll keep the table between him and me."

Ryder could have refused to see us, making our trip futile, but soon we heard scuffling and jangling outside the room. A bald, overweight guard opened the door, and a lean guard with a wispy mustache brought the prisoner in. The wrinkles in Ryder's brownish-gray prison uniform suggested he'd slept in it. I'd seen Ryder on the interrogation videos, but I wasn't prepared for how his presence filled the room. He was anything but feeble. His untrimmed dark hair gave him a wild crown and, as he glared at us, his brown eyes glowed under his thick brows. Tattoos lined his neck and arms. The guards sat him down but left his shackles on.

Jax gestured toward the handcuffs. "Can you remove them?"

"S'better if we don't," Baldy said. "You'll be calling us for help with this one. We'll stay close." The skinny guard grinned at Baldy like they shared a secret joke. They closed the door behind them, but Baldy watched through a small window.

Ryder scowled. He clenched his hands together, banging his metal cuffs against the table. Bags under his eyes and gray streaks in his hair showed how incarceration had aged him. His style of mustache, grown down past his mouth, reminded me of his Locke fixation.

"Where's nosy Nozer?" he growled.

Jax introduced himself, then me, and said, "I work with Nozer. He's unable to come today, but we've spoken with your daughter, Vaughn."

I jumped in. "He means Fawn. Your girl. You named her yourself, didn't you?" It was a guess, but he'd cared about her more than his son. She was the only one he'd mentioned in the interviews.

He looked through suspicious eyes from Jax to me and shook his head. "Don't want her here."

He'd acknowledged her. A good start. "She's not here," I assured him, "but she's spoken with us about you."

"Whatever you tell us is confidential," Jax added.

Ryder sneered. "Don't talk to no one." He rubbed a hand with dirty nails over his mouth.

"I know you care about her," I said. "She's trying to get help for you. She wants—"

Ryder's eyes flashed with anger. "Don't TALK to no one!"

Was he taking a stand or warning me? With a less volatile subject, I'd have pointed out the contradiction: *You're here.* I decided to just go for it. "Someone you know wants to harm her. They want to keep her quiet."

He flinched but maintained his hostile stare.

I glanced at the window to make sure Baldy wouldn't read my lips. "She has a recording."

His right nostril twitched. I smelled sweat. I was getting to him, but maybe not in the way I needed. I felt light pressure from Jax's foot. He sensed it, too.

I opened my folder and removed the suicide note. "Mr. Ryder, this is your writing. We know what these symbols mean. Nags Head is one. And Arrowhead. You sent police looking there. They failed, but we found it." I showed him a page that featured the Arrowhead Mountain Lake map.

Ryder blinked. He seemed confused. His pupils grew larger. He grabbed the note, leaned toward me, and tapped it. "You can't take it, we're not taking it. There's flies in here. I know the answer to all the questions. Might be an arrowhead, might be a horse head, might be a dog sled, but plants need water, and *horses* won't get fed."

Jax leaned back.

Ryder sounded psychotic. Vaughn had called him erratic but not out of it. Then I remembered the candy bar. On the videos, he'd talked gibberish until he got what he wanted. I pulled out a *Milky Way*, pushed it toward him, and tried again. "Fawn is in danger. Where would they take her?"

He ripped the wrapper off the candy and took a large bite, then chewed noisily as we waited. The smell of chocolate mixed with his sweat and rancid breath nearly gagged me in the overly warm room. Then Ryder pointed at the note. "Did *he* send you? *He* wanted this."

"Do you mean Locke?"

Ryder blinked hard. His face screwed up. He jumped to his feet as he leaned over the note and stabbed it with his right pointer finger. "*This* is the truth. It's a record. Tell him to leave me alone!"

Baldy looked in. I waved him away to show things were under control. But they weren't. Ryder's tension prickled the air.

"Please sit down, Mr. Ryder," Jax said. I sensed Jax ready to physically defend me if necessary.

I tried to puzzle through what Ryder was saying. I'd guessed wrong. Locke wouldn't benefit from Ryder revealing locations, not even if they implicated Ryder. Too risky. Locke wasn't the guy who "wanted" this. What had Vaughn said? *Broward's trying to stop me. He visits Ketch an' talks 'im out of it. Ketch caves pretty fast under pressure.*

I had to be firm. "I gave you the candy. I want information. Who did you tell? Special Agent Broward? Do you think he sent us?"

Ryder stood up straight and looked down at me. Then he plopped back down, manacles clanking, his eyes still bright. "Ancil."

I had no idea what he meant. He spat it out, like an insult. I tried again. "He wants to stop Fawn. He told her not to visit you."

Ryder shook his head. "Don't want her hurt. Keep her away."

It dawned on me that Ryder might have lied to Vaughn. Maybe he'd pre-emptively set up the recording to ensure she'd believe *him* if she ever learned about his confession. I had to shift my strategy. He wasn't joining Vaughn's cause. Using her wasn't working. I had to soften his resistance. That meant "believing" him.

"You want us to do what you asked," I said. "In this note, you showed us where they are. You want us to find them, so they believe you. That's what I'm doing. I'm looking for them." I reached for the suicide note. He gave it up. I pointed at the GHG symbol. "Gray Hollow Group. Are they involved?"

His eyebrows shot up. He looked at the door, then at me.

I leaned toward him. "If we find Ella, that's a start. They'll finally believe you. Where did you put her?"

His lips went back, showing a set of yellow, tobacco- and chocolate-stained teeth. His eyes bugged out and his face flushed as he rubbed the tabletop. "In the hole!" He flipped his hand. "Through the gates of Hell, the trail*head* to the abyss!"

His sudden animation gave me an opening. I pulled out our photo of Ella's GHG insignia ring. Ryder scowled. Then the right side of his mouth turned up. He knew what it was.

"She was wearing this," I said. "Did you see it? Did you give it to someone?"

Ryder looked over my head. His eyes seemed to follow something invisible in the room. I stayed silent, hoping he'd feel pressured to say something.

Ryder squinted at me. "Were you at the cabin? Was he there? The headmaster watches. Is he pleased?" His eyes shifted to Jax, then back to me. He waited. A silent minute ticked past. "Did you find others? No, they'd ask me. There's a book about me. Did you read it?"

I took out another photo: the binder that Ryder had stolen, its leather cover emblazoned with the GHG crest. "This book?"

He stared at it. Then he touched it and whispered, "Where's this?"

"I have it."

His nostrils flared. He cursed at me.

I ignored his ire and pulled out a photo of the page from the binder that featured the map where Vaughn said Ketch had drawn markers. He pulled back.

Ketch caves pretty fast under pressure. "Tell me," I said.

He picked up the candy bar wrapper. "Another."

I was getting somewhere. "Earn it."

Ryder leaned forward. "She put the photos in the pocket. She wanted to hurt him." He shook his head and drew his right hand over his mouth. "Hide them! Don't show Fawn."

I leaned forward. "What photos? What do they show?"

His eyes narrowed, and his mouth formed a straight line.

I tried another route. "We're testing the ring. Whoever handled it left his DNA. If it's not you, they'll look at the case again. We'll produce your recording. This whole thing's gonna fall apart unless you tell us where Ella is. Your confession to Broward will be worthless. Prove you know. If you did this, own it! Give us a body."

He sneered and tapped the suicide note. "They pay. This is the record." He stood and went to the door. Just before he knocked on it to be taken out, he looked at me and said, "If you had the photos, you wouldn't be here."

I jumped up. "Wait! What about Fawn?"

"What's done is done. Don't come back." He showed his stained teeth. "Won't get ahead."

Chapter Twenty-Six

I sat in the Wrangler, fuming. "So much obfuscation. That got us nowhere."

Jax was checking his messages. "Maybe it did, Annie. Nozer sent a text." He handed over his phone. I read it. *Hope I catch you in time. Warden doesn't want you talking to Ryder. Some FBI request.*

"Looks like the reduced holiday staff worked in our favor," he said.

I nodded. "FBI request. Has to be Broward. He's invested in the status quo."

"Maybe financially as well as professionally." Jax started the engine. "Let's go. Prisons are full of snitches. He probably already knows we got in."

While Jax focused on driving, I ran the interview through my mind, looking for any lead. Once we were on a highway, I said, "He didn't tell us much, but I think he was referring to Broward, not Locke, when he asked who sent us. The suicide note's a *record* that *he* wants. Makes sense that he's the one paying."

"Wouldn't do Ryder much good in prison."

"Maybe sending money to Vaughn, then. She has a FundMe account. Payments would have to be disguised, though. Money from Broward or through Ryder's prison account would be too easy to discover. What did you see?"

Jax watched the road for a moment before he responded. "He seemed upset about that binder, maybe that you have it. And about Ella. That got him angry. First thing I'd do is check the gate Ella drew. See if there's a hole near it. He mentioned a trailhead."

"Yeah, *head*. And *head*master. I think he was telling us something."

"And his parting shot. You won't get a*head*."

I squinted. "Is the Dacretown gate the gate to Hell?"

"You said Ella, he said gate. He pointed to the GHG symbol, which is *on* a very specific gate. The other symbols are about locations. There's no reason to think her remains will be with Clark's. It's worth checking."

"I'll ask Kip about trails. He and his brothers know that property better than anyone besides maybe my dad." A thought struck me. "What if Dad knows something?"

"Could be. That Gray Hollow Group sounds protective."

"I hate to think he'd cover this up, but he did refuse to help Gregory."

"Not altogether, Annie. You say Gregory hid things there, but that ring was in a safe. Lang told Kip to get it." He glanced at me. "So, he knew about that."

I blew out air. "This is so frustrating. I wonder what Ryder meant by a pocket. There's one in the binder, but I didn't see anything in it."

"Annie, I noticed your shift in there with him. What made you think he's the killer?"

"I don't, necessarily. I just decided to stop pushing against his resistance. He *wants* to be this killer, like it's some badge of honor, so I used that. The interrogation shows issues. Broward clearly fed him details. Ryder seemed confused or vague about some things that, as the killer, he should've known—especially if he's determined to take credit. Vaughn said he had a head injury, so maybe he's just forgetful. And if he wanted to be exonerated, he'd have worked with us. Instead, he shut the door. So, he's either afraid of telling the truth or he's gaining something from his act. I'm leaning toward him being involved, but not with the whole package."

"There's something about photos, and if you had them, you wouldn't need to talk to him. They must be proof of something."

I held up a finger. "Hang on." I called Natra. She answered right away. "Are you near the binder?" I asked. "I need you to look for something."

"I'll get it." A minute later, she said, "I have it. What?"

"Can you look in the pocket on the inside of the front cover?"

I heard her put down the phone. After a few minutes, Natra came back on. "It's a clever design, this binder. I didn't notice it. You could slide something thin into it, like an envelope, but it's a tight fit. If there's something deep inside, I'll have to work on it."

"Ryder mentioned some photos. He said if I had them, I wouldn't be talking to him. I'd guess there's something incriminating, something that might inspire certain people to be looking for them. Try to examine the pocket without damaging the binder, like with a letter opener, then call me if you find anything. We're on our way back. We'll be there for dinner. Any word from Vaughn?"

"None. Ayden and Kip are out driving around to look for suspicious cars."

"Anything more in the boxes?"

"Not so far. Your dad really was a hoarder."

"Maybe more than that. I'm homing in on what I think Kip suspected. And when you see him, ask him if he recalls any significant holes around a trailhead, especially near that gate. Could help narrow the search there."

"Copy."

Jax accelerated to pass several vehicles. He watched in the rearview mirror.

I looked behind us, then asked, "What's up?"

"Not sure. I caught a glimpse of blue, same color as that Audi."

I signed off with Natra and turned in my seat to watch, but the white Chevy van behind us blocked me. "Why would he follow us?"

Jax glanced at me as if surprised I'd ask.

"Slow down," I suggested. "Get that van to pass us. Better yet, take that exit. See what happens."

Jax steered over to the exit. I watched the highway. "That's an Audi, you're right. But it didn't follow us this way."

"Doesn't need to. He knows where we went and where we're going."

"Drive back on the highway. See if we can catch up. I wanna see his face."

Jax maneuvered us back into traffic. It wasn't heavy in this area. He sped up. "If this is Jordan Locke or one of his associates, he won't let us see him."

"Maybe I can get the back license plate. It was muddy before, but maybe this rain has cleaned it."

"I see it," Jax said. "Pretty far up. Should be able to get it on the dash cam." He passed an Equinox and a Rav4. "He's moving fast. Probably figures we're coming up."

"But he's boxed in." I checked my seatbelt.

Jax got some breaks, which put us within two car lengths of being parallel to the Audi driver. He pulled into the passing lane, putting a black Silverado between us. Jax shifted to the right lane. The red Mazda CX-50 in front of us moved up, which made the Audi's plate partially visible. The rain didn't help. I strained to see and lifted my phone for a photo.

Suddenly, the Audi swerved into our lane and knocked the Wrangler's fender. Jax jerked to the right. I dropped my phone to clutch my seat. My heart raced.

We slid off the macadam and spun to the left. I stiffened for an impact, but we remained clear of the traffic. Several drivers honked as they passed. Jax brought the Wrangler to a stop along the side. The Audi was long gone. I breathed out. Jax grabbed my arm. "All right?"

My adrenaline still pumped. "My god! He could've killed us."

"Nah. That was skillful, like a cop trained in traffic maneuvers."

"I didn't get the photo."

"We'll look at the dashcam, but I'm not optimistic. As soon as we were in position, he hit me, then shot away."

"I think he broke his taillight."

Jax unfastened his seat belt and got out. He went to the front to look at his Jeep. He shook his head. A truck pulled up, but Jax waved the driver away and gave a thumbs-up. When he returned, he got in and said, "There's some damage, but not bad. I can hammer it out. I've had worse at home. We can drive."

"You're not submitting a report?"

Jax gave me a hard look. "This guy's no one to mess with, Annie. I don't think he's watching Kip. I think he's watching you."

Chapter Twenty-Seven

We arrived at my place without seeing the Audi. I'd played back the dashcam footage, but it had captured only the last two numbers from the license plate. At least I could tell that it was Georgia. Ayden's truck came in behind us. Despite the cold air, Ayden and Kip stayed outside with Jax to look at the Jeep while I went in to set up for dinner. Natra needed a break. She'd been working all day to pull together the records. When she entered the kitchen, I told her what happened on the road. "That was close. I thought we'd roll over."

"Glad you're okay. That guy means business, whoever he is."

I pulled out soup bowls. "Did you get anything from the binder's pocket?"

"No, sorry. I stuck a long blade into it. If something's in there, maybe deep, we might have to destroy the cover to get it."

"I'm ready to do that. There's no more GHG. This binder's just a historical record now, but obviously there's no packet of photos. Gregory had the binder. So did Ella. Locke must've taken it from her, and Ryder stole it from him. Or Ryder stole it from her or Gregory."

Natra collected silverware from the drawer. "Then Ivy had it, then Clay, and he left it here. Quite a journey. By the way, I found the book about the Lovato murders in your dad's library. *The Nags Head Horrors.*"

"Of course he'd have it. I vaguely remember it. Ryder mentioned it."

"I thought maybe Gregory brought it, but it was published after he died. Got tabs and markings, too. I read some of it. Repeats a lot from the interrogations we saw, but the author, Doug Hershall, corresponded with Ryder. Might be worth calling him. Lives nearby, in Manteo. I found his number."

"Good work." I washed some loose lettuce. "I'd like to see what Dad marked up, but I owe Jax a good dinner and some downtime. How's Mika?"

"Took her to the vet. She'd pulled on the stitches, so they redid them. I decided to board her there overnight. Too much excitement here."

I handed Natra a stack of plates to take to the table and checked the new batch of stuffing in the oven. "Probably a good idea, but we lose our first line of defense. We'll have to be extra vigilant. Ayden brought over a videocam for out back." I prepared a platter of carved turkey. "Did Kip say anything?"

"His brothers went to the property around lunchtime with a map. He said cell service is poor out there."

"Right, I remember. Couldn't call anyone when I was there."

"I found some dog handlers for them, and I think that cop, Terri Frye, was prepared to go over if they found something. She lives about forty minutes from Dacretown. Who do you think this Audi guy is?"

"Well, it's not Clay, but we can't rule out someone associated with him. It could be Broward, because now we know he's aware of us. Could be Locke or someone he hired. We tried to get the license plate number, but no dice."

Natra poured water into glasses. "I've done a victimology for Ella, as far as I can go from records and articles. It gives us better context. I also got more on Locke. Ayden did some digging today, too. Kip helped him."

I heard hammering on metal. I looked out and saw Ayden working on the dent in the Wrangler's front left fender. "Ayden and his tools. Always prepared."

A sharp rap on the front door startled me. I'm so oriented toward the back of my house, facing the ocean, I barely remember the front. No one who knows me would use that door.

Our visitor knocked again, insistent.

I wiped my hands. "Get a gun. I'll see who this is."

I looked through the peephole, then opened the door. A slender man in a black wool trench coat stood on the porch. I recognized him. I'd watched Reid Broward on the interrogation videos, but he looked more imposing face-to-face. Although he wasn't tall, maybe five-foot-nine, his manner said he had every right to be here.

"Good afternoon, Dr. Hunter," he said in a buttery southern accent. "Supervisory Special Agent Reid Broward." He held up his ID. "FBI. I apologize for this disturbance on a holiday, but my business is urgent. May I come in?"

I wanted to say no but didn't think I could. "We're about to sit down for dinner."

"I won't take much of your time, I promise."

I ushered him into the small sitting room I keep for business meetings when I don't want someone in my living area—someone like Broward. It smelled dusty, but the plain furnishings were presentable. I gestured for him to sit in an upholstered armchair and offered to take his coat. He unbuttoned it but waved me off. "This won't take long." He sat stiffly, like he wanted to get this done and leave.

I took a seat opposite him on the couch. Having talked about him over the past two days and even suspected him of orchestrating Ryder's compliance, it felt unsettling to sit with him. He liked to "watch...and catch." He might be in that mode right now. "What can I do for you?"

He moved his hand over his dark gray suit jacket, a gesture that suggested he was armed. "I happened to be with family in Virginia Beach this morning when I was notified of a visit to someone of interest to me, Ketch Ryder. That was you today at the prison, was it not?"

I heard a light footstep in the hall. Natra. She was listening.

"I was there with an attorney," I said. "Confidential business."

Broward leaned toward me. "Now, there's no need to be defensive. As you may already know, I got the man to confess. I have a special interest in him and a long relationship. He responds to me." He held up a hand. "Full disclosure. I've heard your podcast about me. I'm aware you dislike my methods, but they're effective and *legal*. Mr. Ryder's confession was freely given. I don't expect he went back on his statements this morning; he wouldn't do that. He had details we've corroborated. He's our guy. You probably think I exploited his mental state, but he's confessed more than once. His confession is sound."

I sensed he was baiting me to engage, but he'd played a hand. He'd revealed that he knew Ryder wasn't all there. "Again, Agent Broward, our matter was confidential. And, yes, I know your 'guilt whisperer' tactics. Watch and catch, isn't that your phrase? Seems like you've built quite a reputation on a guy who can barely offer a coherent sentence."

Broward snorted. "I wish it were that simple, Dr. Hunter, I truly do. You're getting into the middle of something that is far beyond your skills, whatever they may be."

He'd insulted me. I burned to defend my involvement, but I bit my tongue. "I think I know what I'm getting into."

"Well, let me give you a little help there. The young lady, Vaughn Ryder, is looking for allies. We know about that. We have her recorded calls to him in the prison. She told him she has evidence in some recording, but she's got nothing. Whatever he might have told her was just his way of protecting her. The girl's quest is hopeless, and if I were you, I wouldn't put much stock in her notions. I'm aware she's working with a young man and that he's been a visitor here."

Broward had just signaled—politely—that we were all being watched. I thought of the Audi and clasped my hands together, hoping I looked calmer than I felt. "I'm still not sure why you're here."

Broward pointed his chin, his olive-green eyes intense. "Let me be clear. You made an unauthorized visit to Ryder this morning."

"We followed all the protocols."

"A staff failure, I'm afraid. All visits go through me. You won't get in again. I'm working with Ryder to find his victims. I have full authority in his case, and I want no interference. Currently, except for his attorney—"

"I'm the attorney." Jax stepped into the room. Relief flooded me. Still in his suit from our prison visit, he radiated authority. "Dr. Hunter went in with me, at my request. Whatever business you have is with me."

Broward rose and extended his hand to introduce himself. Jax accepted the gesture. Taller than Broward, Jax drilled him with his dark eyes. Broward retained his pleasant façade, but I sensed annoyance when he addressed Jax. "You're Vaughn Ryder's attorney, according to the prison, with minimal attachment to Ryder. You're a *juvenile* attorney." The snarky tone came through loud and clear.

"Not exclusively. Vaughn Ryder has requested representation for him in the event he's not mentally competent."

Broward cocked his head. "And did you find him to be so?"

"You can contact her for my report."

"Of course. Not authorized to reveal anything." Broward shot me a look before he returned his attention to Jax. "That girl's making a big mistake, working against his wishes. She stands to lose what she's…the girl's interfering with an investigation. But let me assure you—"

Jax's eyes blazed, though his expression remained unchanged. "I'll assure *you* that I will conduct business as I see fit."

Broward looked from Jax to me, an eyebrow raised as if he suspected something more between us. "I had hoped you'd be cooperative, but you'll be stopped next time you try to see him. *Legally.* And he won't request your assistance. Thank you for your time." He hesitated, then said, "You two should be careful. You may soon wish we were on the same side."

He buttoned his coat. He was about to leave when he turned to me. "Let me make you this offer. I'm taking him out tomorrow to a site he claims is a body dump. We've tried it before, unsuccessfully, but he says he remembers now." Broward handed me his card. "You come along, tell me whether he's got a guilty mind. I've been at this a long time. I'm good at what I do. If you're convinced, then hear me out. If you want to go, call me tonight by 10. I'm at the Hilton down the road. Enjoy your dinner." He tipped his head toward Jax and walked out.

I slipped his card into my back pocket and closed and locked the door.

Jax came next to me to watch through the window. "He's not driving an Audi."

I breathed out. "But he's keeping track of us. And he revealed a few things. Kind of careless of him."

Jax looked at me. "I'm sure it was calculated, but he's done, Annie. Aside from the celebrity he's gained from his association with the case, he has no business blocking visits to Ryder."

"Vaughn stands to lose something, he said. 'Lose what she's'…and he stopped himself. That's a leak. She's getting support from someone, and he knows about it."

Jax looked thoughtful. "We need to find out about her FundMe account."

"Should I take him up on his offer?"

Jax half-smiled. "I'm going with you."

"I haven't decided—"

"Yes, you have. You wouldn't miss being in the field with Ryder."

"Is this you helping me decide? I'm not acting on my own?"

"You could take it that way."

I leaned into him. "So, you have a new client."

He hugged me back before he said. "Maybe. She's still M.I.A., and now her funds are suspect."

"As if you won't do *pro bono*. You're as hooked as I am. And until we hear from her, we won't know for sure. For now, let's get you out of this suit, counselor, so you can relax."

Chapter Twenty-Eight

In the main room, Ayden burst in through the sliding doors. Kip followed.

"We saw the Audi," Ayden said. "Natra told us Broward was here, so we went looking."

I gestured to the front. "He drove away in a black BMW, a luxury one, like an X-5."

"Yup, he did, but up the road, the Audi pulled out behind him. Must be his scout. Saw a broken right taillight."

I looked at Jax. "So, the guy following us today works with Broward. With that Georgia plate, I thought he was with Locke."

"Good to know."

Jax went to change. I reported what Broward had said and looked at Kip. "Any word from your brothers?"

"They've been mapping the place. 'Bout three hours ago, Frank called, and I told 'im what you said, to focus around the gate area. Got a couple texts, but he has to go off the property to update me."

"You've never noticed any significant holes there?"

Kip shrugged. "People've been digging there for decades. Holes are everywhere. But if someone hid a body, that would be in a cave, wouldn't it?"

"Could be. Or they dug a hole and covered it. What about a trailhead?"

"Hard to say. I've seen old trails there, and *we've* made trails. There's snow on the ground, so it could be tough."

"Snow won't be a problem for the dogs," Natra said.

"The handlers are there. So's the cold case cop. Frank texted that she was coming to see what they're doing."

"Terri Frye? Wouldn't she come only if there's reason to?"

"I can't reach 'em, Annie. You know what that place is like. They'll call when they can." Kip placed two phones near his plate on the table. "Mine and Vaughn's. Nothing from her yet, either."

"I hope she's all right," I said. "But I have no good news from my conversation with Ketch. He's not inclined to cooperate, so that recording she has might be worthless. He could just say he lied to her to protect her."

Kip sat and shook his head. "It's not what you think. It's not him talking to her. More like talking to himself. *He* recorded it. She found it."

This surprised me. "You've heard it?"

"She played me some, maybe five minutes of it, before we loaded it to my laptop. He lists things he has to do, like buying things and packing things. A gun, I remember that, and rope. Says them over and over, mumbling. Sounds kinda crazy."

"So, it's not something he directly told to Vaughn."

"No. But she told him she has it."

"Yes, on a recorded prison call. Broward knows about it."

Kip shrugged. "I guess that's why Ketch tried to shush her. Told her not to tell anyone."

"Interesting. So, this recording suggests he's just a gofer. Okay, well, we don't have it, but we do have my conversation. Let's talk about it." I looked at Natra. "Are we ready to sit down?"

"Pretty much."

"Wait," Ayden said. He went to the kitchen and brought out a bottle of wine. The label featured a dozen crows sitting on bare branches over the words *Murder Ridge* Zinfandel. I shook my head and took a seat. "You had time to shop?"

"Special order. Just arrived."

Jax sat next to me. I gripped his hand. The aromas from warm turkey and fresh bread grounded me. Across from me, Ayden opened the wine. He raised an eyebrow and smiled. "Seemed appropriate for tonight."

Kip extended his wine glass. I resumed questioning him. "Did you talk to your cousin, Mark?"

He pursed his lips and nodded. "He didn't want me to say anything, cuz it's s'posed to be secret, but I told him we have to know. He finally agreed that since you're Lang's daughter, it's all right. Mark's the sixth member, like you thought. He was twenty-four when Dad died, and he and Kate managed things. She was just out of law school. Lang gave them a hand, but Mark was in charge. You were right, Annie. Mark formed the Skeleton Crew as a kind of substitute GHG. I guess he thought if Dacretown remained intact, he'd bring me into the family biz."

I'd already explained most of this to Jax, but I turned to him. "They protected that Dacretown property near Concord that my family owned." I gestured toward Kip. "Which I gladly handed off." I turned back to Kip. "Did Mark know Ella?"

"He did, but not well. She was gone by the time he got fully involved."

"Right. The year before. Did you ask him about Locke?"

"I just asked if he'd been around, tried to get him to talk. I don't think Mark knows that Locke was Ella's first husband or that Locke sent Dad the letter we're looking for. Seems like Dad only discussed Locke with Lang, like it was seriously confidential."

I looked at Natra. "What do we need to know about Ella?"

She set down her fork and picked up the notes she'd placed near her plate. "I've added this to our chronology. I looked through news articles, but some of this came from the binder, including some pages Gregory removed and put in his packet. Also, Ayden called the cold case officer there, which added some items. I used handwriting comparison to identify Ella as the GHG record keeper. She kept track of taxes, expenses, income, documents, etc. I believe the binder was primarily hers. I estimate the start of her membership in the GHG at around twenty years ago."

I stopped chewing. "Twenty! While she was married to Locke?"

"Yes, since before she met him. Gregory had a brief chronology in his box, and also information on Locke. He shows that Lang had sporadic involvement with the GHG after he left Concord. Once I knew Ella's nickname, it was easier to track her. She grew up in Massachusetts but met Locke and moved to Georgia. Still, she kept the GHG records."

"So, Locke had to know about the group. Maybe he'd seen the binder."

"It seems so. And when they moved to Georgia, it was to Richmond Hill." She gave us all a meaningful look. "Locke also had some wooded properties in South Carolina. Just FYI, Gregory learned that Locke had a rough background. Grew up in an off-the-grid religious cult associated with the community Ryder was in. He was a suspect in a dispute over land that ended up with one man dead and his father gaining the property. I think that's the cabin at Arrowhead. His dad died shortly thereafter, with Locke the heir."

"Suspicious?" I asked.

"Maybe, especially since Locke was arrested for domestic abuse on his first wife. Before the court date, she disappeared. Charges were dropped. So, he was married before Ella. He lived in Georgia but traveled a lot. From Vaughn, we know he was a roving member for this community, which has branches all along the East Coast. He also owned a land management business. His marriage to Ella lasted about two years."

I buttered a roll. "I wonder what she saw in him."

"He's nice," Kip said. "Generous, attentive, charming. He fooled me."

Natra continued. "Shortly after Ralph and Sharon Pryor disappeared, Ella divorced him. That's the first couple Ryder mentions in his confession, although his details are too sketchy to be sure. I rewatched that part of the interrogation, and it's clear that Broward fed him details. Sometimes he even signaled the response with his fingers. But Ryder did seem to know things on his own about where they were killed and dumped. Still, no one found them. Back to Ella. The divorce was contentious—Locke was a suspect briefly in her disappearance but cleared. Anyway, she returned to Concord. A year later, she married Clark Steadman. Second marriages for both."

"So, five GHG members at that time?"

"As far as I can tell, it was four. Gregory, Ella, and the two you know who were later forced out. Lang was in and out. After Gregory died, Mark took it over, and Lang got more involved."

Kip nodded.

Natra looked at me. "I've seen enough of Lang's handwriting to believe he was instrumental in helping Ella leave Locke. There are notes in the ledger. He even hired security for her. There's an expense line for it."

I didn't like this. "He knew her well, then."

Natra glanced at Ayden, who cleared his throat, before she continued. "In the true crime book, Lang highlighted several sections about her. She introduced him to the Lovatos. They found this house for him." She gestured in a circle. "Clark, Ella's husband, was in real estate as well. He worked for your grandfather, Annie."

I crossed my arms and exchanged looks with Kip. The interactions between our families for at least four generations seemed mostly jinxed.

Natra continued. "Ella and Clark lived in New Hampshire, not far from Concord. She was involved there in a safe house for battered women, apparently because Locke had been abusive. A woman who also worked there gave a statement when Ella disappeared. She said Ella had been planning to move to elude a stalker. From Vaughn, we know that Ella met Ivy Ryder through this network and that, around then, Ketch Ryder acquired the binder. And he just added another piece. There were photos."

"Yes," I said, "according to him, if we had the photos, we wouldn't be there talking to him. He said this only after he realized I had the binder, so those items are related. He seemed very surprised I had it. Let me just add some things from our conversation. Ketch doesn't want Vaughn's help. He won't cooperate. He thought someone had sent us. We think he meant Broward, as if he thought Broward was trying to test his adherence to the story. Had a word for him, *ancil*, I think." I looked at Jax.

"That's what I heard, too," he said.

"Seemed like an insult. Seemingly, Broward wanted Ketch to put the drawings in the suicide note, which suggests the attempt was staged. Ryder asked if we'd found others, like there's more than one person involved. He mentioned a headmaster, which fits the 'head' theme. Also, someone is paying for something, and Ryder's protecting that transaction."

Ayden gestured for attention. "I can add something. Kip and I were thinking about Gregory's visit. We read through his notes again. He came here because he believed Locke was involved in the murders. He'd talked with people who knew Locke and looked up the investigation into Locke's first wife's disappearance—the one before Ella. But Lang wanted no part of it. We wanted to know why, so we made a timeline for Lang. We discovered something important. Ella came here soon after the Lovatos went missing."

Chapter Twenty-Nine

I felt heat rise in my face. I looked at Kip, but his eyes were averted. They knew things about Dad I didn't. They'd penetrated my space. In a measured voice I hoped didn't reveal the twist in my stomach, I said, "Okay. I'm listening."

"He's kind of a mystery, Annie." Ayden looked at Natra.

She waved him off. "It's your work."

He returned his attention to me. "There are gaps, but I used those journals you found in the house when you moved in, the ones you used to track Lang around Europe when *he* went missing. You gave them to me when you wanted ideas."

"I remember."

"This case clarifies some of his entries. Also, we found public records, and we have Gregory's notes and Kip's memory from being here. This is all since Lang divorced your mother." He hesitated. I swallowed and urged him to keep going. "Okay, so here goes. You were still in high school when they split, so you lived with your mother in Asheville. Lang went to Boston."

I nodded. "I visited him there. He had an apartment."

"He also had another address. We think he was living with Ella."

My mouth dropped open. *"Dad?* With Ella?" I looked at Kip. "I thought you said Gregory—"

He held up his hands. "I didn't know."

I hugged myself against a chill. Jax rubbed my back. Ayden continued. "That's around the time she came into the GHG. He comments about Merlin in a journal. Remember when we read the journals, and we were trying to figure out who that was?"

"I really don't know him, do I? I was caught up in college and graduate school and then married, raising a kid. He never told me this."

Ayden checked his notes. "I don't know what happened between them, but eventually she met and married Locke and moved to Georgia."

I gasped. "My God, this is all about revenge!"

"Maybe. During that time, she introduced Lang to the Lovatos, who sold him the house, so they must've stayed friends. Shortly after the Pryor incident, they helped her get away from Locke. She came to Nags Head. Gregory mentions that visit."

I stared at Ayden. "They were killed as payback for their assistance."

Kip finally looked at me, his expression guarded. "We think Lang knows exactly what happened. That's why Gregory came here. He wanted Lang to do something."

I tapped my finger on the table, trying to make sense of this. "Well, why *wouldn't* he?"

"He said it was too dangerous."

"For *whom?*"

Jax pressed on my arm. I looked at him, then back at Ayden. "For *me?*"

Ayden nodded. "Makes sense. You'd just had Kamryn, so for both of you. When Ella disappeared with Clark a year after the Lovatos, Lang had to know Locke was involved. Locke certainly knew about Lang. And Ella was here again, right after the Lovatos went missing. She and Lang must've talked about Locke."

I went still. I had to process this. Ella probably had hoped to do something before Locke came for *her*. And then he did come for her. I felt sick. "Why didn't *she* go to the police here? She didn't need Lang. She had the evidence. That would've been her best move."

"Unless she *didn't* have it." Ayden leaned toward me. "Let's follow the photos, now that we know about them. What do they show? Something that Locke wants no one to see. Suppose they show what happened to the Pryors. Ella nicked 'em, so she had them the first time she came here. Ryder learned about them, probably from Ivy, so Ella took them to New Hampshire."

Natra passed the bread basket. "Do we know if Ryder actually saw them?"

I looked at Jax. He shook his head. "He didn't say he did. He only said if you had them, you wouldn't be there. That implies he knows what they show."

I leaned on my hands. "So, he heard about them. Would Locke have told him? Seems unlikely. So, Ivy saw them or heard about them from Ella. We know Ivy had the binder. So did Ryder. Vaughn looked through it, but she didn't say anything about photos. Somewhere along the line, amid all these transfers of the binder, they vanished."

Ayden dipped a piece of bread his soup. "Let's say Ella hid them in the binder. Gregory had the binder once. Maybe he saw them, and she fessed up to what they were."

I glanced at Kip. "Did our dads discuss photos when Gregory was here?"

Kip shook his head. "I wish I could remember. They argued about stuff Dad wanted to leave here. Lang resisted. Said it wasn't safe."

"Can you ask Mark? That might tell us whether Gregory had them. If he found them in the binder and brought them here…but that makes no sense. He'd have talked with Ella about them, wouldn't he?"

Kip grabbed his phone and worked on a text.

To the others, I said, "If Locke threatened Gregory because Gregory was investigating him, it's fair to say he was worried about *something* Gregory knew or had."

Natra scanned her notes. "Right after the Lovatos disappeared, Ella's expense ledger shows that PIs were hired in Georgia and North Carolina, as if she were looking into Locke's movements. She didn't make notes or file their reports, not that we found."

Jax cleared his throat. "May I suggest a simpler angle? Let's shift the narrative. Ivy meets Ella, who describes her abusive first husband and mentions the photos she has. Ivy realizes Ella's ex is Jordan Locke. She tells Ketch about the photos. He spots an opportunity to please his hero. He steals the binder. When Ivy grabs it from him, Ryder tells Locke, who realizes Ella's a threat. He kills Ella and Clark but doesn't locate the binder. Ivy has it, but she doesn't have the photos. We can eliminate them getting lost in those transfers."

Natra moved in her seat. "That's why Locke would contact Gregory instead of hunting down Ivy. Ryder never had them. And if Ella didn't have them when she came to see Lang, the wild card is Gregory. He had the binder once."

"But why wouldn't *he* take them to the police?" Kip asked. He and I were passing a hot potato back and forth. *One* of our dads should have done something. Where would this potato come to rest?

Kip's text tone sounded. He looked. "It's Mark." He read it out loud. "*Gregory had an SD card. Said he left it in a safe place.*"

A chill ran down my back. Somewhere in my house, a tiny memory card held some dark and terrible images.

I got up. "A safe place." I strode to the key holder, retrieved the key to Dad's office, and marched down the hall.

Chapter Thirty

I grabbed the lock code and went straight to the safe. When I struggled to get the painting off the wall, Jax came behind me and lifted it away. My fingers trembled. I had to try the combination several times before I heard the lock click. The others gathered while I took everything from the safe and placed each item on the desk.

I started with the spiral-bound notebook. I opened each page but found nothing inside. I handed it to Natra. "We need to see what Lang wrote in this." I picked up the zippered black pouch and dumped out the money. Some change clanged against the desktop.

"Wow!" Ayden said. "He left that behind?"

"Among other things." I glanced at Kip, who leaned against the door frame. He already knew the safe's contents.

I turned the pouch inside out. Nothing.

Next, I focused on the keys. I looked at the bottom of the box, in case the SD card was taped to it. Then I stirred through the keys. I opened the envelopes containing Dad's documents but found no card. Finally, I examined the revolver. I returned to the safe to feel along every inch before I asked Natra, "Have we been through all the boxes in the attic?"

"Pretty much, but we weren't looking for an SD card. I can check through Gregory's stash again."

"I don't think he'd put it there. Too risky. If Lang found Gregory's packet, he'd've just destroyed it."

Ayden folded his arms. "Gregory wouldn't hide it in the safe, either, would he?"

"Hang on." I retrieved the box with Ella's ring from my room. "Dad had to know this is evidence. Why would he have it if he wanted nothing about Ella's abduction in the house?"

"It's GHG property," Natra suggested. "And valuable."

"Then why not tell Gregory to put it in the archives?"

She offered another reason. "Maybe Lang just wanted something of hers."

I breathed in. Then I removed the plastic bag from the box. With a pencil, I turned it over. We'd already examined it. Nothing was in this bag but the ring.

"The box, Annie," Jax said. "There's a false bottom. See it?"

I did. The box was two inches thick, but the silk lining inside covered a platform.

Natra held up a hand. "Gloves!" She left the room.

Kip wrapped his arms close, as if expecting an explosion. My heart felt like it could trigger one. Ayden used the pencil to better examine the ring.

Natra returned and handed me a pair of purple evidence gloves. She put a white sheet of paper next to me. Ayden opened a thin-bladed pocketknife and offered it. I fumbled to pull the gloves on. Finally, I was ready.

I pressed the platform. "Cardboard." I leveraged the knife blade between the platform on the left side and the box's inside wall. "Feels glued in." I ran the knife around the platform, but it didn't lift. I held up the box and shook it. Nothing rattled.

"I'm going to get this thing out, even if I wreck it."

"Wait," said Ayden. He held up his phone. I let him take several photos. My thumping heart heated my ears and made each second a minute long.

Ayden stepped back and nodded.

I pried the platform from its position. "If it's in here, that Gregory was clever. Almost hiding it in plain sight. Lang would never throw away this ring, and he'd never look under the platform. This was the safest hiding place in the whole house."

The platform resisted but finally gave way. Silk also lined the true bottom, but I noted a two-inch slit along the back side. I touched several spots. An unyielding object was under the lining.

I grabbed an envelope opener from the desk drawer. With it, I tried to force the object. My hands felt uncoordinated.

"Want me to do it?" Natra asked.

I held up a hand to ask for patience. "I'll get this. Something's here."

Kip's text tone sounded. "My brothers." He read it. *"Found something. Dogs alerted. Digging turned up plastic. They're bringing lights. Heading back in."*

"Wow!" Ayden said. "What if she's there?"

Kip blinked hard. I realized we might be on the verge of finding Ella's remains. She was a Hawkins, his kin. He'd been caretaking that property—and maybe her—for five years.

I looked at Ayden. "We might need your Vermont contact to connect with them."

"Copy."

I pointed to the box. "Let's finish this first." I renewed my effort. Once it was clear I couldn't move the object, I looked at Jax. "Close your eyes, counselor."

He shook his head. "That box is past saving as evidence."

I cut the silk. Ayden took pictures. I pulled the slinky fabric away. Taped to the bottom of the box was an SD card.

Chapter Thirty-One

We took it to the conference area. I removed the tape that held the memory card in place. Fortunately, a plastic sleeve protected it. The room seemed to grow warmer as I used tweezers to extract the card from the sleeve. I held it for a photo before I slid it into the card reader. "Let's hope the files are still intact." I gestured to Kip. "Sit with me."

I believed he was now going to see what a man he'd thought was a friend had done. He was going to see what his father had viewed. This would be difficult. He took a chair next to me. The others leaned in around us. Ayden took photos while Natra took notes.

I looked up to the large screen. Two folder icons appeared, labeled *Photos* and *Maps*.

"Good start." I pressed on the *Photos* folder. Four subfolders appeared, labeled *Target, Seize, Dom, Prize*. I hit the first one, *Target*. Multiple images filled the screen, too small to clearly see the contents. I tapped on one to enlarge it, then another. The photos featured a man and a woman walking together on a street. A brief video showed them entering a house.

"Looks like surveillance," Ayden observed. "I think that's the Pryors."

Natra pulled out her file folder and showed us pictures from the missing persons reports.

"It's them," I said. "Whoever took these was watching them. They're the targets."

I enlarged a few more, which showed the house from different angles, a gray BMW, and more images of the couple. "Any victimology?" I asked.

Natra picked up her tablet. "In their mid-forties. Two kids, one in college, one married. Lived in the upscale Richmond Hill development of Buckhead. He was an administrator at the Savannah College of Art and Design, and she was a victims' advocate. She advised clients on what to expect at trial, reported on victim intimidation, and accompanied them to court. Second marriage for both. The kids were hers. Low-risk victims. Disappeared from their home. No one knew of plans for them to travel. No evidence of a break-in. Their BMW was gone, never recovered. Their medications and corrective lenses were left behind. Nothing in the house indicated they were killed there. A neighbor's surveillance camera picked up a car and a van, but cops couldn't identify them. No bodies found."

"Thank you." I tapped the last image, which showed the house at night. "I guess they've arrived." I moved on to the *Seize* folder. A dozen images featured the Pryors in their home, seemingly taken by surprise. They sat on a patterned couch, looking scared. I took a breath before I opened the *Dom* subfolder. This contained two more folders, labeled *Male* and *Female*. I opened the *Male* folder and wished I hadn't. Kip gasped. Jax moved closer. I hugged myself. No one said a word.

The photo images featured a shirtless Ralph Pryor bound and gagged. In one, blood streamed from a wound near the top of his head, and his face was bruised and swollen. One eye was shut. In another, he'd been stabbed in several places. He looked like he was suffering. The photographer had grabbed an image of a bloody bat. Another photo showed Clark on the floor, eyes shut.

Jax pointed at an image. "Look. Two sets of legs next to him. Three perps at least."

"You're right," I said. "One to use the camera and the others to hurt 'im."

"We might get some images with faces. There's a video in this folder. Let's see it."

I turned to my left. Kip looked pale. "Kip?"

"I can take it."

I wasn't so sure, but I opened the video and tapped *play*. It showed the same ordeal from a different angle. I could barely watch. I tried to focus on the men involved, not the victim. The camera stayed low, so no one's face fully showed. One glimpse from the side indicated a man with a mustache. Could've been Ryder. The camera caught another participant looking almost feral, as if he were experiencing primitive rage when he brought down a hammer. He noticed he was being filmed, growled, and waved a hand for the cameraman to move away. The dim lighting made it difficult to see clearly, but Ralph's pleas came through loud and clear.

"There might be four people," I observed. "One for stills, one for video, and two to handle the victim. No wonder Ella was scared. We'll get a screenshot of that guy and any other whose features we can see."

"It's a club," Jax said, "maybe a network."

"The hunting club," Kip said. "Jordan called it that. Ella would know there could be victims wherever he had business. Vaughn told us he traveled."

"I've seen enough of this video." I pressed *stop*. "Ayden and Natra, you can view it for info, but no more for me." I left that folder, then paused. I stared at the one labeled *Female*. "I'll pass on this one. If Sharon got the treatment Ryder described for the Lovatos, we know what to expect." No matter how prepared Kip might be, I wouldn't expose him to brutal rape scenes. Such images were part of our work, but Kip didn't have to imprint them on his memory. I wished I could erase what he'd seen of the beating.

"Seems likely Sharon's the target," Jax observed. "She might've investigated abuse claims from Ella."

I nodded. "I think these murders are about payback for Locke's humiliation. He had a list, maybe triggered by Ella leaving. Somehow, he persuaded these men to participate."

"Righting wrongs," Kip added. "That's what he always talked about, how important it was."

"I noticed something," Jax said. "The location where they're assaulted is a different house or different room. The couch and paint color on the walls are different."

"Ryder said the Lovatos were taken to another house," Ayden added. "Maybe the Pryors were, too."

Natra raised a finger. "And there's no evidence they were hurt or killed in their home. There would've been blood."

"We should get these photos to law enforcement," Jax said. "Not local. Higher up."

I nodded. "First thing tomorrow. I can't imagine why Dad didn't do that."

I closed the *Dom* subfolder and hovered over *Prize*. Natra gave me a warning look and shook her head. Jax squeezed my shoulder.

"It's okay," Kip said. "I don't need to see it." He got up and went to the table to pick up his phone. "I'll try to contact my brothers."

"You can go in my apartment," Natra told him.

I moved the images from the large screen to the computer screen. Diminishing them made them less oppressive. Jax took Kip's seat next to me.

"Not sure I want to see this after a meal," I said. "We know they're dead. Maybe we should—"

Jax breathed out. "Let's see what we've got and then make a plan."

I tapped on the *Prize* folder. It held images and another subfolder, labeled *Trophy*. In the images, both victims were clearly dead, bruised, and stripped of clothing. The side of Ralph's head appeared to be caved in. I swallowed back the gorge that rose in my throat.

"Like Clark, maybe," Natra observed. "If that Vermont discovery turns out to be his skull."

I looked at Ayden. "Did you send your drawing to Terri Frye?"

"I did, boss. That's why she's interested in the Dacretown search."

Ayden's phone rang. He looked at it. "Sidney Karro, the local guy. Maybe he found Kip's laptop. Be right back." He walked away and took the call.

I enlarged five more images. The bodies were being trussed with ropes and wrapped in plastic. I pointed. "There's Locke, I think." The photographer had caught a blurry image of the side of a bald man's face as he bent over Ralph's body. "Ella must've been shocked when she found these. Imagine knowing you married this scumbag."

Three more images showed the wrapped bodies next to a hole, but they'd been switched to bags—multiple bags. I suspected they were now dismembered.

"I don't see anything that places them, geographically," Jax commented. "Maybe the maps will help."

The last item was the folder labeled *Trophy*. I braced myself and opened it. "Oh, my God!" I put my hand to my mouth and jumped up so fast I knocked over my chair. I crossed the room and went out to the balcony. The blast of cold air helped. I wanted to vomit. I opened my mouth and gulped in deep breaths. Tears filled my eyes. The ultimate trophy—the *prize*—was Sharon Pryor's head. A hand had held it up by the hair to show the jagged flesh where it had been sawed or hacked off the body. I rubbed my face hard.

Jax came out and wrapped his arms around me. I trembled against him. "How could they keep this secret? Any of them? Gregory, Dad, Ella. How *could* they?"

He didn't respond. There *was* no adequate response.

Natra opened the slider. "Annie, come back in and look at this."

I shook my head. "I can't."

"You need to see this."

I took a deep breath of cold air before Jax and I followed her back inside. She had a photograph up on the large screen. She pointed at it.

Three men stood together, raising beers over a fire. Their blood-spattered faces were all clearly visible. Ketch Ryder had looked straight at the camera and grinned.

Chapter Thirty-Two

Kip entered and saw the photo. He blinked. "Isn't that…?"

"Yes," I said. "He's part of it. This is proof. He's in the photos Ella stole from Jordan Locke."

Kip nodded and crossed his arms. "The hunting club."

Jax snapped his fingers. "Hunting club. The maps. Let's look at that folder."

"Wait, wait!" said Kip. "I have news."

We all turned to him. He held up his phone. "They have a skull. They couldn't send photos, but JJ said it's in a plastic bag with hair remnants the right color and some earrings." Kip ran his fingers over his throat. "Like…maybe…"

I nodded. "All those names with 'head' in them. That was their game. Maybe it started with Buckhead. Was this at a trailhead?"

"Yeah. An old trail we didn't maintain, but it was near the gate. They had to quit. They'll go back tomorrow."

"So, Ryder got one right. The headmaster must've trusted 'im."

"Or he did it on his own," Ayden suggested. "Some things are different about this one."

Natra opened the *Maps* folder. Four regional maps popped up.

Jax studied them. "They're marked with Xs. Look at the South Carolina map. That's near that area where we had your other case."

"Devil's Fork. I recognize it." He meant a case we'd solved two months earlier, thanks to a series of poems and tattoos. I enlarged it. "I doubt Locke missed *that* name."

Jax peered at it and pointed at an X to the north. "That's where Caesars Head Park is."

"And there's Hilton Head." Natra used a laser pointer on a second map. "But it doesn't go as far north as OBX, so no Nags Head."

Jax tapped the table. "This memory card's date is before the Lovatos. It's about the Pryors. So, Buckhead, Caesars Head, even Hilton Head. Those make sense. 'Head' is clearly the headmaster's theme. They could be preplanned burial locations. The fourth map is Arrowhead Beach in North Carolina."

"Not far from here," I said, "But did they go after the Lovatos just because they were in Nags Head? Seems too coincidental that they were also Ella's friends."

"Maybe they wouldn't have been targeted otherwise. Think about it. Ella went to them when she left Locke. Maybe he discovered they'd sheltered her. He'd suspect she told them things about him. By then, the game was in motion. Nags *Head* would draw his attention. Too good to pass up. They'd done it once and gotten away with it."

"I can't fathom why Dad did nothing. Ella came here right after that incident. She must have been terrified."

"But we don't know what she told Lang or showed him," Natra offered. "And now that I see that photo of Ketch, which she'd also seen, I wonder if we got the chronology wrong. Maybe she went looking for Ivy. It wasn't just a chance meeting. *She* initiated it. We know she hired PIs. I mean, Locke doesn't clearly appear in *these* photos. She wants to nail him. Maybe she did her own undercover work."

Ayden came in, waving his phone. "Sid says they stopped the Audi driver. Pulled 'im over. Broken taillight. Get this. He's GBI! An agent. He admitted he's been parking near your house but said it's official business."

I looked at Jax. "Georgia Bureau of Investigation. Would he ram us?"

"He might if he had to protect his cover."

"Why's he watching *this* house, though? He's not just an assistant to Broward. He's from a different agency."

Jax cocked his head at Ayden. "Did this agent say how the taillight got broken?"

I squinted at him. "What're you thinking?"

"We can't assume anything."

Ayden nodded. "Said he backed into a pole."

I snorted. "So, he lied. He hit us. I saw it break. We have the video. Maybe he's lying about other things. Did you get a name?"

"Yeah. Eric Skinner."

Jax wrote it down. "This is my part, Annie. I'll pull in some favors and check his credentials."

I felt surrounded. FBI. GBI. Locke. Clay. "I hate to say this, but what if Locke's got enough clout to get law enforcement on his side?"

"Or in the club," Kip said. "Vaughn told me Broward threatened her. I thought he was just protecting his media image. Maybe he's protecting Locke."

"That would explain why it wasn't easy to take these photos to law enforcement. You don't know who to trust."

"You going out with Broward tomorrow?" Ayden asked. "He could be just tryin' to get you into a trap."

"I'm not sure, Ayden. These photos and videos complicate things. Still..."

Jax crossed his arms. "We're going, if only to call his bluff."

A chirp sounded at the table where the food still sat. A text to Vaughn's phone. Kip ran for it and picked it up. "It's Vaughn, for me. She wants me to pick 'er up. She's on the boardwalk."

"In Duck?" I asked.

He nodded.

"Where?"

He texted her, then waited. He read her response. "'Just walking. Want to keep moving. Got away.'"

"Why wouldn't she just come here?"

"I don't know, Annie, but I'll go."

Ayden got up. "I'll drive. Tell her to find the Super Wings store and stay at the red chair. She can't miss it."

Jax held out a hand. "Wait. How do you know it's her?"

CHAPTER THIRTY-TWO

Kip frowned. "It's on her phone. She knows we're waiting to hear from her."

"And someone could be with her, making her send the text. Why wouldn't she call and talk to you?"

"Good point," said Ayden. "Text her back. Tell her to call."

Kip seemed reluctant.

"Kip," I said. "You're not sure what her agenda is. And if it's not her, then someone's trying to get you out alone."

He nodded and typed in a text. He got a response and read it. "'Too risky.'" He looked torn. "I'll just go, drive by. There can't be many people out. Don't we wanna find out what's going on with her? Why she just took off?"

There was plenty I wanted to find out, but rushing out without a plan was a bad idea. We decided that Ayden would drive Kip to the location, and Jax would follow. Natra and I would arm ourselves and watch for someone trying to get in. Now I really wished we had Mika here.

Shortly after they left, my phone rang. I looked at the caller ID.

"Scotland! Shona. Finally, some news."

Chapter Thirty-Three

I grabbed the phone and accepted the call. "Shona? Is everything okay?"

"Holding steady, Annie. Lang's sorry he hasn't called. He's been quite ill. I'd like to set up a video call with you, if it's convenient, so you can see him, but please keep it short. Talking makes him cough, which worsens his condition."

"He hasn't improved?"

"Not yet. We've made him more comfortable, but it's temporary. He has good days and bad."

"Okay, I understand." I gestured for Natra to prepare the computer for a videocall.

"I've asked him the questions you've sent, but he wants you to stop pursuing this."

"I can't, Shona. We've got people in danger, including me. I'm hoping Dad can help us figure this out. With or without him, I'm staying on it."

"He said you'd say that. Can you get on now?"

"Ready on my end."

I sat at the computer and Natra stayed to the side, ready to take notes. She started a recorder. When Dad finally came on, I was astonished at his appearance. As he lay slightly inclined in bed, he looked thin and pasty, much worse than when I'd seen him just a month ago. He hadn't shaved, and his hair had turned white. Shona was right. I had to be careful.

We exchanged greetings. Dad's voice sounded raspy. I didn't bother to ask how his work was going. I got to the point.

"Dad, we're being watched, maybe stalked. Kip is here. He got into your safe and took Ella Steadman's ring, but I took it back."

Dad held up a hand. He wanted to talk. "Give it to Mark Gardiner." He coughed. It sounded like his lungs were coming out.

"It has to be processed—"

"Did that…nothing on it."

This surprised me. "You had DNA analysis done?"

"Private lab." He coughed again.

"Did Gregory Hawkins know that?"

He put a crumpled tissue to his mouth and nodded.

"Do you know what else was in the ring box?"

Silence. Dad blinked as if I'd confused him.

"Under the platform that supported the ring was a memory card with photos, maps, and videos. We think Ella took them from Jordan Locke. They show a couple from Georgia, beaten and brutally killed."

Lang looked distressed. He shook his head. "Ella…no…she…it was stolen."

I felt instant relief. Dad didn't know. He hadn't covered this up. "Gregory must've taken it from Ella. He didn't tell you?"

"Said…he saw it."

"Why didn't he take it to the police?"

He coughed so hard he had to sit up. With a wave, he indicated he couldn't say much more. "A threat," he choked out. "A…recording." Dad coughed again. Shona showed her face to give me a reproachful look. Dad nudged her away. "Hunting trip. Gregory…talking on it. That's in a note. That envelope. Kip said Gregory…*cough*…left it…there. Locke…said…" He turned and coughed. I cringed. I saw red in the tissue. Dad was coughing up blood.

But we were nearly there. "We haven't found the envelope, Dad."

He took a breath and whispered. "Safe."

"Not there."

"Attic…" More coughing. He clenched his fist and moved it back.

I was crushed. He meant I should pull the stair back. I'd already looked there. "Not under the stair tread, either."

Shona's face came on. "No more, Annie. He can't help, not right now."

"Please, just—"

"No."

I had to give up. "Okay. If he remembers something else, please let me know as soon as you can."

"I'll see what I can do. No promises."

I wanted to tell Dad we'd found Ella's remains, but I wasn't yet sure. He'd take it hard if he learned she'd been buried in Dacretown, *his* property—the place that had made him so ill. If he'd been in love with her, this would be especially hard to hear. The news had to be delivered with care. I realized he'd probably used every resource he had at the time to find her.

"Dad, I'll talk to you when you're better. Please rest now."

He gave a weak wave. His lips formed a message. I thought he said *burn it.* Shona ended the video.

"He looks awful," I said to Natra. "I shouldn't have put him through that."

"At least now you know he wasn't aware of the memory card. He didn't see the images."

I nodded. "And he knows we've got trouble here. Maybe he'll think of something."

Natra stood. "Let's check the attic again. I didn't see a safe or lockbox up there, but he said *attic* not *stair.* It's worth looking."

I removed the SD card and placed it into the sleeve before we went up the steps. I stopped at the trick stair tread and pulled it out again, just to be sure. I ran my hand around inside and pressed on the bottom to check for a hidden compartment. Nothing. I continued into the hurricane room. We'd done a good job of organizing and emptying it, but there were still a few boxes.

Natra came up behind me.

"Wait," I said. "This is the *safe* room. Gregory told Kip he'd put the letter somewhere *safe.* He didn't mean Dad's office safe. He wanted to hide it in a safe spot, like with the SD card." I looked around and up at the ceiling. "What was he thinking?"

Natra hugged herself. "It's cold up here."

"Yes, sorry. Ayden didn't have time to look at the register."

I went over to it and bent close to tap on it. I had a thought. I pointed to the other one. "Tap that one."

She did. It sounded hollow.

"Something's up with this one. Doesn't sound right." I gripped the metal louvers and pulled. It didn't budge. "These screws have glue around them. Kip noticed that. But why?"

Natra used her phone flashlight to better illuminate them. "Are they screwed in?"

I pulled again. The register plate moved. "Dad made a pulling gesture." I looked around and spotted the knife we'd used to cut through tape. I grabbed it. "Stand back." I stuck the blade behind the top of the register and pulled it toward me.

"You're gonna break the blade," Natra said. "I have a better idea." She rooted through a box until she came out with some twine. "Saw this yesterday." She knelt and threaded it through the louver slots. I grabbed a piece and mirrored her at the other end. We braced ourselves.

"On the count of three," I said. "One-two—" We pulled the cover off a gaping hole.

Natra peered at it. "Clever. It's not for a duct. The fake screw heads covered magnets, strong ones."

I pointed. "And there's the white envelope. In a safe place. A safe in the safe room. Dad *did* tell us. Even if Locke looked up here, he wouldn't have figured this out."

I reached for the envelope. It had the GHG seal. I used the knife to slide under it and open the envelope. Inside was a blue business-style envelope. "There it is. Locke's letter to Gregory. Finally!"

Natra stopped me. "Don't touch it. We need gloves. We've lost the ring as evidence, and the SD card has been handled. If anything contains Locke's uncontaminated DNA, it's this."

"You're right. Let's get some."

A noise from downstairs made us freeze. We looked at each other. Someone was in the house.

Chapter Thirty-Four

I went to the top of the stairs to listen. I heard a low voice. Male. My heart raced. Natra came up behind me. I put a finger to my lips and whispered, "You armed?"

"No. You?"

"No. Looks like Vaughn was bait. It'll soon be obvious we're up here. The door's open, the light's on."

"Maybe I can get into my apartment."

I shook my head. I heard a rustle of papers. "More than one. I think they're in the main room. They might see you in the hall." No one had to say it: all the notes were sitting on the table. They'd see our chart.

I stepped back, shut off the stairwell light, and closed the door. As quietly as possible, I turned the lock. It wouldn't keep them out for long if they came up, but it gave us a delay we might need. I pulled out my phone and texted Ayden and Jax to return ASAP. Then I strode over to the register vent we'd just pulled off and put it back in place. The magnets snapped into position. I pointed up at the trapdoor.

"Call the cops?" Natra whispered.

"Ayden and Jax will get here first. After our recent issues, I don't want cops probing our work. If the intruders come up the steps, I'll make that call."

Natra opened a wardrobe to grab the waterproof coats I'd stored for weather events. I accepted one before I pressed the button on the remote that lowered the folding stairs. I cringed at the sound of the motor and hoped the closed door muffled it. Natra went up. The steps creaked. I followed. When I reached the platform, the cold ocean wind shocked me, despite the coat. I closed the stairs while Natra opened the latches on a box that contained an emergency escape ladder.

"It will get us only to the balcony," I said. "And they're in the main room. The curtains will hide us, but they might hear us."

"I'll risk it. I'm fast. You stay here. I'll get out to the road and intercept Ayden."

"Stay clear of the house. We don't know who might be outside."

We hooked the ladder to the railing, and I watched Natra step over and go down. Once she hit the balcony, she raced to the steps. I stepped back to avoid being seen.

A flash of light came from the beach. Maybe Natra's phone. Or maybe an accomplice. I couldn't see far in the dark. I listened for sounds that someone had forced the door and come into the attic, but the ocean's rumble thwarted me.

Ayden's truck came flying into the back driveway. A dark figure came off the beach toward it. In the front of the house, car tires screeched. I opened and went down the trapdoor steps. A door downstairs slammed, followed by familiar voices. Ayden and Natra were now inside. I opened the attic door and descended, bumping into Natra at the bottom. Her face was red from the cold.

I raced to the main room. The table we'd used for planning was empty. Ayden stood there. "Looks like they took it all, boss. The binder, the chart, the notes."

"And the SD card." The rolling whiteboard showed the side where we'd placed our recent chronology, but our primary chart remained hidden. "I can't believe this. They must've been waiting outside when you left."

"That's everything," Kip said. "We lost the photos and Dad's file. They cleaned us out."

"We've got the letter."

Kip gasped. "You found it?"

I turned to him. "Yes. It's safe, but we aren't. They'll soon realize what we know."

"What does the letter say?"

"Haven't read it yet."

Natra rolled the whiteboard out. "We also have our analysis."

"But nothing that gives it legal substance." I looked around. "Speaking of… where's Jax?"

Ayden turned toward the sliding door. "He was right behind me."

I recalled the screeching tires. "He must've followed them. Ayden, come on. He needs backup. Natra, you and Kip try to find how they got in and lock it."

I changed coats and pocketed my phone before I went out. We jumped into Ayden's truck and went out to the main street. "I don't know which way," I said.

"Hang on." Ayden jumped out to look at the street. He shook his head and got in. "Hard to tell, but I think north. That's where Vaughn supposedly was."

He made a right and accelerated. I gave him a brief rundown of our close encounter and asked about Vaughn.

"She wasn't there, Annie, and before we could fan out on the boardwalk, you texted your SOS, so we raced back. Lucky we didn't get pulled over."

"She could still be there, then."

"You got me. Maybe it was a ruse, a way to divide and conquer."

I watched in the rearview. No one followed. "That occurred to me. Keep your eyes open on that side, in case Jax stopped somewhere. I'll watch on this side. She might be near where she left Kip's car."

"Copy, boss."

My text tone drew my attention. "Natra. Kip got another text from Vaughn. Says she's hiding in the woods."

"That narrows it down if she's near the boardwalk. But Jax first, right?"

"Yes." I considered a plan, then texted. *Have him tell her to stay where she is.*

We passed the main tourist areas, the shops at Scarborough Lane on the right, then the Soundside Shoppes and a realtor on the left. Except for near a restaurant, the lots were empty. I gripped the car seat. We had to go slower in this area or risk a ticket. Near the Super Wings beach store with its red roof and multiple blue gables, Ayden crept along. "The Red Chair's behind this."

"Park for a second. I can jump out and look."

I ran to the boardwalk to view the oversized red chair where many tourists take photos. Vaughn wasn't there. I ran back. Just as I got in, my text tone sounded.

Kip left. Took your gun. Couldn't stop him.

I read it to Ayden. "These two, Vaughn and Kip. Like herding cats. She must've told 'im where she is."

"If she's anywhere near here, we'll see her. And his car's white, easy to spot."

"Let's keep going."

We passed more businesses, including the township offices. The Duck Town Park came up next on Ayden's side.

I pointed. "That parking lot in there is secluded. It's also in the woods. Maybe we should check it."

"Good place to get trapped," Ayden said. "There's a large open lot ahead. We can park there and take the boardwalk back. Gives us a clear escape route."

I agreed. We passed Nags Head Hammocks and the stark white Duck Church. On the right was ABC Liquors and a small deli, closed. Then Kitty Hawk Kites on the left. I strained to see ahead.

"Stop here?" Ayden asked.

No sign of the Wrangler. "Let's go to the end of the boardwalk and turn around. It's not far. We can search the area back to the woods."

Ayden pressed on the gas. We passed the parking lot on the left for the Waterfront Shops. I sat up. Just beyond the large blue and white sign for the shopping center, I spotted the Wrangler. "There it is!"

Besides Jax's Jeep, only a silver Tahoe, a white Passat, and a black Escalade were in the lot. Ayden turned in, parked, and jumped out. He looked inside the Wrangler and opened the door. I joined him.

"Empty," he said. "And unlocked."

I looked around. The shops were all dark. "Why would he park here?"

Ayden pointed toward a large building. "Let's get on the boardwalk over there and head south to the park."

"Maybe he saw Vaughn here." I felt a stab of panic that quickened my heart. "Or what if they forced him to stop and then took him?"

Chapter Thirty-Five

I could barely think. Things were quiet here, too quiet. It *felt* empty. No one was outside on a cold Friday night in November. I texted Natra. *Wrangler at Waterfront Shops, empty.*

We took the ramp to get on the boardwalk but saw no sign of Jax in either direction.

"To that park?" Ayden asked.

"Yes, but let's drive back to the Wee Winks lot. It's closer."

We got in his truck. As we neared a small lot on my side, I said, "Pull in here for a sec. There's a chapel back in the woods, perfect for hiding."

Before Ayden had fully stopped, I saw movement near the path—a figure that resembled Vaughn. I got out and ran toward the chapel. The sound of running feet on the boardwalk drew me onto the ramp and out to the open walkway. Despite the small lights along this path, I saw no one. Ayden caught up.

"I think Vaughn's here," I told him. "I heard someone run south, just one person. I don't want her to get past us. Drive down to the park, and I'll go this way. I'll meet you in the lot over there."

"We shouldn't split—"

But I took off. The boards sounded hollow as I pounded along. A slick spot made me slip. I rounded a corner, looked over the side toward the water, and kept going. Two ramps to my left led down to the secluded parking lot. I took the first one. "Vaughn!" I called. Then I heard footsteps behind me. I looked back. A slender teenage boy strode up. He showed me his gun. "Keep going."

I turned to run, but he grabbed my coat and pushed me against the railing, jamming his body against mine. I yelled and tried to wriggle free. A tall, stocky man appeared and put tape over my mouth. I recognized him. He'd been in the campfire photo with Ketch Ryder. The man holding me was part of Locke's hunting club.

He jerked me toward the lot. The lights were dim under the overhanging trees. Twenty feet away, another man had Vaughn in a bear hug. She struggled to avoid the tape. I felt my phone slide out of my back pocket. No! I struggled but couldn't break the grip on my arms. I heard a thud nearby, as if they'd tossed the phone. My captor forced me toward a black panel van. I managed a solid kick into his knee, but he flung me through the seatless van's open back doors. I hit the floor.

Vaughn came in behind me, but she yelled and put up a fierce fight. The boy struggled with her. He closed one of the back doors. She pushed him against it and scooted toward the open door. The kid grabbed her hair. She clasped her hands and pushed straight into his stomach. He swore and fell back.

Vaughn leapt out. The kid yelled her name. She shouted back, "You're an idiot, Clay!"

This kid was her brother.

I got to my knees to follow her but heard a distinct *click*. I looked back. The man who'd gagged me, now in the passenger seat, pointed a semi-auto at me. "Don't move!"

Clay pushed Vaughn back inside. She kicked him hard with both feet. He howled and grabbed her jacket as she jumped out again. She swung around and slugged him in the jaw. He let go. I heard a man shout outside. Then Clay got in with me and slammed the second door closed. "She got away," he mumbled.

The driver opened his door, but headlights shone in the window.

Ayden! I had to warn him. I reached for my phone and felt the empty pocket.

"Someone's coming," the driver said. "Let's go."

He gunned it, jerking the van around before racing out to Duck Road. I guessed he'd swerved around Ayden. But Ayden would pivot and follow. I couldn't see out the window from the floor, but I felt the van make several hard turns. I sensed they'd taken a residential street. Clay watched out the back. "He went straight," he said.

My heart sank. If Ayden hadn't seen them enter this street, he'd lose us. He'd see the empty road ahead and would double back, but he'd have multiple side roads to consider. With my phone gone, he couldn't track me.

Still, Vaughn had gotten away. Maybe he'd see her, and she'd tell him where they were taking me. Kip, too, might connect with her. I kicked myself for separating from Ayden. I knew better. Jax had warned me.

Gun Guy ordered me to stay down. I couldn't see, but from the ocean sounds I believed we were going north. If these people had abducted Jax, maybe I'd end up with him. We'd gotten out of scrapes together before. Counting Clay, the two men in this van, and one I'd heard outside, there were at least four. With Locke, five. At least. The odds weren't in our favor.

The driver looked in his rearview mirror. "Hey, kid, how'd she get away? She's just a girl."

"She hits hard." Clay kneaded his left hand. "I think she broke my finger."

The two men in front exchanged glances. One snorted as if this was funny. "We should make you walk back."

Clay didn't respond. He seemed peeved. He was just a skinny sixteen-year-old no more than five-seven. His black baseball cap, which sported a pair of crossed rifles embroidered in gold, said he wanted to seem strong, be bigger than he was, maybe heroic. I imagined that Clay had aligned with Locke, a high-status member of his community. He wanted to please the man. He'd gotten a truck. Clay probably viewed Vaughn as a traitor. He'd given Kip the binder to try to strip her of an ally.

I'd watch for an opportunity to work on him. For the moment, he was steamed. He'd had one job; he'd failed. That didn't sit well with teenage boys.

"Slow down," Gun Guy growled at the driver. "Don't draw attention."

He must have seen a patrol, maybe Karro. I tensed up, prepared to jump up and pound on the window, but Gun Guy told Clay, "She moves, deck 'er."

I believed the kid would do it.

They turned, then turned again. I listened for the ocean, but Gun Guy increased the volume of a Country Western song he'd selected, maybe to thwart me.

The images from the photos and video spooked me. Gun Guy, at least, had participated in this brutality. I had to stay alert. My life might depend on a split-second opening. I believed they were taking me to the headmaster. The gag itched. I wriggled my mouth to test it. The tape was tight, but they hadn't bound my hands or feet. Yet.

I thought the van was moving in a southerly direction. The Outer Banks stretches a long way. I remembered Kip saying Locke looked like a pirate. Ocracoke, Blackbeard's former hideout, was across from Hatteras at the southernmost point. But that would be highly inconvenient for an operation focused on my house. They had to be closer. Maybe Kill Devil Hills or Nags Head. Locke liked his name game.

I stretched my neck to try to see. The windows were too high. I glanced at Clay and wondered if I could rush him, maybe bull my way out the back. He glared at me and made a fist.

They took more turns, which kept me off balance, before we seemed to get on a road with several moderate curves. That wouldn't be Kill Devil Hills or Nags Head. The main roads through there are fairly straight, with stoplights. I figured north. More isolated.

Locke had met me. He knew Dad. I prayed they didn't have Jax. Locke tortured *couples*. He probably knew his crew had grabbed our notes and the SD card, but I still had something he wanted. That letter to Gregory might buy me time. I tried not to envision what he might do to me. This righter of wrongs—wrongs against *him*—probably believed his atrocities were justified, even necessary. Ella had stolen from him, abandoned him, maybe reported his abuse. Anyone who helped her had to be punished. Dad had tried to protect me from all this. I should've done what he asked, just looked for the letter and left Kip out.

The van slowed. It made a left turn and crawled along. My heart quickened. We had to be close.

"Got the clicker?" the driver asked. Gun Guy handed him something. They paused, then moved. I figured it out. They'd stopped at a gate. We'd left Duck, and I didn't think we'd gone to Kill Devil Hills. The Currituck Club? Seemed about the right distance. Then it hit me. Of course. Hunt Club Drive in Corolla. *Hunt Club.* This road curved around for over four miles, sporting high-end secluded properties. A perfect place for a command center. Many of these properties were rentable, especially off-season. Some sat behind tangles of trees and tall shrubs, completely shielded.

The van entered a lighted garage and stopped. The door rolled down. Gun Guy hustled me into a house. With the hard barrel of his weapon poking into my back, he urged me down a dark hall with several closed doors, up a set of steps, into another long hall, then left and through a door on my right. We were in a mansion.

I found myself in a room furnished as a sitting area, with a table, buffet, and a scattering of chairs that smelled of mildew. This was a rental. Locke's crew would do what they'd come for, clean the place, then vanish. There were two small windows. We were on the second floor, but the windows gave me a little hope. There might be something below that could break my jump. Then I realized that Gun Guy intended to stay in the room. I couldn't escape. He stripped off my gag, pulling out strands of hair.

I held my mouth for a moment to reduce the burn. Then I asked, "Where am I? Where have you brought me?"

He jerked his head toward the chairs. I sat down. I knew how they silenced people who knew too much. The items they'd grabbed from my house showed I knew way too much. I cringed.

Vaughn had escaped. Certainly, she'd contact Kip. Jax was out there somewhere, too. Unless he was here, a captive.

The door opened. Clay Ryder entered. He looked even more fragile than he had in the car. No wonder Vaughn had bested him. He gestured with his head for Gun Guy to go.

"They're not leaving her with you," Gun Guy said. "You lost the other one."

"Jordan wants you." A slight tremor in his voice suggested insecurity. Clay lifted his shirt and displayed a 9-mil stowed under his belt. "I have this now.

She's not goin' anywhere."

Gun Guy narrowed his eyes, glanced at me, then left.

Clay shut the door. He put his left hand into his jeans pocket—the hand he'd claimed was injured. It wasn't. *He'd let her go.* This could work in my favor.

"Doesn't look like she hurt you too badly," I said.

Clay raised his chin. He pulled a folded piece of white paper out of his pocket. A sharp rap on the door startled him. He shoved the paper back in his jeans and opened the door. A bald man with a black mustache and a single gold earring entered the room.

Chapter Thirty-Six

Jordan Christopher Locke stopped, cocked his head toward me, and smiled. His head-to-toe black clothing signaled he'd been "in the field." He was tall and hefty, dwarfing Clay. His earring sparkled.

"Lang Hunter's daughter," Locke said. "We meet again. What a treat. And so clever to think you know the game." His Georgia accent softened his imposing impression. He turned to Clay. "Heard you lost your sister. That right?"

Clay looked at the floor. "S-s-sorry, sir. Thought she was coming with us."

"So, she tricked you."

"Yes, sir, sorry, sir."

Locke raised his head to look down his nose. "She nick your truck?"

Clay shook his head and peeked at his boss from under the brim of his black cap. "No, sir. It's in the court, ready to roll. I could go back and—"

"Need you here. We'll get 'er. Got an ancil out looking. She'll learn a lesson she won't forget. I'll need you to help me with that. For now, stand outside the door. Got some business in here."

"Yes, s-sir." Clay went out. Just as he pulled the door behind him, he shifted his eyes toward me. He'd conveyed something. *And* he'd nearly shown me something he didn't want Locke to see.

Locke pulled up a chair to sit directly across from me, two feet away, legs spread. I saw the multiple rings on his fingers Kip had described. He showed even, white teeth in a nasty smile. "Scream if you like. No one's gonna hear you." He leaned closer. "Now, tell me, dahlin'. Why'd you wanna go an' meddle with the plan? It was perfect and I never even told 'im to do it."

"I don't know what you mean," I said.

"Shu'ah you do. I know you went to the prison, you talked to his girl, you even brought in *my* friend, Kip. What an interestin' dinn'ah that musta been. But Ryder's not innocent. He was the'ah all along. He's a lunkhead and his daughtah's no bettah. Not worth all the trouble."

He waited, his eyes gleaming with amusement. I stared at him.

"All right," he said. "Act all superior, just like yo'ah daddy would. Never quite liked him. Can't trust a man who won't drink with the boys. But you know how this works. You have people you care about. We know whey'ah they live. You know what we do. Got a whole gang o' ancillaries makin' this all work, includin' cops. We git you in a situation that only *we* can git you out of, and we'll do that only when you join the game. So, you'll do what Ah say." His right hand formed a fist.

Dread swept through me. My daughter. My father. Jax. My team and everyone they cared about. Lang and Gregory had understood. They'd complied. A rush of heat from my chest through my face likely gave Locke the sign he sought.

"Fo'ah leverage," Locke continued, "we'll get you on tape proving yo'ah knowledge of the doin's and yo'ah part in a coverup. We'll make you an honorary ancil, like a brand."

I pressed back against the chair, unable to shield my disgust.

He cocked his head. "Oh, that's how we managed Gregory Hawkins. He spent plenty a' time with the boys, drinkin' and sayin' things we made so deliciously complicit. Even Lang. He knew things. Did things. Nev'ah took it to the cops. Ah know he has items the *bitch* stole. And *you* have things Ah want. Ah hope we can come to an undah-standin'."

I narrowed my eyes. He made it sound like an easy transfer: the items for my life. I knew better. "You kill people."

"Nothin' you can prove, dahlin. That's the beauty of it. Ah'm a lawyah mahself. Ah kin work the system. Got plenty o' ancils, some leveraged and some, well…let's just say, they embrace the reckonin'. No one was innocent. They all deserved it."

"I haven't done anything to you."

"An' I'll make sure you don't. You can't hide from us. We see you. We hunt, and we'ah good at it."

He was telling me his "ancil" network was beyond my ability to bring to justice, or to escape their control. I persisted, anyway. "Ketch Ryder's already turned on you. His bloody little drawings helped us find some of your victims. Looks like he's getting out of the game."

A quick twitch near Locke's mouth exposed a flicker of annoyance. "*His* victims, Ah assume you mean. Oh, yes, Ah've been told about the dig today. Got ancils up they'ah, too. They'ah's not much ta find."

"That was your wife. You had reason to kill her. She knew things. You'll be a suspect."

"And yet, Ah have a solid alibi for the day she disappe'ahed. Surely you know that."

"Meaningless, when you have…ancils."

"Good, good, you'ah speakin' the language. But you ovah-estimate me." He peered at me. "If, as you say, they found her, whe'ah was she? Ah don't own that land. Who hunted they'ah?"

So, he knew about Dacretown *and* that Ella had been buried there. "Gregory wouldn't have killed Ella."

He tilted his bald head. "Are you so sure Lang wouldn't? He's got secrets you don't know."

I swallowed, then reminded myself that Locke was a manipulative, lying predator. But he was also right.

"She told me everythang," he continued. "You know she almost married 'im 'til she learned things about 'im. She jilted 'im. Many a man has killed a woman fo'ah less."

I looked at his ringed hands—wrestler hands Kip had called them—then back at his smirk. "Sounds more like her response to *you*."

Locke's face hardened. "Lang *Hunter*. Don't you find that amusin'?"

"He didn't hunt."

"Didn't he? Or maybe he just didn't hunt dee'ah."

I decided to cut the crap. "What do you want from me?"

He sat back and put his hands on his thighs. "Let's get to it. He'ah's what you'll do. You will create a report from yo'ah visit to Ketch. You will find him competent. You will confirm that what he's told Agent Broward is the truth. And then you'll leave 'im alone. That's a start."

I made a face. "I didn't assess him for—"

He stood and raised his voice, his big hands formed into fists. "*You* will do what Ah tell you! Unless you want yo'ah team to find *yo'ah* pretty little head." A vein in his forehead bulged.

This wasn't a negotiation. I was watching what Ella had witnessed—a self-important narcissist who exerts control over those around him. His sycophantic ancillaries affirmed this. Anyone who questioned him would be dealt with. If words failed, he'd pummel them. My stomach clenched. I'd gone too far.

Yet, he wasn't acting like a man who'd already gained an advantage. Maybe he didn't realize I no longer had the photos and Gregory's file. He *needed* me to do this. He was worried.

"All right," I said. "I'll make the report and send a copy to Broward."

He leaned toward me. "That's mo'ah like it. And we'll help. You'll do it right he'ah. But first, you'll make a recordin', so you won't be tempted to back out." He went to the door, opened it, and said, "Have Pete bring the equipment."

A man downstairs shouted. Glass shattered. I jumped. Locke shot me a nasty look and stepped into the hall. I heard more commotion downstairs. Locke told Clay to stay in place, then slammed the door behind him. He strode with heavy steps away from the room.

I went to the door to listen. It sounded like chaos out there. Several men were shouting. A shot was fired, and more glass broke. Sounded like a window. I tested the knob. It turned in my hand. I opened the door.

Clay pushed me back into the room and closed the door behind him.

Chapter Thirty-Seven

"Let me go, Clay," I said. "You don't want to get tangled up with this crew. I can help you." I steeled myself to run him over.

He held up a finger. "Shh!" Then he pulled the folded paper from his pocket and shoved it at me. "Take this. Get out of here. They're gonna hurt you." He pointed to his left. "Go that way, last room. There's an open window and a tree you can jump to. Run behind the house, cross through the woods to the next street. Look for an F-150, bronze."

Then he was gone. Something had happened.

I entered the dark hallway, followed his directions, and found the open window. A streetlight illuminated a live oak with thick branches that spread every which way. Rain had slickened the bark. If I jumped just right, I could use the closest branch to shimmy to the ground, but if I missed—

"Hey!" Behind me, a light switched on.

The van driver came at me, his right hand raised. I didn't cower as he likely expected. Instead, I stepped to his left and slammed his nose with the flat of my hand. When he jerked back, I kicked his left foot forward and pushed him with my full weight. He fell on his back.

I climbed onto the sill, but the guy was up. He grabbed my hair. I launched backward into him. We fell to the floor. He let go, and I jumped up and stomped on his throat. He grabbed my foot, but I put my full weight on him, choking him. He struggled to throw me off. I lost my balance and jumped to the left. When he got to his knees, I pushed his head back and kicked him in the groin. He yelled and curled into a protective crouch.

I ran to the sill and pushed off. I hit a branch but failed to find purchase. I grabbed for anything but slid too fast. A twig slowed my momentum, but I fell and hit the ground hard. I lay for a moment, dazed. My left wrist and hand hurt. But I had to get up. *They're gonna hurt you.*

Van Man leaned out the open window and shouted, "Get her!" I pushed myself up and ran to the side of the three-car garage, then took off into the dark backyard. A light came on. Gun Guy came out the mansion's back door, weapon ready. I ducked into a shadow. He looked around. I waited. My wrist was killing me. I pressed it against my chest and willed myself to stay quiet. He went back in. I held my arm close and moved through the yard. Tripping over a tree root, I went to my knees. Pain shot through me. I felt something wet on my face and realized I'd scraped my head. But I was alive and almost free.

I spotted a sign that signaled a walking path through a wooded spot. I couldn't just plunge ahead. There were golf courses here, with sand traps and small lakes. But I had to go. They'd likely urge Clay to fetch his truck, or worse, call him a traitor. They might follow me.

Darts of pain slowed me. I stayed in shadows. The air was so crisp I could hear the commotion at the mansion as if I were in the room. I thought the entire area could, although many of these houses were empty. Careful about noise, I strode between two houses to a street. To my relief, the streetlight was burned out.

I barely understood what had just happened. There'd been a plan. Clay had let Vaughn get away. And now he'd helped me escape. There'd be consequences. They'd surely hurt him, maybe execute him without a second thought. He had to know this. I considered going back, but my injury made me useless. I had no gun, and no phone to call police.

Down the street, a set of lights flashed once. Truck lights. Maybe Clay had run, too. I clamped my injured arm close and strode in that direction, but pain doubled me over. A door opened. I couldn't move. Soon, I saw black shoes next to me.

"Annie! I got you."

I looked up. Kip grabbed me around the waist. The truck's engine started, and the vehicle came toward us. Kip helped me get in. I moved with difficulty to the middle of the bench seat. Vaughn, at the wheel, urged Kip to hurry. We took off. I kept my arm close, but the pain still took my breath away.

"You scraped your head," Kip said. "You're bleeding."

I nodded. "Might've broke my wrist, too."

"We'll get you back to the house."

Vaughn looked at me. "Did you get it?"

"What's going on?" I asked. "Why are you here?"

She gave me a look. "Isn't it obvious? Did you *get* it?"

"Get what?"

"The list. Clay was s'posed to give it to you."

With difficulty, I extracted the folded piece of paper from my pocket. "This?"

Vaughn nodded. "That. And now we gotta get Clay."

"We can't," Kip said. "They'll see us."

"There's at least four guys," I warned. "They know I got out. They're armed."

"They're not gonna shoot. Jordan said no shooting. Everyone on this road would call the cops."

"Someone's shooting," I said.

"Whatever. I'm not leavin' him. Everyone, strap in. It's gonna get wild!"

I pulled on a seatbelt as Vaughn accelerated. Kip helped me buckle it. When Vaughn turned right, I saw the sign for Hunt Club Drive. The truck lurched. She swore at it and pushed it into a higher speed. "Stupid truck," she mumbled. "Why'd he drive this thing here?"

I sat up. "They know this truck. They'll shoot us."

"They don't know I'm driving."

"They'll think *I'm* driving."

"I talked Clay into this. Not leavin' 'im behind."

I pressed back against the seat. Kip gripped my right arm. We approached a mansion fully lit on all three floors. Had to be Locke's. Just as we passed the driveway, a black Escalade sped backwards and rammed the back of the truck, spinning us. The truck tipped left. I clung to the seat with my good hand and prayed we wouldn't flip. Vaughn moved her weight to the right, bumping me and sending shooting pains through my wrist. The truck returned to all four wheels. Kip breathed out. The SUV pulled forward as if to make another try.

"Get out of here!" Kip urged her. "We can't do it this way."

"There!" I pointed to a male figure running in the street two houses up, chased by a taller figure. "That's Clay."

Vaughn sped up and bumped the tall man, throwing him to the grass. He rolled. As she reached Clay, she slowed. He vaulted into the open bed. The SUV rammed us again. Kip looked back. "Clay's getting knocked around."

"He knows where the grab bars are." Vaughn tore off, going south. The SUV followed.

"There's no outlet this way," I said. "You'll get stuck at the gate."

"Got a plan."

The Escalade came up tight behind us. To Kip, Vaughn said, "Tell me when you see the street."

"It's coming up."

She lowered her window and shouted, "Grab something, Clay! Hold tight!"

"Here!" Kip pointed. Vaughn made a hard left, screeching the tires. The Escalade shot past. I heard noise in the back, as if Clay had fallen. We came to a small traffic circle with a white gazebo. Vaughn flew around it, pushing me into Kip. I moaned. The Escalade had recovered and followed.

"He's coming!" Kip shouted.

Now facing the SUV, Vaughn veered, then knocked into its left side, forcing the driver into sand on the right. It wouldn't stop him, but it would slow him down. At Hunt Club Drive, she turned right and looked in the rearview mirror. "Good thing he's a kid. He'll survive the bumps."

She sped to the north end loop. Wrong way. We were going in circles. If others followed, we'd be trapped. But Vaughn turned right onto what looked like a dirt road. She flipped off her lights.

"What're you doing?" I asked.

"We got this. Don't worry."

Kip patted my arm. "It's okay, Annie. We know a way out."

Vaughn bumped along on dirt and gravel, then stopped. Kip got out.

"He's closing the chain," Vaughn told me. I heard Kip say something before he got back in. "Clay's gonna stay back there," he said. "He's okay. He says, just go."

Vaughn took us out to pavement, turned on her lights, and turned right. I recognized the main route, Highway 12, and let my breath out. Kip patted my arm. "You okay?"

"Still alive. Thank you." I didn't want to admit how much my head and arm hurt.

Vaughn accelerated, ignoring the speed limit. I made a move to get my phone to text my team but remembered I'd lost it. "Can we stop where they grabbed us so I can find my phone? I think they tossed it in that park."

"I have it," Vaughn said. "Clay threw it so they wouldn't get it. I'll give it to you when we get there."

I looked at Kip. "Did you see Ayden?"

"He's back there."

"Back where?"

He gestured with his head behind us. "The house. He broke windows to distract them so you could run. Clay opened a window to let 'im know you could get out."

I shook my head. "We can't leave him there."

"He knows the way out." Kip directed Vaughn to slow down. "We're almost there." He pulled out his phone and texted someone.

I looked around. "We're going to the Duck House?"

"Yup."

"No. We need to go—"

"Natra's there."

"Why?"

"Safer for everyone, at least for now."

Vaughn arrived. Kip's Range Rover sat tucked along the side of the house. Vaughn pulled into the double-wide driveway. The garage door opened. She drove in and parked next to Natra's Bronco. The door closed behind us.

Vaughn jumped out. Kip opened his door, but I stopped him. "How did you end up with Vaughn?"

"Long story. Let's go in. Your arm okay?"

I moved it and stiffened. "I'll need help."

He gave me a hand. I grimaced against another shot of pain. Natra opened a door into the house. It looked light and warm inside. She helped Kip get me to the nearest chair. Vaughn came in, supporting Clay, and handed me my phone.

I tapped in the code. There were so many messages waiting to be opened that I laid it face down on my thigh. I had to get steady.

"I brought the first-aid kit," Natra said. "Figured someone would need it."

"My brother, too," Vaughn said. "Someone shot at 'im. Skinned 'is arm."

The sleeve of Clay's jacket showed a bloodstained rip. He removed his jacket and cap and nodded toward me. I wanted to hug him. He'd shown immense courage. I figured he knew his safety here was temporary. The vengeful Jordan Locke, hopped up on his private sense of justice, would not forgive him. Or me. We'd humiliated him. He'd punish us both if he got the chance.

Natra showed Vaughn the first-aid items. "Help yourself. There's more in the bathroom down the hall, and hot water on the stove."

With a wet cloth, Natra dabbed at my forehead. "Bad bump. This'll hurt. You must've scraped something sharp."

"A tree. And hurt my wrist. Have a brace?"

"Not here, but an elastic bandage and a splint will give it support. And I have some meds." She handed me a pill and a bottle of water. "This is strong, so don't drive."

I took the pill before I asked, "Did you hear from Jax? Or Ayden?"

"They haven't checked in since they left."

"They're together?"

Vaughn looked over at me. "Jax followed us, me an' Clay. We couldn't lose 'im, so we pulled over."

I was confused. "Followed you from where?"

"Your house."

I looked at Natra.

"It's complicated," she said. "Let's get everyone—"

Her phone rang. She answered it. To me, she mouthed, *Ayden.* Then she said, "They're all here. Come back…. What?" She listened, then ended the call. Her expression told me the news was bad.

"They're still at Locke's command center. Jax went in and hasn't come out."

Chapter Thirty-Eight

My heart stopped. I could hardly breathe. "He went in the *house*? Where Jordan Locke is? Why?"

Vaughn stopped working on Clay. "My attorney? I have to go back!"

"No one's going there," Natra said. "We wait for what Ayden can tell us." Vaughn pouted.

"But he went in for me, and I'm *here*," I said. "We can call the cops, get them over there."

"Ayden will make the call when he and Jax are clear," Natra said. "Don't want them arrested, too."

"He went for the map," Clay said. "I told 'im about it. A master map. He wanted to get it."

I looked around. "Someone needs to tell me what's happening. Here's my part. I saw Vaughn near the boardwalk in Duck and chased her to the park. Ayden came from the other side in the truck, but they caught me before he got there. They took me to a house in Corolla. I met Jordan Locke, who ordered me to prepare a false document about Ketch Ryder and to say things on tape that would muzzle me about their murders. Thanks to Clay, I got away. But how does everyone else know about Locke's place?"

"From me," Vaughn said. She cut a piece of adhesive tape and applied it to the thick pad of gauze that Clay held against his left arm. He flinched. Without his shirt, he looked *really* thin. "Sorry about fleeing your party," she continued, "but Clay was in trouble. Told me I had to come, but it was a set-up. I went to a place in Duck to meet 'im, parked where you could see it, and left my phone so you could track the messages. Figured you could do that, but I deleted most of 'em in case *they* got the phone. They took me to see Locke. They blindfolded me, but I tilted my head and watched the street signs. That's how I knew where he was."

"Jordan wanted me to talk to 'er," Clay added. "Get 'er to stop helpin' Ketch. I showed 'er the map Ketch marked where he'd buried people."

Vaughn broke in. "But it wasn't Ketch's map. He marks them differently and makes weird notes. It was Jordan's map, his handwriting. I pretended to take it all seriously, believe it, you know? Told Jordan I'd drop it and give 'im the tape I had and never see Ketch again."

"I thought he wanted a key," I said.

"The passkey to open Kip's laptop. He thought Kip would tell me. When I said I don't know it, they were gonna use me to get Kip like they used Clay to get me. Jordan also wanted to know what *you* told me. Oh, and he sent Broward to talk to you, by the way."

I peered at her. "Locke sent Broward? They're working together?"

"Seems so. Or he's one of the ancillaries, as Jordan calls them—the ancils. That's his security buffer. People he makes do his stuff. Anyway, you have something Jordan wants. I said I hadn't seen anything, but I thought I could get Kip to find out more." She looked at him. "Didn't mean it. Just wanted to make 'im think I'd help. I needed to get alone with Clay, to tell 'im the truth. But Jordan kept watchin' us. It wasn't till the house was quiet that night that I managed it."

"She woke me up," Clay said.

"I told 'im about what Kip knew and the stuff you had, Annie, that proved it." She tousled her brother's dark blond hair with affection. "He didn't know he was being groomed to help with murder. He wanted to see what you had, though. This morning, Clay told Jordan he'd break into your house and get the stuff."

This startled me. "Break in? Is that why he sent his crew? You told him?"

Vaughn looked confused.

"It wasn't Locke's guys we heard," Natra said. She pointed to Clay and Vaughn. "It was these two."

"*You* set us up?" I asked.

Vaughn crossed her arms. "I sent Kip a text to come and get me. I wanted him to bring help, so, yes, it was a set-up to get you out, but not to *rob* you. To protect the stuff."

"But Locke knew what you were doing," I said. "Did you tell him what I had?"

Vaughn shook her head. "Just that you'd worked stuff out on all these charts. Jordan wanted some photos. He was planning to bust in and force you to give them to 'im. I said he should let us do it. Since I'd already been inside, we could pretend I was introducing Clay to you. That way, we'd get the stuff first, before he did. But we told Jordan we couldn't get it, so he thinks you still have it."

I felt both anger and relief. "And do I?"

"It's over there on the table," Natra said. "The binder, the memory card, our notes."

Vaughn continued. "When you came and chased me, Clay made sure I got away, cuz the stuff was still in the truck. Jordan's guys were there, so he had to pretend to be with them." She rubbed her arm and looked at Clay. "Got a little rough, I guess."

He shrugged.

"I got Kip to come, and he showed me this place." She waved her hand around. "We brought Clay's truck here, so they wouldn't find the stuff. Then Kip called Natra. When she came, Kip and I gave her the stuff and took the truck to Locke's place, to be there when you got out."

"How did you know that back way?" I asked.

"Jordan," Clay offered. "He showed it to all his ancils. The chain has a broken link. It's for construction trucks, I think."

"And why is Jax over there?"

Natra took this part. She'd placed a splint on my wrist—sprained, not broken—and wrapped it with tape. "Jax followed these two after our break-in." She gestured toward Vaughn and Clay. "They pulled over in Duck and told him what they were doing. Locke's guys were waiting in the park for Clay and Vaughn to return."

Vaughn broke in. "I told Jax I saw the Audi parked south of there. He wanted to get a picture of it, so he went on foot. We moved the truck, and Clay went to the park. When he didn't come back, I went looking. That's when you showed up, Annie. Jordan's guys were there, so Clay had to act like he was with them."

Natra continued. "Jax saw Ayden drive into the park and the van leave. That's how they ended up together. Vaughn told them you were in the van and where it was going. Then Kip arrived."

"Jax went with Ayden to create a distraction," Vaughn said. "Kip and I went to wait for you."

I sat back. My head pounded. "I can't follow it all."

"Doesn't matter," said Natra. "We have the documents. Ayden will watch for Jax."

"We have Jordan's list, too," said Clay. "It has his plans, his supplies, the people he used. I saw it there, so I grabbed it."

"Let me see it."

Natra pointed. "On the table."

She helped me up. The painkiller was kicking in. I went to the table. Natra had everything laid out in her usual organized way.

"What we've pieced together," she said, "is that when Ketch was arrested for using a victim's credit card, he saw an opportunity to please or *be* Jordan. You saw that. It was no feat for Broward to get a confession. Ketch was ready. Once committed, he elaborated. Broward won fame and Locke got unexpected protection. But Gregory Hawkins intruded. He knew Ella and he dug deeper. Locke sent Ella's ring with a threat, so Gregory went to Lang for help. Lang tried but failed to get evidence from the ring. Gregory had the photos that Ella stole from Locke, of course. We don't know why he didn't take them to law enforcement, but Lang said Locke had a recording that leveraged Gregory."

"But Locke has nothing on *us*," I said.

"Right. We have the card, the ring, the binder, two skulls that might be Locke's victims, Locke's letter to Gregory, and now Locke's personal to-do list." She tapped it.

I looked more closely at this piece of paper. In tiny handwritten print was a series of lists. One was a grudge list, labeled *Targets*. The last names of each of our victims was on it. So was *Hawk* and *Hunt*, and some others. I shuddered and looked at Natra. "This is ugly."

She pointed to a list called *GS*. "This looks like a list of map coordinates or codes. We think it means gravesites. We'd need the specific maps to be sure."

"It's in the house back there," Clay said. "A master map. The one I thought Ketch made."

"So, if Jax gets it, that's one more piece, especially if Locke's markers match the skull locations we've already found."

I leaned over Locke's notes. "Things to remember," I read. "Surveil sites carefully; don't charge gas or food near sites; use rentals; spread parts in separate places; supply of gloves and footies; hairnets; transport tarps; weather reports; encryption software; burn barrel; scanner; rope and gags; saws and knives; clean-up wipes; feed ancils; set alabis; record the party. Alabis?"

Natra squinted at it. "Probably meant alibis."

"But he's an attorney. He should know how to spell this."

"So he says."

I looked at the *Prep* list and declined to read it out loud. It featured instructions for removing heads and disposing of bodies.

Natra pointed to another list. "He hasn't updated what he calls the 'status.' Thinks nothing's been found."

"I told him we found Ella. He brushed it off, but it affected him. He didn't like hearing it."

"There's some on the other side," Clay told us. "I think it's about Ketch. That's what Jordan calls him."

I turned it over. The label read *Lunkhead.* I swallowed hard before I read the short list out loud. "Feed monster, water plants, erase challenge."

"That's me," Vaughn said. "I'm the challenge."

"As am I." I read it again. "Water plants. Ketch said this. And he mentioned someone paying. Is that what he means?"

CHAPTER THIRTY-EIGHT

"Yeah, yeah," Clay said. "The plants are the ancils who protect him."

"Is Ketch a plant?"

"More like the monster," Vaughn said.

"Then who's getting money?"

No one had an answer. Vaughn looked like she really didn't know. "Broward?" Natra suggested.

"But how would Ketch benefit, then? I had the impression it motivated him to keep his confession intact." To Natra, I said, "We need to contact the author of that book, Doug Hershall, to see if Broward gets any proceeds and, if so, how it's set up."

Natra frowned. "No dice. I called 'im, but when I mentioned Broward, he hung up. I tried again. No answer."

"That's a red flag. Where's Gregory's letter? Did you take it from the safe?"

"It's still there. I locked up the house, put on the alarm, and came here."

"We need it," said Kip. "I want to know what Jordan said to my dad. I'll go get it."

Natra shook her head. "They could be watching the house."

"I'll go with you," Vaughn offered. "I'll stand guard. Be an ancil cracker."

"Wait." I picked up my phone and sorted through the multiple messages until I found those from Jax. He'd asked where I was, urged me to call him, said he'd found Vaughn. Distressed—like I felt now about him. All were sent before he went to Corolla. I looked through Ayden's. He'd also asked where I was and urged me to contact him. I wanted to call him but couldn't risk noise. I texted. *Report status.*

I told the others what I was doing. We waited. Ayden responded. *Still watching. No sign of Jax. Guys getting into cars.*

"Into cars. They're heading out." I looked at Kip. "We have a ten-minute head start. You and I, let's get that letter."

"Annie!" Natra protested.

"I want as few as possible at the house. Everyone else, wait here. Let's go."

Chapter Thirty-Nine

Kip drove. Cold air seeped through the now-soggy cardboard over his broken window. Ayden kept me updated, although my wrapped, immobilized wrist made it awkward to text back. An Expedition and an Escalade had left the command center. I watched behind us. The few cars that were out on the road looked benign.

Kip glanced over at me. "Annie, I'm sorry about—"

"No apologies. You couldn't have known. I'm taking you to fetch that letter because it's rightfully yours. You should read it first."

"Thank you."

"Kip, here's the thing about Locke. He doesn't come at you straight, like a rattler. He's a constrictor. He wraps around you till you can't move. If Clay hadn't helped me escape, Locke would've had me trapped, probably like he did with our dads. I'm beginning to get why they kept quiet."

Kip nodded. "So, you heard from Lang?"

"I did, when you were gone. A brief video call. He really is quite ill. I took full responsibility for what we're doing, so he'll be upset only with me. He didn't know about the memory card. Ella told him it was stolen, which suggests that Gregory took it from the binder pocket before Ryder grabbed it. Anyway, Lang processed the ring. There was no DNA. Maybe there's some on this letter, so I'll ask you to handle it with gloves."

"I will. There should be some on the paper Clay took, right? The lists?"

"Maybe, but it's likely contaminated. Also, there's handwriting analysis, but since Jordan's not in the photos or tapes, we still can't prove his involvement in murder. First, we have to get him arrested. Ketch is our best bet, but I doubt he'll cooperate."

"There's still Vaughn's recording."

"Could help, but that's in Delaware, right?"

"And on my laptop."

"Right. Which we also don't have. We need something forceful. Physical evidence, a witness, something like that. Do you have my gun?"

"Yes."

"Keep it close." I held up my wrapped hand. "I can't steady it."

I didn't see anyone near the house. "Just be careful. They might be parked behind." Kip turned in to my drive and went behind the house. No one else was there. I entered through a garage door on the lower floor to disengage the alarm. After sorting through tools, I gave Kip a screwdriver.

"In the attic, remember the register? You noticed the screws. The cover hides the safe. You'll need this to pry it from the wall. That's where the letter is, in a white envelope. I'll grab evidence gloves for both of us. Now, quick! They might be heading here."

When he was gone, I texted Ayden. *At the house.* He didn't respond. My wrist had started to ache, despite the meds. I listened for activity from the beach and for the sound of vehicles on the road. Every beam of light that passed chilled me. The ancils could be here any minute. I wished I knew where Ayden was. I called Natra to report our status and ask about him.

"Nothing yet," she said.

I sent Jax another text. No response. I felt in my back pocket for Broward's business card. To my relief, it was still there. I had an idea.

Kip returned. He patted his jacket. "Envelope secure."

I engaged the alarm and shut the garage door. To my left, lights shown down the driveway. We were trapped. I gestured. "Follow me." I made my way up the dune and slid in the sand to duck down behind it. Kip did the same. He peeked over the rise. "It's them. Black Expedition. They'll see my car."

"It'll distract them. Let's go."

I led the way down the dune onto the beach and toward the water's edge. The harder sand there would help us go faster and the darkness would hide us. "I have an idea, and we can get there by walking." I pointed toward a distant pier, lit up for the holiday. "We're heading there." Broward was at the Hilton in Kitty Hawk. It was down a ways, but I often walked to it. The place should have guests, given the local post-Thanksgiving fairs, which made it relatively safe. And I had things to say to Broward. I'd missed his deadline, but I thought he'd take my call.

We walked fast. After ten minutes, I had to stop. "Out of breath. Need a sec."

Kip looked behind us. "I see a light moving on the dune, like they're looking for us. Should we call the cops?"

"Good idea." I called Natra to tell her what happened and to ask Karro to run by the house to check suspicious activity. "Tell him we moved to a hotel due to the break-in, and our doorbell camera shows someone's there."

"I already called, just in case. The available law enforcement is responding to a situation in Corolla—I'd guess for Locke's place. Where are you?"

"On the beach, heading south. They can't follow by car, and we're well ahead. We're nearly to the Hilton, where Broward's staying. He's either with them or he's a reluctant accomplice. I'm gambling on the latter, which means he might be open to cooperating. We have the evidence, he has the means to use it."

"He might just arrest you."

"We can't do this on our own. Law enforcement has to make the case. If I read him right, he's not like Locke. He's uneasy. He has a relationship with Ketch Ryder. He's protecting something. I'll use what I know and see how he responds. If you hear from Ayden or Jax, tell them where we are. But don't tell Vaughn. I don't want her barging into this."

"I think this plan's too risky."

"Got a better one? I'm listening."

"No. Keep in touch."

I ended the call and looked at Kip. "Let's go."

As we walked, he asked, "You want to see Broward?"

"Yes."

"Didn't Vaughn say he's with Locke?"

"She said Locke sent Broward to me. That could mean he's compliant but not aligned."

"I don't see the difference."

"If he sees a way to extricate himself and still keep his reputation, he'll take it."

"What if he tries to take everything we have and bury it?"

"He could try, Kip, but we have a good lawyer on our side." I didn't add that this depended on Jax getting out alive. "I won't show him everything. Just enough to read him better."

With my good hand, I grabbed Kip's arm to steady myself. "Tell me again about Ketch Ryder's recording. How much did you hear?"

"Enough to convince me he's just a sideline guy, an ancil."

"Tell me what you remember."

"He was talking to himself, repeating what Locke told 'im to do. Called himself Lunkhead, I remember that. Said something like, 'he wants ropes, he wants bags, he wants a saw.' Everything was about what someone—a headmaster—wanted. I guess that's Locke."

"He used that word with me, too."

"He also said, 'make it look like her group did it. A reckoning.'"

"Her group? The Gray Hollow Group?"

"Maybe. He wanted to get the book back, to use it against them."

"Hmm. The binder. If he had it, he could've planted it to implicate them. Why would he record this?"

"Because at the end, according to Vaughn, he said, 'in case Fawn needs this.'"

"He made the tape for her?"

"With her in mind, I guess. He didn't give it to her, she found it. I mean, he was coherent."

"When did he make it?"

"Just before he was arrested."

I considered this. "Like he wants the world to think one thing about him, but his daughter to know something else. Or hedging his bets against Locke. Maybe he didn't know at that point he was going to confess. We need to get that laptop."

We walked through the parking lot. I spotted Broward's BMW. "He's here."

Kip pointed toward the Audi in a corner spot. "So's the GBI guy."

"Let's go in."

The lobby felt warm and bright for the holiday. The aquarium in the middle caught my attention. I felt like those fish. Several groups in the Aviator Tavern toward the back were enjoying quiet dinners, and the place smelled like fried seafood. I directed Kip to a quiet, empty area on the other side of a two-sided fireplace. "No one's over there. I'll wait. You go read the letter."

He nodded. "I came all this way to get it and now I'm not sure I'm ready."

He went over to a chair, got out the evidence glove, and sat down. Glancing at me, he opened the white envelope and pulled out a smaller blue envelope that contained Locke's warning to Gregory.

I watched Kip's face as he perused the contents. He looked away once, and his shoulders hunched, as if fending off what he'd learned. Gregory had died five years ago, but I knew the loss likely remained raw. Kip wiped his face and sat up. I went over to him. Without looking at me, he held the letter toward me. I donned rubber gloves and took it. Kip got up and walked over to the glass doors that led to the outside veranda.

My turn. I sat down.

Chapter Forty

The letter showed the same tiny handwritten print as the lists. That was good. Forensic linguistics technology could link them. It could also eliminate alternate suspects. I took a deep breath and read the message. Having met Locke, I could hear his arrogant voice.

Recognize the ring? You know how we got it. Stop looking. You're on tape with us and no alabi for that day. We have photos of the "Hunter" digging there. Ancils watch. Keep looking and we'll finish you and bury your sons, one by one. You know we can. Burn this. Move on. Or the reckoning will come. We're everywhere. We see you. You can't hide from the headmaster.

I cringed. I could hear Locke's voice saying these things. This had to have been brutal for Gregory, and even for Dad, the "Hunter." Both were connected to Ella, who'd obviously been "reckoned" with. Locke had misspelled *alibi* again—an idiosyncrasy that could help sink him. Dad had seen this letter. He'd wanted to burn it, as Locke had ordered. And he'd often dug holes in Dacretown. I'd witnessed this myself. "Digging there" confirmed that we'd found Ella. The threat to Kip and his brothers was clear. And the line about "the reckoning" linked it to Ryder's tape and Locke's threat to me. But the note wasn't signed. The envelope had been sealed, which could be good for us, but it had no stamp. It must have been hand-delivered.

I folded the letter and placed it in the envelope before I went over to Kip. I put my right hand on his shoulder. "That's gotta be hard, knowing your supposed friend made this callous threat."

Kip nodded. "He played me, never cared about us."

"That's what someone like him does. I'm sure he's played a lot of people.

I suspect most of the loyalty he's acquired was coerced. I'm going to call Broward."

He looked at me. "Maybe we should wait 'til they identify the skulls."

"There's no waiting. Everyone I know is at risk, including you. This letter confirms that Locke was involved in Ella's death, and that he's aware she was buried where one of his ancils photographed my dad digging. That's Dacretown. Locke could still set Dad up for it. Broward's a soft spot. I'm going to poke him and see what he does. But I want you to stay apart." I pointed to a cushioned wicker chair in a cozy alcove area. "You can either stay out of sight or you can help. If you want to help, I need you to watch." I handed him the letter. "Keep this with you."

"I should stay with you."

I shook my head. "There's a chance this could go wrong. I need you to be able to slip away if necessary and let the others know."

"Okay. I'll watch."

Kip went to the alcove and took a seat, his expression glum. He didn't understand what I was doing, but sometimes my clinical training is my best ally. I needed a one-on-one interaction.

I pulled Broward's card from my back pocket. I wasn't as sure of this move as I'd sounded to Kip, but I had to find leverage. Based on the clues I'd collected, including Broward's behavior at my house, he seemed my best bet. I found a seat on an L-shaped couch in a quiet corner and called him. He answered quickly.

"Agent Broward, this is Dr. Hunter. I'm in the lobby. I know it's late, but I'd like to discuss something with you. Will you come down?"

He hesitated. Then he said, "I have a suite on the fifth floor. It's private."

"It's down here or it's off."

"I'll be right down."

This confirmed my hunch. He didn't take charge.

I nodded toward Kip, but my heart raced. This could go so wrong. I held my breath and rubbed the bandage on my wrist to calm myself. Surely Broward knew what had transpired this evening on Hunt Club Drive. Locke would have sent him orders. He had to be surprised by my call and equally so by my presence here. He'd likely be calling Locke to apprise him of this development.

Or maybe not.

His stiff manner during the meeting that Locke had ordered suggested he wanted to make his own decisions. Maybe he'd hear me out first. I had a lot riding on it.

Broward entered the lobby dressed in the same gray suit I'd seen him in earlier. He came right over to me. His face registered concern and he touched his forehead. "Something's happened to you. Your face. Are you alright?" Pretense or genuine? I didn't know.

I dismissed his question and gestured for him to take a seat near me, at an angle. I placed my phone on a round table in front of me. I'd already silenced the ringer to avoid interruptions. Despite my worry for my team, this meeting required a fine balance. "I'm going to record this," I said. "I invite you to do the same. Mutual protection."

"All right." He prepared his cellphone to record and placed it next to mine. Then he looked at me expectantly. "I'm all ears. Is this about tomorrow? My offer?"

"No, it's not. I think you know that I've recently been with Jordan Locke."

He blinked but showed no expression. At least he didn't say, "Who?"

I continued. "I'm aware that he sent you to see me about Ketch Ryder."

Now his face flushed a little. His head came forward slightly. All good signs. He wasn't prepared.

I continued. "You said you hoped I'd see the wisdom of us being on the same side. I'm here to invite you to side with me."

He squinted and looked around. Kip turned his face away, but Broward didn't look that far. Returning to me, he asked, "What are you proposing?"

"I have items that would implicate someone else in the murders that Ketch Ryder confessed to you. I'm willing to show them to you, but only if you're willing to admit that Ryder lied."

He was on the spot. If he were true to his law enforcement oath, he'd accept the possibility. If he were loyal to Locke, he'd readily say yes just to see what I had. If he wanted to cling to what he'd gained from the confession, he'd anchor in that narrative. I watched him carefully. I'm good at reading microexpressions—flashes of truth that leak even from the most stoic façades.

Broward clasped his hands together and narrowed his eyes. "Is this another stupid test?"

He'd shown his hand. He knew Locke. He didn't like him. I'd guessed right. A gate had opened, but the path forward remained bumpy.

"Here's what I think, Agent Broward. You've been leveraged. Someone is paying someone else to maintain Ryder's confession, and you're in the middle of that."

A twitch near his mouth revealed stress. "Dr. Hunter, this really isn't the best place—"

"I'm not done."

A text came onto my phone. Before I swiped it away, I saw that Natra had sent it. But I was at a crucial moment. "We have located the remains of some victims. One is the former wife of Jordan Locke. We have a letter from him with an item taken from this victim that was used to thwart an investigation. We have other items from this victim that strengthen our case against Locke."

I could almost see Broward's mental calculation: stick with Locke and stay leveraged but safe in the status quo or move toward me and freedom but at a cost.

"What do you want from me?" Broward asked.

"Several things. I want you to persuade Ketch Ryder to tell you what he *actually* knows."

Broward shook his head. "I don't think I can do that."

"I'm not negotiating. With you or without you, I'm going to make a case against Jordan Locke. You have an opportunity to be part of this and be free of his corruption, maybe even salvage your career. Or you can go down with him and his pirate ship."

Broward looked at his hands. Then he cocked his head. "We should bring Agent Skinner into this, from the GBI. He's been investigating Locke undercover. He's in this hotel. But he won't talk out in the open. Are you willing to go into a more private area?" He nodded toward the empty conference room off the lobby. "I can arrange for us to meet in there. People can see through the glass, so it's public, but they can't hear us."

I considered this. "Leave your phone here. Arrange it, and then you can call him where I can see and hear you."

Broward turned off the recorder on his phone and went to the front desk. I signaled a thumbs-up to Kip. This information reassured me. Skinner was a buffer. I felt less vulnerable. If Skinner was working an investigation and Broward was with him, we were near a positive resolution. Kip looked concerned. He pointed to his phone and mouthed something. I reached for mine to check the text, but Broward was on his way back.

"The room is free for our use," he said. "May I call him now?"

I looked up. "You sure you trust him?"

"More than I trust you. I suspect there's another shoe about to fall with you, and I'm close to arresting you for obstruction of justice."

I stood. I had one more card. "You can do that, but I think the author of that book about Ketch Ryder, the one who turned you into a super-agent, will have some things to say."

Broward's face went white. His eyes widened. I'd hit the mark. I silently thanked Natra for her research. *That's* who made the payments.

Broward held up his phone.

I gestured. "Go ahead and call. I'll be interested in what he can tell us."

He placed the call.

The front entrance doors *swooshed* open, and Jax strode in. He looked around, saw me, and came over. "Stop, Annie! Don't say anything more."

Chapter Forty-One

Broward stepped back and went for his weapon. Jax held up a hand. "You're not shooting anyone in this lobby, Broward."

"I could arrest both of you right now," he said.

Kip came over before I could gesture for him to stay put. Jax grabbed Kip's arm and leaned in to say something I couldn't hear. Kip looked at him in surprise and went out the front door.

"Jax," I said, "Agent Skinner from the GBI is on his way here. We're working something out. He's—"

"He's not Agent Skinner," Jax said. "I checked. He stole Skinner's credentials." He looked at Broward. "His name's Lossky. He's one of Locke's partners. They've decided you're expendable. I heard them. He'll persuade you to go with him, then orchestrate an accident."

Broward looked from Jax to me. His alarm seemed genuine. "Then I should leave."

"He's about to be arrested. Keep your meeting. Don't give him any reason to run. We have his car blocked, but we want this to go as easy as possible."

I pointed to the conference room. "Here. We're gonna meet in here. We'll keep 'im talking."

Kip ran back in. He carried his laptop with the skull decal. Jax directed Kip into the conference room. "Get it ready." Then he noticed my injuries. "Are you all right, Annie? Can you do this?"

"I can." I entered the conference room and sat where I could watch the lobby through the large window. Jax encouraged Broward to enter, then sat at the head end. "Ayden's out there," he said to me, "blocking the Audi."

Broward took a seat across from me. Pale and sweaty, he looked distinctly uneasy. Jax leaned toward him and said, "Act as if I was here all along. I'm Annie's attorney, protecting her rights. Your career is over, Broward, but your life depends on this. If you cooperate, you can possibly stay out of prison. But one move to alert him and all deals are off."

Broward looked at me. The other shoe had dropped. His face relaxed, and he nodded. "I'll cooperate."

Kip had the tape ready when "Agent Skinner" arrived. Jax opened the door, introduced himself as an attorney, and invited the man to enter. I nearly did a double-take. He was Hammer Man in the video on the SD card. He'd been there. He'd growled at the camera. He'd also been with Gun Guy and Ketch in the campfire photo. I looked at Broward. He was watching me. I nodded, hoping to convey that Jax was right. It was difficult for me to shake Skinner's hand. This was a member of Locke's hunting club. His hands had done terrible things. I felt Jax's foot touch mine. Steady. We were nearly there.

Skinner took a seat. I noted the bulge under his jacket. I figured he was jumpy and might shoot his way out if he felt cornered. "What's all this about evidence?" he asked. "Do you have something to show me?"

Jax took the lead. "My clients have come into possession of some damning items. They have documents, photographs, and audiotapes. We've come to Agent Broward because he's been involved in this case. He says you're working it with him."

"I am. Been on it for some time. The whole team has. So far, though, our target comes up clean. If you have evidence, I can get it to the right people."

I'll bet, I thought. I glanced at Kip. He stared at his computer screen as if he didn't dare to look at me. The room prickled with tension.

Skinner sat down, and Jax cleared his throat. "We have a tape we'd like to play for you. It's just part of the collection. This is from Ketch Ryder's daughter. He made it for her."

Skinner nodded. "We know about that tape. It's nothing. Just a story he made up to reassure her." He looked at Broward. "Right? He told that to you."

Broward nodded. "He did. But now that we have it, I'd like to hear it for myself."

Skinner shrugged and gestured for us to continue. Jax nodded to Kip, who tapped the *play* button. Ryder's voice was clear. I already knew what to expect, but it was still fascinating to hear him mention the list of items the "Headmaster" wanted him to procure. *Headmaster.* I wanted to vomit. But I noted a slight upturn on the right side of Skinner's mouth. He was amused. One thing I hadn't realized was on this recording was Ryder describing the binder and how he got it. "Took it from Hawkins. Photos not in the pocket. He has them. Will get them."

Vaughn was right. This recording said a lot.

"Can't really make much of this," Skinner said. "How is this evidence?"

Jax remained calm. "It's part of a package. We have papers, a map with burial sites, some photos, and—"

Skinner frowned. "A map?"

"Yes. Just acquired it. The markers and codes on it match other things we've discovered."

Skinner's upper lip curled. "Oh, we've seen maps. They—"

"I'm sure you've seen this one."

I heard activity in the lobby. Through the window, I saw three men in uniforms. I tried to remain calm. Jax gestured for Kip to pause the recording. I was sure everyone in the room could hear my heart. I could hardly breathe.

Skinner turned around to look. He didn't miss a beat. "Ah, convenient." He nodded toward Broward. "Good thinking." To Jax, he said, "I'm afraid your clients here will soon be under arrest."

Two officers came to the glass door. Skinner got up and opened it. "Please come in," he said. "This woman and this young man have committed multiple crimes. They have several stolen items on them and more at another location."

I looked at Jax. He motioned for me to stay cool and rose to his feet. "Officers," he said. "I'm Jackson Raines." He offered his credentials. "My colleagues in Georgia called you for assistance, and a member of our team met you outside. This is Neil Lossky, a.k.a., Agent Eric Skinner. He's impersonating an officer and is a suspect in several murders."

Skinner shot Jax a fierce look and reached for his weapon. The deputies grabbed him and pushed his face down on the table. In seconds, they had him in handcuffs. He protested that he was an undercover operative. "You have the wrong man! I'm an agent." As they moved him out, he struggled and yelled to Broward, "You're a dead man!"

The door closed. I leaned against the table. Jax put his hand on my back. "By now, they have Locke in custody, too, Annie. All that noise triggered calls from multiple neighbors."

I sat back and looked up at him. "Thank you. I was so worried about you."

Broward rose to his feet. He looked weary. "You really have the map?"

Jax nodded. "I do." He pointed at Kip's computer. "It was with that."

"I assume I will be arrested as well."

"Yes. But since you cooperated, you get the courtesy of some dignity. You can pack your room. An officer will go with you."

"Thank you." To me, Broward said, "Good work, Dr. Hunter. You're observant."

I raised an eyebrow. "As you say, watch… and catch."

"Touche´. Yes, I had a professional compromise I deeply regret. Locke used it. Since I think Ketch Ryder is implicated, I facilitated his pose. I have things to bargain with, but getting him released won't be on my list. Go back and see him. I think you'll agree."

I shrugged. "What I'll see is a man with a disorder that you and Locke exploited. He was needy and pliable. There wasn't any outing with him tomorrow, was there?"

"No. That was Locke's idea. But you have the map. You don't need Ryder."

"He's a witness. And this will change things for him and Vaughn."

"She won't like what she learns. Locke secretly set up her FundMe account, using her gullible followers to get money to her. 'Feed the monster, water the plants,' is how he put it. That funding will now dry up." He looked at each of us. "That was the deal. A percentage of the fame and fees I earned for getting Ryder's confession was channeled through the book author to her, as you discovered. That's what Ketch required to keep up the façade."

"That's why you didn't call him out on his copycat embellishments," I said. "You didn't care that he was lying."

"Right. Locke ensured that I cooperate. Ketch was never going to change his story. It was for her. If Vaughn owes you for your services, I doubt you'll get paid."

He nodded to Jax and went out. Jax followed him and beckoned for an officer to accompany Broward to his room.

Kip closed his laptop. "I came here to get a letter. Never expected all this. Thought I was gonna blow it when I saw that guy from the video."

"Me, too," I said.

He gave me a sidelong look. "Maybe we don't have to tell Lang all this? I mean, we got it figured out."

"Kip, he'll want to know about Ella. I'm sure it's been agony for him. And you should be the one to tell him."

"Even that I didn't burn Locke's letter?"

"We can't burn it. He knows that. It's evidence. And it gets him off the hook. He'll be relieved. We can say I found it and wouldn't give it to you, which is true. Show it to Jax."

Kip slid the envelope over to me. I carefully opened it. Jax read the threatening message and looked at Kip. "That's rough. I'm sorry."

"Where did you find my laptop?" Kip asked.

"I knew with that sticker it would be easy to spot. Clay told me where Locke's bedroom was. I figured he'd keep things of value there. Ayden kept them busy by breaking a couple windows, and neighbors did the rest by calling cops. We managed to get away before they came." He looked at me. "Clay tried to keep track of you, but he ran, and we lost you. Natra told us you were coming here. By then, the sheriff here knew about Lossky."

I pushed away from the table. "Glad you came when you did. And you got a map?"

"*The* map. You saw Lossky blanch. He knew what I had: everything the hunting club did and what they planned next." Jax helped me up.

Outside, I hugged and thanked Ayden before Kip got in his truck.

"You got hurt," Ayden observed.

"Can't feel it, thanks to meds. It'll heal. I should've listened to you. I'll work on that."

He held up his hands. "Us splitting up probably saved my life. And yours."

"Maybe. Thanks for the diversion. That was a good idea. See you back at the house."

I went to the Wrangler and called Natra. "We're all safe. Arrests have been made. Ayden and Kip are on their way there, but I'll stop at the house to check for damage. Everything good with Vaughn and Clay?"

"We ordered pizza," she said. "They're coming up with names for this house. We've got the Hide-Out, the Quack Shack, Fowl Play, Duck Stoop, and Safe and Sound. I favor Duck Stoop."

"It's cute, but I like Safe and Sound. I'm sure Ayden will go for the Quack Shack. So, you don't need me there?"

"Kip can fill us in. Go home. Chill. Be with Jax."

"Thanks. Call you later."

When Jax and I pulled into my driveway, I looked up at the house. My doubts about living here felt resolved. It was *my* house, and Dad was the father I wanted. He'd sacrificed a lot to protect me, and I'd solved his most personal vanishment case.

"I wanted to celebrate this house with friends," I said to Jax. "Not exactly like this, but it does feel like I gathered the right people to heal this place. It finally feels safe."

Chapter Forty-Two

Our case debrief session involved just Ayden, Natra, and I. We'd had to wait for developments.

Kip had taken Vaughn to Norfolk before driving home to Concord, and Clay had accompanied her to Delaware. They had a lot of catching up to do, and Clay had statements to give to the cops. He knew a lot. Vaughn had taken the news about her FundMe account in stride. She had enough for two more semesters, she said, and thought she could get a scholarship to finish. She wasn't as upbeat about losing her mission to exonerate her dad. Jax had returned to Georgia with my promise that our next holiday together would be quiet. He'd just smiled. He aimed to check Locke's assets and sue on Vaughn's behalf.

I made my famous seafood chowder for an early dinner. Ayden contributed *19 Crimes: The Banished* red blend. Mika was back with us, healed and happy, and Natra had caught up on our case file notes. We'd given our collection of evidence to a task force commander assigned to the multi-state case, keeping copies for our files. They were working to link recovered unidentified remains to the markers on the map. Two ancils were helping in exchange for deals, and Gregory's notes filled in some holes. Other families with missing loved ones would finally get news.

Ayden and I were packed and ready to fly to Concord for the forensic meetings regarding the skulls. All discovery thus far confirmed our suspicions about their identities.

"How's your wrist?" Ayden asked. "Your forehead's healing."

I held up my wrist guard. "Still tender. I can travel."

"Did you pack the ring?"

"I gave it to Kip, for Mark. That's what Dad asked. If they need it for evidence, they can get it from Mark."

"And he's not implicated?"

"I doubt it. He helped with the dig that unearthed Ella's remains. Kip said Mark was floored by the allegations against Locke and truly upset about Ella."

Natra had Mika lie down. "That master map Jax got from Locke's house had everything, all coded in his pinched handwriting. That hunting club was spread across four different states."

"Five, if you count Dacretown. But the evidence for Ella's murder points to Ketch. I really think he did it, maybe on his own. That accounts for the shift in pattern we noticed. He hated Ella for helping Ivy. He used the club activities as his cover. No doubt he told Locke and got his blessing, maybe gave him Ella's ring. Locke does have an alibi for that day, as he said. And speaking of 'alibi', my forensic linguistics associate ran our samples through her software. She thinks the match on Locke's misspellings will stand up in court as part of the evidence bundle."

Ayden broke off a chunk of fresh bread and dipped it in his chowder. "My contacts told me Neil Lossky rolled over on Locke for a deal. Between that and our evidence, Locke's done. No more hunting club."

Natra poured more wine all around. "So, what shall we do for Christmas? We have more vanishment cases from your dad's pile."

Ayden grinned. "I'm ready. I have some ideas."

I raised my glass. "To the Nut Crackers. Natra, while we're in Massachusetts, pull a few for us to consider. Maybe a simple one for a change."

She shook her head. "Nah. Not for us. We work only on hard nuts to crack."

II

SHORT CASES FROM THE NUT CRACKER INVESTIGATIONS

Short Cases from the Nut Cracker Investigations

Note for Collection:

The Nut Crackers team began with a short story, written for the 2019 Writers Police Academy anthology, *After Midnight*, which benefited law enforcement. It launched a context that I shifted for the series, although it's still based on actual case investigation. That same year, I entered a Master of Fine Arts program. I proposed to my mentor that I use my fictional Nut Crackers team to address actual cases for a blended effect between fiction and narrative nonfiction. He allowed it. I used the cases to show Annie Hunter's consulting style, how she met her team members, episodes from her podcast *Psi Apps*, and how the team undertook investigations. I also worked on a novel, *I Scream Man*. Just after the completion of my MFA, I sold *I Scream Man* and two more novels, *In the Damage Path* and *Dead-Handed,* to Verena Rose at Level Best Books. The current collection includes the fourth novel, plus five short stories. In order, they are:

"The Case of the Staring Man" (the inaugural short story)

"Every Body has a Story: *Psi Apps* Podcast #4"

"The Girl Without a Face: *Psi Apps* Podcast #9"

"Rodanthe Man: *Psi Apps* Podcast #10"

"Missing Parts" (for the *People are Strange* anthology, never published)

The Case of the Staring Man

Our case began with a ghost story.

I'd heard the tale. Barry Ross's office was in Suite 332 in the Hotel Ashton. His business was tanking. One day, his secretary tried to enter the bathroom. Something blocked the door. It took hotel security several tries, but they finally pushed in and found Ross's blood-spattered body sprawled inside. He'd shot himself and fallen against the door as he died.

Or so the story goes.

The medical examiner's finding of suicide canceled insurance payouts, so Ross's wife mounted a legal challenge. She thought he'd been killed. The M.E. insisted that the position of Ross's body sealed the deal. No one else could have been in the bathroom. The court supported him, and the death certificate remained unchanged.

Three months passed before the first ghost report. A maid was cleaning 332. As she wiped the bathroom mirror, she saw the reflection of a man in a brown suit staring at her. She turned. He was gone. She quit.

Other tales followed over the next two years. A woman who'd rented 332 fled at 2 a.m. when she awoke to a staring man at the foot of her bed. Another guest had entered after check-in to find a man in the room. She'd gone to a hotel across town.

For me, this was just a strange local tale. Then Ross's wife called. She wanted an independent analysis.

I'm Annie Hunter, a forensic psychologist who consults on unique investigations. I call my business Nut Crackers, because I take on cases considered hard nuts to crack. Also, my partners are…let's just say, unique. I do the shrink-wrapping, but for special demands, I subcontract. My team is like that insurance group with the annoying ads: we know things cuz we've seen things.

Science is central, but we use whatever helps—including paranormalists. As a certified death investigator and licensed PI, I specialize in psychological autopsy, or a postmortem analysis that unwraps clues about a decedent's state of mind. It's victimology on steroids. I also accept "night work," where I investigate haunted crime scenes or tackle demonic possession. I've infiltrated vampire clubs and spent the night alone where Lizzie Borden gave out whacks. All in a day's—or night's—work.

Some call me *She*lock Holmes, but I reject the title. For me, emotional nuances play a greater role in crime than cold, hard facts. Holmes never dreamt of the depravities we see, and some make no logical sense. That's why they're hard nuts to crack.

Back to Connie Ross. At a slender five-foot-seven, she'd overlooked nothing in her effort to show poise except a crimp in her brown hair from electric rollers. Otherwise, her tan skirt and blazer, with a red rose lapel pin, were professional.

Natra, my info officer and confidante, took an unobtrusive seat. A top cadaver dog handler and Eastern Band Cherokee, she could often be found practicing knots or studying tool marks on bone. Today, she'd replaced her jeans and scuffed boots with heels and a blue silk blouse tucked into a black skirt. She poses as my "assistant" to watch how clients sit, gesture, and talk.

Connie Ross denied that her husband had killed himself. "He wasn't depressed, he was happy!" We hear it all the time. Relatives of suicides cannot bear certain truths. I prepared to listen to the first but least fertile layer.

Suicidal people can be riddles. Once they've resolved to end their lives, they don't flag it. They want a way out. They might as easily be scared or ashamed as suffering a psychache. But with the family's resistance, we gain potential for misdirection. Red rose: *sub rosa*.

"There was just a month left before the suicide clause on his policy expired," Connie continued. Her fierce brown eyes said *she* would control the narrative. "Even if he was depressed, he would've hung on. He wouldn't leave our son and me without money. I tried other agencies. They think it's a lost cause. I've heard you accept challenging cases."

"We do." I leaned toward her. "Do you have his computer?"

She patted a bag.

"And did he use his own gun?"

"Yes. But there's something else."

"Toss it in. Let's see what we stir up."

"Three weeks before he died, someone shot at our house. It was late at night. The police dismissed it as kids messing with guns, but I'm sure it's related to his death. Afterward, Barry kept his Glock loaded and ready, as if he expected it to happen again. He even carried it."

"Did he tell you why?"

"No, but I think I'm being followed. I catch a silver Lexus out of the corner of my eye. I've seen it several times, including near our house."

"Plate number?"

"I'm too scared to get that close."

Natra raised an eyebrow. She knew I would take the case.

After agreeing to our terms, Connie gave us Barry's laptop and insurance policy, the autopsy report, and other papers from the slender case file she'd acquired. The police had not searched his laptop, she said, but his partner had, and he'd found nothing of note. She had no photos or death scene sketches, since it was coded as a suicide. She didn't know what had happened to the gun.

I promised to look into it and walked her out.

Next, I texted Ayden Scott, our primary PI. I'd alerted him earlier about a potential client. *This one has a...* I added the ghost icon. Like me, he loved what we called 'night work' or the 'midnight shift'.

I returned to hear Natra's thoughts.

"A locked-room mystery," she said as she sorted through the file. She meant a device in detective fiction in which it seems impossible for someone to have entered or escaped a closed crime scene.

"I've heard of others," I said. "Tough but not impossible."

"Mrs. Ross is hiding something."

"I agree. See anything?"

"The autopsy findings. A shot to the leg and a shot to the stomach. Painful and slow. One shot could be accidental, not both. We should track down the business partner. Who's on board?"

"First, we'll see if Ross *could* have been murdered. If we can't reconstruct this as a possible homicide, we're done. We have a ghost story, so we'll use our paranormalists. Also, the re-con team. That's you, me, and—"

"Me, I hope!" Ayden burst in. He wore a black OBX T-shirt and an eager grin.

Natra rolled her eyes. She knew that the tall PI with the outdoorsy tan and shaggy blond hair had a thing for me. He signed all his notes to me with "one day…" He was my type in all the wrong ways, better at striving than arriving. But once focused, he'd work this case to the bone. Plus, he was a skilled artist.

"That was fast," I observed. "Stalking me again?"

Ayden winked. "Protection detail."

I brought him up to speed.

He crossed his arms and nodded. "Sounds like the midnight shift. Check with your voices yet?"

He meant what I called "meditating with mentors." As I walk the beach, I imagine intrepid investigators from earlier times "speaking" to me. Often, their cases yield an insight. It's an altered mental state that I'd honed as a kid and decorated later with solid research. Forensic pioneers such as the first French detective or the first private crime lab director guide me.

But I needed no trance for this one. It came to me at once, and my associates needed no introduction to my favorite nineteenth-century pathologist.

"Alexandre Lacassagne investigated the case of a man found dead in bed in a locked room. In his hand was a pistol. Looked like a suicide. But Lacassagne spotted things that were off. The eyes were closed, atypical for a gunshot suicide, and he saw no close-range powder burns."

Natra shrugged. "How does this help? Our decedent was disturbed when they pushed the door open. We can't know his original position."

"Like Lacassagne, we accept nothing at face value. That's our theme. In this case, he asked colleagues to alert him when someone died, and then he'd place a gun in the decedent's hand. He saw that a recently dead hand could be made to grasp it, and that rigor would tighten the grip. So, the guy *could* have been murdered and posed. Closing his eyes suggested remorse, which meant the killer probably knew him. The obvious suspect was the victim's son and heir. He had a key to the room and a motive. Eventually, he confessed."

"I still don't see how it connects. Our guy was leaning against the only way in or out."

"We need to see if someone else could've been in the bathroom with him and gotten out with the body against the door."

Ayden sat on the arm of the couch and tapped his jeans. "Can we get access? I'll bring a mannequin."

Natra nodded. "Just rent room 332."

Which we did.

* * *

Paranormalists Peter Fleming and Gail Holtz met us there around 11 p.m. They brought dowsing rods, crystals, and an assortment of cameras and recorders. Natra, now back in jeans with her long hair braided, helped them to set up. Her black Doberdor, Mika, nosed into their bags for treats. We used Mika for finding buried remains, but she came on paranormal cases as well. Dogs see things that we can't, and she's fiercely protective.

Ayden had gotten an independent M.E.'s opinion on the autopsy report. "There was no bullet trajectory analysis," he told us, "but she agrees that the bullet placement is suspicious. Better yet, she gave me a little gossip. The M.E. who did this report is suspected of accepting bribes for falsified findings. We don't know if this case was one of them, but we can't rule it out."

I nodded. "Great work."

Ayden beamed. Natra shook her head. What I called incentive she called teasing.

Natra also had a report. "The bathroom floor was retiled. They couldn't get the blood out of the grout, so it's all new, and the walls have been painted. Otherwise, no significant changes."

"Too bad," Peter said. "The blood might be what anchored the apparition that people saw. Any reports of sightings after the alteration?"

"The manager was reluctant to discuss it, but I put a request on our site. Someone from the public might know."

I put my hands on my hips. "Time for action."

The bathroom was tight. Ayden liked it more than I did, although he at least smelled like ocean air. I held the faceless unisex dummy while he stuffed its various pockets with weights to equal Ross's 163 pounds.

We'd learned from the hotel's night engineer that the death event had been pegged around the time of our summer festival's fireworks, so the shots were buffered. Had this been planned? Loud fireworks protected the incident from immediate discovery, but why would a suicidal man care? State of mind always mattered in alleged suicides.

In the other room, I heard Peter's deep voice as he dictated the set-up to document the date, time, conditions, and protocols. "We have recorders to pick up electronic voice phenomena, or EVP, and we'll ask questions to try to get a name and perhaps a reason for the haunting. In addition, we'll use dowsing rods to acquire answers to 'yes' or 'no' questions. After a sweep of the place to detect naturally occurring anomalies, our medium will ask if Ross is present. He might be persuaded to be filmed with infrared cameras."

Gail, a former ad exec, was the medium. In other cases, I'd watched how the tall blonde would hold a dangling crystal or a pair of bent metal dowsing rods that she said were sensitive to paranormal activity. Before she'd met Peter, a history professor, she'd never even thought about ghosts, but eventually she'd had enough training to hone her second sight. I'd seen my share of hokey mediums, but my team wanted to document things correctly. Better to accept a long, fruitless night—and there had been many—than to create a sketchy report based on wishful thinking. They laid out pens and a stack of white note cards for corroboration exercises.

I didn't always agree that their results were paranormal, but I've seen enough to accept that some cases have an added dimension. Our remote viewing sessions had located missing people, and I'd gotten my own creepy EVP. The ghost sightings in this room by unrelated people lent each incident more credibility.

We were ready for the reconstruction.

I closed the bathroom door. With some difficulty, we placed "Barry" against it, slumped like a man who'd just been shot. Ayden twisted the "wounded" leg away, and Barry fell over. He wasn't cooperating, but we finally got him in place.

From the other side, Natra pushed on the door. It didn't budge. She pushed harder, moving Barry slightly, but she couldn't get in.

Peter gave her a hand, and they succeeded. Now, the hard part.

We repositioned Barry and tried to get out without disturbing him, as we thought his killer would have done. But neither of us could exit and also keep him in place in a way that blocked the door. When the dummy had leaned away, Natra had easily pushed in, so we'd failed to replicate the original incident.

I thought about Lacassagne. We had to show that it *could* have been a homicide before we could proceed. What would a killer have to do to stage this as a locked-room suicide that would convince investigators?

"We got a voice!" Gail called out.

We left Barry on the floor and gathered at the table. We each grabbed a notecard. Our protocol was that Gail would play the results, and we'd each write down what we thought we'd heard. She held up the recorder and pressed a button. We heard her ask several questions, among them, "Can you tell me what happened to you?" To this, I heard a scratchy two-syllable response. Mika barked. I made a face at Natra before I wrote what it sounded like to me.

When we were ready, Peter held up his card: "Murder." Gail nodded.

Natra shook her card in the air. "Mm-mmr," she'd written.

Mine said "Tazer" and Ayden offered "Earner."

Gail shrugged. "The 'er' part seems clear. Most of us heard it."

As we listened again, we all heard "murder," but suggestion had tainted our perception, so it didn't count. Mika pointed her nose toward the ceiling. Dog-confirmation worked for me. We had to keep trying. I beckoned to Ayden. "There's something we're not doing. Maybe the ghost will guide us."

"Always willing to share a tight space with you."

"Mind on the case, Blondie."

"We'll turn off the lights in here," Peter said, "and see what we get with infrared."

Ayden and I repeated everything we'd just done, with the same results. We even stood the body up. We still couldn't get out while leaving Barry propped against the door. Frustrated, we finally joined the others in their séance mode. Ayden perked up. He wanted to see the staring man.

"This might be helpful," Gail offered. She held up her purple crystal, dangling on a silver chain. "I've been hearing something that sounds like edge or ledge. Mean anything?"

Mika whined, jumped up, and wagged her stubby tail. Natra reached toward her and froze. "*Wedge!*" She held up her hands in surprise. "I don't know where that came from, but that's what I got."

And that's why I always gathered diverse participants. There's nothing like psycho-braiding to pop a juicy "aha!"

Natra grabbed two foam pillows off one of the double beds. Standing them between the door's edge and frame, she made a space large enough to squeeze through. Ayden went in to lean the mannequin against the door. He worked his way through the gap without disturbing the body and pulled the pillows free. The door closed. He pushed. The door resisted. He pushed again and finally got in. "There we go!"

"Okay," I said. "Good enough. Our locked room mystery is solved. So, by using a removable wedge in the door, a killer *could* have shot Barry Ross and squeezed out. *Now* we can investigate."

Ayden set up to take measurements and snap photos, while Natra checked her request on our team-sourcing site. We like this phrase better than 'crowd-sourcing.' We had several dedicated amateur sleuths we could count on.

Peter tapped the camera. "Shall we look at the video?"

We did, and saw nothing from their work thus far, but we gathered around the night-vision trail cam to watch in real time. Peter set up the specter detector, a sensitive device that resembles a telegraph and dings when "something" taps it. This work often takes hours and produces only dust particles and the occasional bug. Still, people had reported apparitions here, so we took shifts. With her crystal, Gail tried to coax the staring man to answer questions.

By 3 a.m., Ayden had left with the mannequin, Mika was softly snoring, and Gail had given up. She and Natra talked quietly while Peter and I watched the camera. The Ghost Hour, we called it. Around the world, 3 a.m. is the most active time.

Suddenly, Mika raised her head and lifted her ears. On the lens, I saw a bright flash. It zipped across the room and disappeared. Mika whined. I thought I heard a tap on the door. I opened it, but no one was there or anywhere in the hall.

Peter studied the recorded image. Too large and too fast to be a random dust particle floating near the lens, it was a bright, opaque ball with a tail. Gail tried again with her questions, but after an hour, we had nothing more. On the recorder were two scratchy sounds that bore a resemblance to a voice. Peter promised to clean them up.

We'd seen no man in a suit, but we'd opened the door to our next step.

Back in my digital lab, we found Joe Lochren at work on Ross's computer. A former cyber-detective, he was our primary digital expert. Since Joe looked as if he'd just come from central casting for a cop show, I sometimes used him as a front man. We let him work his private cases on our high-end equipment in return for his assistance with ours. He also knew my ex, a SLED agent in South Carolina, so he could trade favors and access data files.

Joe turned the laptop toward me. "So far, it's mostly business stuff and some legal porn. A couple things stand out. Did Connie Ross mention that her husband was seeing a shrink?"

I crossed my arms. "No."

"Secret number one," Natra said.

Joe pointed. "Maybe she didn't know. I found an appointment schedule with Dr. Lilian Kaufman hidden under a game app, including one that was set for two days before he died. I looked her up. Definitely a shrink."

"That potentially supports suicide."

"Also, on Ross's life insurance policy, a Ron Keiser witnessed his signature. Is that a lead?"

"That's his business partner."

"Wait!" Natra went to my desk to pick up the file. "I saw that name." She flipped through the few papers until she found it. "Here. The M.E. interviewed Keiser. The notes are sketchy, but Keiser said that Ross had been depressed." She looked at me. "His business partner knew this, but the wife didn't? And the M.E. didn't mention it when Connie Ross challenged his ruling?"

"Keep digging," I said. "Look for erased files. It's time to scrape off the topsoil. Connie knows more than she's saying."

I divided our tasks. I'd take on Connie. Natra would continue the info mining, and Ayden would locate Keiser. I couldn't help but think that the word I'd heard on Peter's recorder sounded a little like this name.

I was used to people withholding information. I do it myself, so I recognize secret keepers. There's a subtle tension in their posture that suggests they're carrying a box that could fall and spill its contents. This behavior is always a hurdle. My process depends on gathering information from people who were close to decedents. However, these very people often have agendas, from deflecting guilt to hiding a death scene alteration. Connie Ross had the added incentive of a payout and possible damages against the M.E. She did *not* want this to be a suicide.

Connie was ready with coffee. After chit-chat about the re-con, I got to the point. "Do you know the name Lilian Kaufman?"

The widow ran her hand over her mouth as if deliberating. For me, it was a "leak." She was blocking her mouth from blurting something she'd regret.

"She's a therapist," I offered.

"Right. Yes, I've heard of her."

"Did you know that your husband had appointments with her?"

Connie's pupils dilated as if she were nervous, but then she surprised me. "Barry didn't speak about clients, but I believe she was under investigation for insurance fraud. It was in the papers. Barry investigated fraud, so there's nothing mysterious here. Perhaps he was role-playing a patient to get close to her. He found that to be an effective method."

Interesting. But then why hide his appointments? And from whom? "Did you have access to his laptop?"

"Only after…he was gone. His partner had his password."

"The same partner who told the M.E. that Barry was depressed?"

Surprise, then anger. Connie put down her cup. "How do you know this?"

"It's in the report."

"That was… Ron said the M.E. misunderstood him. He'd corrected it. You must have the original report."

"I see." I didn't, actually. "Do you trust Ron Keiser?"

"He was…he's been a good friend. He made the funeral arrangements and found a lawyer for me."

She hadn't said yes. I tried again. "I might need to speak to the lawyer, but if there's anything I should know about Keiser—"

"Ron thought Barry had ruined the business, so he was angry."

"Angry enough to shoot him?"

She raised her chin. "I brought this to you because it's knotty. Your kind of case, according to your website. I want the money, yes, but I also want my son and me to be safe." Looking down briefly, Connie added, "The person who did this might have wanted to hurt *me*."

I pressed, but she offered only her suspicions. I told her I'd be in touch.

Connie was a different kind of locked-room mystery, but I'd learned things. I sent Joe a text to see who might have accessed Barry's laptop. If he'd hidden appointments behind an app, he'd wanted no one to know. I wondered how many threads we'd find in this "knotty" case. Connie didn't seem to like that I'd discovered something she didn't know. Or possibly she just didn't want me to follow that lead.

But now I would.

* * *

Ayden's text was just two words: *Sweet spot*. It's his code for our meeting spot away from the office: Sweet T's Coffee House. He was there on the deck, ready with my favorite Kona blend. The ocean breeze was calm enough to sit outside.

He showed me his artsy-but-accurate drawing of the death scene from the killer's point of view, and said, "I've had some thoughts."

"Go ahead."

"Why was Barry in his office so late? And who would he allow in at that hour? A client? Doubtful. A mistress? Maybe. His partner? Definitely. And Keiser's new office is a long way from a hotel room rental. It's lavish. If he was on a sinking ship with Ross, he's rebounded. His secretary blocked me from seeing him, but I'll try again."

"Think he's crooked?"

"We have the ingredients for rat-atouille, if you know what I mean. I asked Joe to look up his financials. Keiser had access to Ross's computer, so maybe Ross was hiding the appointments from him. But you can't rule out that Keiser planted them to back up his story about depression. He had access, postmortem."

"But police didn't search the computer, and no one benefited from the life insurance. Connie's attorney would have flagged a big payday for him." I told Ayden what I'd learned from Connie, including Keiser's revised narrative to the M.E.

"Keiser found her an attorney? Maybe *he's* in on it."

I squinted at him.

Ayden leaned over his tablet and sketched a stick-man scenario. "Put it together: someone shoots at the house to provoke Ross into arming himself. Ross dies with *that* gun. No payout to Connie. Maybe Keiser took out an earlier policy, so the suicide clause had expired. He's an insurance consultant. He'd know how to find one. Keiser sets Ross up to seem suicidal. Maybe even sends him to investigate the therapist so he can use the appointments as proof of depression, which he then tells the M.E. He doesn't correct the report; he only tells Connie he did."

I shrugged. "Too easy to discover, especially with Connie looking for PIs. If Keiser is so clever, why would he stay in the area where his post-failure success is visible? He's not worried."

"Got another idea?"

I sipped my coffee. "Lilian Kaufman. I told Joe to look for anything related to her. If Barry was checking for fraud, she had a lot to lose, so she's a suspect, too. In fact, given how tight that wedge space was, a female would have an easier time getting out."

"But not posing the body."

I nodded. He had a point. I was athletic, but I couldn't move it.

Ayden raised a finger. "Let's put them together. Maybe she paid Keiser off."

"Now we're getting complicated."

He shrugged. "Comes with the territory."

"You explore Keiser, and I'll see the therapist."

I brought Natra her favorite lunch of crab salad. On our team-source site, she'd posted the original news story about the suicide and asked for tidbits. She'd revealed nothing confidential, nor why we were interested. What she got, she said, was a mix of trolls, off-topic comments, and more ghost stories. "Room 332 has notoriety, so some could be fabricated. A couple of posts were interesting." She handed me a printout.

One was from a regular poster who called herself Vivica. We'd found this moniker on a list called *Names for Girls Most Likely to Become Morticians.* Our team sourcers often adopt unique identities. Vivica offered details of a recent "staring man" sighting that was consistent with those before the renovations.

The second post was from "Matty2+" offering cryptic guidance: "Check a yearbook. Cliques have ties that bind."

I looked at Natra. "That's suggestive."

"I've discovered where Barry went to high school and college. I've just brought up a yearbook website. And FYI, Joe found no red flags for Keiser. Seems his current business is legit and flush. Also, no one else accessed Barry's laptop remotely."

"Let's look at the yearbooks."

Natra showed me a webpage of yearbook photos. Barry's senior class had numbered around 100. We quickly found him. Connie was there as well, so possibly they'd been high-school sweethearts. As Natra scrolled through, I said, "Stop!" We both scrutinized a photo of a freshman with large eyes, straight blond hair, and an expression of disdain beneath her posed smile. Lilian Monroe.

Natra pointed. "Maybe Kaufman's her married name. How many girls are named Lilian with one 'l'?"

"Connie had to have known of her, but she acted as if she didn't. Ties that bind. I wonder what that means. See if Joe can identify the source of this tip. I need to meet Lilian Kaufman. Find out whatever you can about her."

* * *

I sat in my Jeep at the address for Lilian Kaufman. Her practice appeared to be in her home, or rather, her ocean-side mansion. If she were committing insurance fraud, she was doing it well. But from a news article, Natra had learned that she'd gotten a nice divorce settlement.

Barry's secrecy about these appointments bothered me. Since Keiser had access to his computer, this caution was likely aimed at him. But why? If it was just an insurance investigation, it should have been a joint effort.

My options were: 1) depression: Barry was secretly seeking help; 2) deflection: Barry was secretly investigating Lilian; or 3) desperation: Barry thought Keiser was aligned with Lilian, perhaps preparing to abandon their sinking ship. He wanted to know.

I leaned toward number two, with Lilian taking a warning shot at his house. Would she risk his family? Connie had hinted that this was about hurting *her*. Was there some "ties that bind" feud?

I scanned the area but saw no silver Lexus. Feeling a prickly sensation, I glanced up at the second floor. A lace curtain moved.

My phone dinged. Natra sent a scanned photo of Ron and Connie having lunch.

I texted back, *When?*

Team source. No date. In YB, B & R were voted 'most likely to succeed.' Seemed to be friends.

Interesting. Connie knew Barry from high school, and Barry knew his future business partner, Ron. Connie apparently knew Ron well enough to meet him alone. A clique. And in the same school was a woman who might be at the heart of this mystery.

Time to make my move.

* * *

The woman who entered the reception area was an older version of Lilian Monroe, as we'd suspected. I introduced myself and stated my business. At the mention of Connie's name, her eyes narrowed. When I asked Dr. Kaufman about her association with Barry, she said, "I know why she sent you."

"She didn't. Your name was on Barry Ross's computer."

Lilian shrugged. "He asked me about my records. I referred him to my accountant."

"So, he wasn't a client?"

She leaned toward me. "Perhaps you should ask more questions about your *own* client."

I cocked my head. "Why do you think she sent me?"

"Not very bright, are you? Isn't it obvious?"

"She didn't know about his appointments. He hid them."

A disdain-frosted smile played on her face. "Think about that, Dr. Hunter. Why would he need to?"

She said she was busy and told me to ask her attorney for anything else. As she walked out, I saw her reach for her phone. This meeting was clearly over.

* * *

I called a dinner meeting in my office. When I arrived, I smelled pizza. Then I saw Ayden and Natra peeking through the blinds at something outside. I went over and scanned the area. Ayden showed me: a silver Lexus parked a block away.

"I think it followed me," he said. "An hour after you left the shrink. Maybe she hired someone to kill Barry, and now she's sent him after us. I can't see the license plate. Want me to go confront—"

"No. Let's use the law of approach/avoidance."

Natra cocked her head, so I explained. "We stay back. Make them come closer. Let them believe they're in control."

"I think he's seen us watching," said Natra.

"Good. He'd expect *us* to approach. When we don't, he'll make a move."

Ayden touched his concealed holster.

Joe arrived as I was placing colored magnets on our wallboard. Natra took a seat, but Ayden stayed near the window, watching.

"Peter cleaned up the voices," Joe said. "Want to start with that?"

"Did you listen?" I asked.

"Not yet. I followed protocol, but I'm curious."

I passed out note cards and sat at my desk. Joe went to the computer and pulled up an audio file. We listened to the brief burst. I shrugged, and Mika made a quick little yap. Joe played it again. Not as scratchy as the "murder" one, it sounded to me like "stopping." I wrote this down.

When we were ready, we showed our cards. Joe had heard what I'd heard, but Natra said, "Sock him." Ayden looked at each of us before he waved his card with a flourish. "*Stop* him."

I hugged myself. "That's chilling. But who? I wish he'd given us a name."

"Maybe he tried," said Joe. "Peter couldn't clean up the other one."

"It's too ambiguous to be confirmable. Back to square one."

I returned to the board. "Okay, we have four players. We know that Connie, Barry, and Ron were high school buddies. Connie—blue—married Barry—red, and Barry partnered with Ron—green." I moved the magnets into place. "We'll use yellow for Lilian. She seems to know Connie and Barry, and she's sour on Connie. She thinks it's obvious why Barry hid his appointments, so we're missing something."

Joe gestured for attention. "Someone deleted files from Barry's laptop regarding Lilian Kaufman."

Natra sat up. "After he died?" This would point to Ron.

"No, before. It looks as if he discovered evidence of fraud, but then the files were deleted."

I nodded. "Might've felt threatened."

"Then why not take the evidence to police?" Natra asked. "Maybe Ron found and deleted them."

Ayden crossed his arms. "I think Ron and Lilian were hooking up. That's why Barry hid the appointments. But Ron figured it out, confronted him, and shot at his house as a warning."

I wasn't settled on this. "But Barry seems to have removed the files, so why kill him? And why shoot at the house? Ron is friendly with Connie. Why risk hurting her?"

Joe held up a hand. "Wait. The files were deleted *before* the shot at Barry's house."

Silence descended as we stared at the magnets. There were too many unanswered questions. Natra went to the board and pushed the red magnet away, placing blue with green. "We have an undated photo of Ron and Connie together. Possibly this was to make postmortem arrangements, but maybe *they* were hooking up."

I shook my head. "Then why would Lilian think Connie sent me and say the reason should be obvious? Why would she care about what Ron was doing?"

"Maybe Ron was cheating on Connie with Lilian."

I tapped the board, and Barry's magnet dropped to the floor.

"That's interesting," said Natra. She looked at Mika, who only stared at the pizza box.

I replaced the magnet. I was sure we all had the same thought. Was Barry trying to help?

Natra rubbed her chin. "Lilian seems to be the key." She grabbed a marker and drew a primitive sketch. "The yearbook featured photos with some cutesy blurbs. This one was on a photo of Lilian."

I looked. Lilian had written, *Knot what you think*. I shrugged. "So?"

Joe jumped up. "Ah! Knot! The game app, the one Barry used to hide his appointments. It was for tying knots!"

Then I remembered. "Connie called this a 'knotty' case."

We stared at the board before Ayden moved Lilian's magnet next to Barry's and described an intriguing scenario. "Maybe it's *these* two. Hidden in an app for knots—knot what you think."

I nodded. "That's why Lilian thinks Connie sent me. And why Barry would hide it from Ron, who's close with Connie." I pointed to the blue magnet. "But Connie wouldn't stage a suicide that would cut her out of the money. She said that whoever was involved might have wanted to hurt *her*. Seems like a lot of double-crossing going—"

I froze. The others looked at me.

"Pull up our team site," I said to Natra. I pointed Joe toward the other computer. "You, too. I have a hunch we've been set up."

Natra opened our team-source site.

"Search for Matty2+. See if she left any other messages."

Ayden squinted. "What's up?"

"It's here," said Natra. "Several weeks ago."

"I have it, too," said Joe. "I'll check the source."

Mika jumped up, alert to the sudden excitement. She cocked her head.

Natra read Matty2+'s post: "Does this group take any case?"

"Did someone respond?" I asked.

"Yes. Another poster quoted our website: We take hard nuts to crack."

I grabbed my head. "I can't believe I was so stupid. The clues are all there! I interpreted them wrong."

"Same source for Matty-two-plus," said Joe. "But dead end. It's a public computer."

I wrote on the board as I talked. "It's not two-plus, it's two-*cross*. Bear with me. All this high school stuff just gave me an idea. I think Matty is

Connie. She said that Barry thought role-playing was an effective way to fool people. That was a behavioral leak. *She's* role-playing. She's pretending to be a client."

Natra held up her hands. "I don't follow."

"Matty! A character in *Body Heat*. Two-cross is double-cross. In that movie, a high-school friend poses as Matty and manipulates everyone to get her husband whacked and get his money. She picks an inept attorney who's easy to dupe. He's the fall guy. She makes him think he's working with her when she's actually working *him*."

Ayden, with whom I'd once watched this film, picked up the lead. "So, Connie sent us the yearbook lead."

I held up a finger. "Hang on." I wasn't yet ready to admit I'd been played. I called a competitor who'd take any case just for the money. We had codes for speaking that protected our clients.

"Had any recent suicide investigations?" I asked.

"Nope."

Two others said the same thing.

"Confirmed," I said. "Damn! Connie told us she'd shopped around, but she hadn't. She'd checked us out online and exploited my attempt to be unique. I can't believe this! Take nothing at face value. I set the theme for this case, and I violated it. I let her make me a pawn!"

Ayden crossed his arms. "So now we know. Her game stops here. Now you can do what you do best. It's behavior. Interpret it. What's she up to?"

"I saw it in her eyes that first day. She wanted to control the narrative. Red flag." I took a breath to calm myself and went to the board. "She's not the killer. She wants the money. But she wants something else, too, so she put on this charade to use us to get it. We focused on what she *said* she wanted, which blinded us—me—to other motives."

Natra chimed in. "Lilian said Barry had reason to hide his appointments. She also said she knew why Connie sent you. This is about Lilian and Barry."

Ayden held up a hand. "I still say that a woman couldn't have moved Barry's body. We're not there yet."

"I agree," I said. "Lilian's the knot, and she's not what we think. Connie wants us to know that."

"Can't leave Ron out," said Joe. "I found an account on Barry's laptop with links to Lilian's business, managed through the attorney Ron offered to Connie."

"So, it *is* knotty." I moved the magnets as I talked. "This is speculative, but it fits. Barry marries Connie, but she has an affair with Ron. Barry or Ron or both get involved with Lilian, possibly while investigating her for fraud. Ron's first, which means he cheats on Connie. Barry discovers the relationship, so he hides the files. When *he* gets involved with Lilian, he erases the files. But Ron thinks Barry's a threat to Lilian, or a rival, and tells him to back off. Warns him with a shot. Barry ignores him, so Ron kills him. Connie is furious, because Ron not only cheated on her but also robbed her of the insurance money. She wants to get back at him *and* Lilian while also getting the money, so she puts out breadcrumbs for us, the Nut Crackers. She figures my business slogan makes me easy to manipulate."

"But Ron made the whole thing look like a suicide. He told the M.E. about Barry's depression."

"Maybe," said Joe. "Didn't Connie give you the file? If she wanted to lead you to Ron, maybe she fabricated his report to the M.E. That would explain why the M.E. didn't use it in court. There was no such report."

I nodded. "Makes sense."

Ayden chimed in. "If Connie knew that Ron was hooking up with Lilian, she might've sent Barry to investigate, so he could erase Lilian from the picture. So, this gives Ron reason to punish Connie."

Mika rose with a sharp bark. Whining, she trotted to the door and stood still.

Ayden touched his holster and glanced out the window. "Car's gone." Before I could stop him, he was out the door. Mika dashed out behind him, followed by Natra. Joe stood and drew his Glock.

I went out. The ocean breeze had picked up. I looked around but couldn't see where they'd gone. I strode to the other end of my wraparound porch to search in back. Just as I rounded the corner, I heard a weapon click near my head. I raised my hands and froze. This wasn't how I'd envisioned the law of approach/avoidance working for me.

"Consider this a warning," said a man behind me. "You have a lot to lose. Delete this case and tell your client there's nothing you can do. Case closed. We go away."

I heard footsteps to my left. I knew it was Joe, but I couldn't warn him.

Then Ayden was on the right, aiming his Smithfield .45. "Back away from her," he ordered. "Gun down!"

"Shooting me risks her. *You* back away. Now!"

A dark blur jumped the railing and plowed into the man behind me, knocking him over. His shot went wild. Mika went for his arm. I grabbed his gun and ordered the growling dog to stand down. Natra ran up and pulled her back. Joe had already called the police.

* * *

After a search turned up more evidence, Ron confessed. He'd killed his partner to eliminate Barry as a rival and to punish Connie for sending Barry after Lilian. We hadn't untied the knot quite right, but we'd figured out the threads. Joe provided the files for Lilian's fraud investigation, which also implicated Ron. Just like in *Body Heat*, Matty2+ reaped multiple benefits, and I got wiser. We might have been used, but we'd cracked this nut.

Every Body Has a Story: Psi Apps Podcast #4

"My body, if the devil will catch me, will be in the room above the one of my mother."

Hello. I'm Annie Hunter. Welcome to *Psi Apps*, my podcast about my most distinctive cases. I call it *Psi Apps*—like psy-ops—because I cover a range of topics related to my work in forensic psychology. This includes cases with rumors of the paranormal. These can be the most intriguing, although this doesn't make me a ghost hunter. So, instead of P-S-Y, it's P-S-I, as in a type of weird energy. The 'app' part is my application of forensic psychology to crimes that have a creep factor. They're not *all* spooky, but I don't hesitate to include those that are.

I should point out that I've never seen a ghost. I tend to be skeptical of the reports I hear. I've been hired by people to evaluate mediums and haunted spots, and I usually find other explanations for supernatural claims, including downright fraud.

But not always.

Those rare incidents that suggest possible paranormal forces keep me hooked. My podcast helps other investigators to find me. If you've landed on my site, you might know I run a PI agency called the Nut Crackers, because we tackle hard nuts to crack. They're usually twisted tales that other investigators avoid. This leaves a clear field for me.

So, one day, I got a call from a colleague in Rome, Lorenzo Conelli. He wanted help with a case. Here it is:

Residents of a small town in a mountainous region of Italy were curious about the lack of activity at an isolated stucco house with an overgrown garden. At times, they'd see a young man wandering around. He'd go to town once a week and come back, but he'd speak to none of them. The *farmacista* who filled the man's monthly prescriptions said his name was Marco. He'd lived in the derelict house for a decade, taking care of his mother. Although he'd dutifully pick up her medication and other items, it had been some time since he'd come in. A concerned neighbor finally went over to check.

As she approached the front door, she sensed an eerie stillness. She considered turning around. She didn't know these people. Surely, they had relatives that were aware of them. But an odd smell made her think the garbage had been sitting awhile. Maybe someone needed help. She stepped to the door and knocked.

No one answered. She waited and listened before knocking again. She wished she'd persuaded a friend to come with her. She walked around and saw an outside door to the garage slightly ajar. She thought she could at least shut it to keep animals out. She put her hand on the metal knob, then stopped. The foul odor was strongest right here, a mix of urine, vomit, and alcohol.

The neighbor pushed the door open and saw a dark form on the dirt floor. She thought it was a man. He lay near the bumper of a silver Fiat Punto, too still to be alive. Blood smeared his staring face, and an amber liquid seeped from his slackened mouth. The woman ran home to call the *polizia*. Conelli had been on the forensics team that responded.

When I answered the call, I smiled at the Italian twist in his greeting: "It's-a Lorenzo." He described the events at the isolated house. The man in the garage was the homeowner, Marco. His death was an uncontested suicide from an overdose of drugs and alcohol, but "dere are *complicazioni, zome* difficulties." He hoped I could analyze Marco's mental state during the period leading up to his demise.

"I don't speak Italian," I reminded him.

"I will help-a. But I dought of you becuza of…eh, de udder case you haf—dee one where dee woman scribbled many notes on-a her wall. Hyper-graf-i-a, you say. Dat is…eh, dee kind of evidenz we have."

I perked up. Narrative tracks were my specialty. I'd presented on a case about a woman with hypergraphia, a compulsion to write, which was a symptom of her schizophrenia. "Do you have any interviews?" I asked.

"*Mi dispiace*, so sorry. No relatives and-a no *amici*, no friends. Even, eh, heez neighbors did-a not know heem. But he wrote…extenzively. Wiz pictures. It iz your kind of …*astuccio*…eh, kind of caze-a."

He was right. "I'll look at it, Lorenzo. But when you send the report, don't include any opinions from your team. I want to develop my own sense of it."

He sent me the translated case file in digital form. The first few lines told me this would be rough, but with some effort, I could make my way through it. Despite my rule against eating at my computer, a case from Italy begged for pizza and *un po' di vino rosso*. Well, okay, maybe I do speak a little Italian.

An ID showed Marco's age, 36. A brief bio said that he'd lived with his mother, supported by her pension payments. His father had died when Marco was 25, and he had no siblings. A pile of books in one photo told me that someone in the home liked to read, and I was able to make out some titles that showed a religious interest. *La Sacra Bibbia* was there, and *Papa Steven VI*, about the pope who dug up the body of his predecessor, dressed it up, and put it on trial. Boxes of drugs like butalbital, diazepam, and lorazepam suggested stockpiling for suicide. Marco's tox report matched them.

The photos of the trash-stuffed home told a disturbing story. I could almost smell the fusty magazines and food-crusted dishes. Marco's writings covered one dingy plaster wall of a sitting area. It looked like he'd used a black marker to record his messages. From these mini-essays, I pieced together a disjointed chronicle of his thoughts and feelings as he'd evolved toward self-annihilation.

One drawing featured the head of Christ wearing a crown of thorns. I thought I saw the telltale reddish brown of actual dried blood running down the face. Nearby was an attempt to duplicate Caravaggio's *Cristo alla Colonna*, which suggested that Marco identified with being bound, helpless, and prepared for punishment. Another Caravaggio, *David with the Head of Goliath*, had to have been chilling to draw. Goliath's frozen expression of defeat on the severed head dangling from David's hand was not the kind of art one might choose for cozy home décor.

Two narratives next to these drawings suggested the despair of a creeping depression. Marco hinted at *peccati*—sins—but gave no details. He'd copied numerous Bible verses and drawn multiple crucifixes bearing bloody figures expiring in agony. Most of the verses featured grisly episodes from the Old Testament or descriptions of the crucifixion of Christ. Marco seemed to be obsessed with painful death. I wondered if he'd thought he should be punished for something.

A scribbled passage with a sharp upward slant directed those who read *this* note to the second floor. In one bedroom, it said, they should open a sealed wardrobe, but *si prega di maneggiare con cura*—please handle with care—lest the picture of the Virgin Mary he'd nailed inside come loose. "*Stai attento!*" He'd supplied a date from three years earlier.

Curious, I scrolled to the photos of the wardrobe. Whatever was in there had to be the reason Lorenzo had called me. The first photo looked like a dark clump of clothing, so I moved on to the second one.

Shades of *Psycho*! I stopped chewing and looked closer. Sitting inside the wardrobe, illuminated by a crime scene processor's bright flashlight, was a mummified female corpse. Her head leaned forward over bony hands that clasped a Bible. The white hair, drawn back into a bun, looked like a wig, and the nose on her stiffened face had sunk inward, pulling the lips away from stained, yellow teeth. A close-up showed that the eyes had shrunk in their sockets.

Marco's mother, I surmised. Being closed up tight had prevented more typical decomp that would have liquefied her by now. Instead, her skin had hardened into a grayish shell. A notation told me that the team was analyzing DNA to prove the familial association, but she'd lived with Marco, and she hadn't been seen in a while. I expected they'd prove the connection.

I pushed my plate away, no longer enticed by greasy cheese. It wasn't the corpse that erased my appetite but the hints of a twisted relationship. The more I read, the more I realized that it did resemble the attachment between the demented Norman Bates and his controlling mother in Robert Bloch's *Psycho*. Bloch had modeled his character on an actual person, a mentally impaired mama's boy named Ed Gein.

He'd lost his father, brother, and mother, making him a lonely recluse in an isolated Wisconsin farmhouse. Free to indulge, he'd dug up the bodies of deceased women from the local cemetery. Each time he'd removed nipples, skin, and genitalia, he'd felt closer to his mother. Then he'd seen a woman the same size as his mother, so he'd killed her. He'd enjoyed the greater pliability of her skin. When he spotted a woman of similar size three years later, he'd killed her as well. From these bodies, Gein had made a skin suit that let him "become" his mother whenever he wore it.

That's twisted.

The forensic team had its work cut out. Calculating the manner of death in a mummified corpse would be a challenge. Natural mummification takes place when bacterial enzymes are inhibited in certain types of environments. If the date scribbled on the wall was any indication, the woman had been entombed in this cramped cell for three years. The manner of death could be any of the NASH categories: natural, accident, suicide or homicide. If homicide, Marco was the chief suspect. Since he was dead, the results mattered more for science than for law.

Although Marco had seemed despondent over his mother's passing, his grief clarified nothing. Lots of matricidal killers feel remorse. Most often, such cases involve delusional schizophrenia: A young man, resentful over his dependence, blames his mother, while the mother chafes at the burden of his care. They get on each other's nerves, feeding tension until the son vents it with a gun or a knife, even a machete. My job in Marco's case was to carefully consider evidence about his mental state during the days leading up to his mother's death.

The neighbors had been interviewed. No one knew him. All they could offer was that Marco had made regular trips to get his mother's pension payments, groceries, and medications. I noted that he'd continued doing this after her death, so he was guilty of fraud. This might explain the scribbled reference to his sins.

Or not.

Another wall note told a longer tale that offered key details for my report. To study this one, I poured another glass of wine. (I suggest that the reader do the same.) Marco described why and how he'd sealed his mother into the wardrobe. He'd wanted to "prevent any severing of the umbilical cord between them." He could not let death corrupt her, he'd said, so he'd put her into this vault. In his mind, having her corpse nearby would allow him to enter the room each day and talk to her. He'd been heartbroken that she'd died alone in her bed, but he'd done his best to clean and prepare her. He'd washed her, powdered her "delicate parts" ("as you did with me"), put on fresh underwear, and picked out a blue dress with matching shoes. He'd powdered her face and arranged her long hair before placing her in a comfortable position in the wardrobe. Writing *"Totus Tuus"* (Totally Yours) under the picture of the Virgin Mary nailed over her head, he'd sealed the closet with silicone. He'd hoped that "one day I could open these doors and see you again, relaxed and untouched." But he'd admitted in this note that he'd never had the courage to do it. He couldn't bear to see her dead. But he did like having her in the house.

Okay, I'll say it. I cringed at the image of him working lovingly on his mother's corpse. Marco's self-described need to remain in the womb, dead as it was, repulsed me. I couldn't fathom what it had been like for him, as a man, to be so pathologically entwined with his mother.

I returned to the wall writings. One text was drenched in grief: "I absolutely couldn't accept that she wasn't there anymore." He described his fear of growing up and living on his own. In other words, he'd been intelligent enough to understand his stunted development but still unable to mature. Yet Marco had been a caretaker. From the photos, it was clear he'd tenderly chosen clothing for his "beloved" and had meticulously prepared her for preservation.

On the other hand, if he'd killed his mother, hiding her body would facilitate his ability to use her pension money, as well as escape arrest. He'd been allowed to retrieve the checks each month without challenge. So, for three years, he'd been sufficiently deceptive to be able to act as if she were alive.

Still, he'd written that he'd tried several times to kill himself. He'd viewed these failures as "God's rejection." Despite his Catholicism, he didn't seem to notice the contradiction in his belief that suicide, a sin, would be his ticket to heaven. Another lengthy text listed instructions, typical of many suicide notes, which implied that Marco had thought he'd die in his own bed. "My body, if the devil will catch me, will be in the room above the one of my mother."

There were other writings to sort through, but I noticed something. Given his firm religious orientation and his belief that God had rejected him, writing on the wall had presented an opportunity for Marco to confess to murder, if he'd done it, and to purify himself. He hadn't. This omission was glaring. He'd repeatedly tried to kill himself and had repeatedly failed, so he'd seemingly pay any price, including a terrible confession, to earn God's embrace. This *absence* of an expected behavior was significant.

This wasn't a clear case of an anguished son. There certainly were criminal acts involved. I saw no evidence of true hypergraphia, which can signal schizophrenia or temporal lobe epilepsy. No journals or tablets had turned up filled to the brim with writing. The thoughts Marco had expressed were sometimes strange—"I won the devil's assaults for fifteen times"—but not necessarily psychotic. Marco's depression accounted for why his physical surroundings had deteriorated. He'd functioned well enough to collect the pension, feed himself, and pay bills, but this seemed the extent of his ability to survive. He'd expressed no anger, let alone murderous rage.

After DNA confirmed the mother's identity and an autopsy located no physical trauma on her mummified body, I completed my report. Although Marco fit the profile of a person with a serious disorder who might commit matricide, his narratives supported a finding of natural death for the mother and a psychic collapse for him. He was probably not a murderer. He seemed more likely to have been a tragic example of the lack of mental health resources in remote areas for barely functional individuals. The rest of the team concurred.

The Girl Without a Face: Psi Apps Podcast #9

"I have a friend in Chattanooga. He sees part of you walking three feet behind."

Hello, and welcome to my podcast. I'm Annie Hunter. I'm an investigative forensic psychologist. On this podcast, I discuss disturbing crimes with unique twists. So far, I've talked about my methods. I've also mentioned my team, but I haven't told you how I invited them to join me. With each one, a bizarre crime was involved. Let me warn you: the one I'm about to describe is graphic. It's hard to believe someone could plan it, let alone *do* it.

This episode features my data diver and info chief, Natra Gawoni. I don't know how I managed before I met her. She can find information in the most obscure sources. Once, we had to figure out a killer's route from symbols in his poems. She not only nailed the locations from her literary and geographical research, but she also anticipated his next moves.

Natra's also my personal confidante. Older than me by eight years, she's like a big sister. It doesn't hurt that she's a phenomenal cook. I'm grateful that she lives basically next door, in an apartment on the north side of my six-bedroom house on the Outer Banks. She still visits her ex-husband now and then, but they fell apart after losing their teenage daughter to an opioid overdose.

Her roots in the Eastern Band Cherokee endowed her with waist-length dark brown hair, a sense of Native culture, and an instinct for story. This is valuable for incident reconstruction. When she spots a hole in my logic, she balks like a horse at a creek it won't jump. "You're missing something," she'll say. "You have to address this." Invariably, she's right.

Natra's remarkably intense about research. When she's not wrangling data for me, she's focused on some forensic project, like examining saw marks on bone. She wants to be prepared, because I often need resources at a moment's notice. You wouldn't know from her slight figure that she's a top cadaver dog handler, sometimes carrying a heavy pack for hours in the field. Zealous about training, she's claimed a patch of my zoysia grass to work with her Doberdor, Mika. I call the dog a Labradobe. She might have a Doberman's short tail and black-and-tan coloring, but she's got the *don't-you-want-to-be-with-me?* eyes of a Lab. (I'd give Natra the same look should she ever decide to quit.)

Here's how we met:

I had just started investigative consulting as a psychologist, so I worked *pro bono* to develop credentials and contacts. I performed psychological autopsies on questioned deaths, investigated missing persons cases, and offered clinical assessments for court. Detective Aaron Brasse had a possible missing person, and he'd figured it wouldn't hurt to have an expert opinion, especially one at no cost to him.

Brasse told me the basics: twenty-one-year-old Imani Kuta, from Tanzania, had lived with her uncle, Mosi Kuta, so she could afford to go to college. Over a period of two weeks, friends noticed her absence from class and notified authorities. No one had filed a missing-person report, and Imani was an adult, so police couldn't do much. The friends had persisted. They learned that while Mosi Kuta had told them Imani had gone home, Imani's mother had denied it. Frantic over reports from Imani's friends, the mother had contacted the local police, putting her in touch with Brasse. She'd begged him to look for the girl. When Brasse had questioned Kuta, the man was evasive.

Now, Brasse's the kind of guy who sizes you up before he makes his move. He knows that his six-foot-three height can intimidate, so he's developed a quiet approach that invites his interviewees to lean toward him. This elicits better responses.

But Kuta had remained uncooperative, and Brasse had no probable cause for a search warrant. That's when he invited me to work on the case. I learned from Imani's friends that she'd been wary of her uncle. Then I acquired some revealing information from Imani's sister, Leyla.

"She got pregnant a year ago," Leyla confided. "I think he raped her, then forced her to get an abortion. She felt so ashamed. She didn't report it because she had no other place to go. She just wanted to get through school. I'm afraid he's done something to keep her quiet."

I'd just given Brasse my report when he learned of a disturbing discovery a month before along a riverbank eighty-five miles north. Picnickers had found the head, torso, and right leg of a dismembered Jane Doe, wrapped in separate plastic bags. Brasse suspected this could be Imani, but the victim's face and torso had been completely skinned, and the eyes and ears were gone. Only the red muscles and some white tissue showed. A state anthropologist had estimated the victim's age to be between eighteen and twenty-five. She wanted to make a clay bust from the skull to help with identification, but she thought this process could destroy valuable evidence.

They'd found a solution. I can't explain the mechanics, but the procedure is worth describing. Technicians at a prototyping center developed a 3-D model layering hundreds of successive CT scans of the victim's head. From the results, a forensic artist had sketched a likeness, adding the ears. Posters were made. Brasse saw one. He thought the Jane Doe resembled Imani closely enough to order a DNA analysis on the remains. A match was made to saliva from an envelope Imani had licked. Brasse got his warrant, but the search got him no further. He told me about the results.

"It was clear that this young woman hadn't packed up and gone home. We found her Bible, her passport, and her purse with her ID and credit cards. One of our guys spotted an open box of gray garbage bags the same size and color as those used to wrap the parts."

"Sounds like a solid case," I told him.

"Except for one thing. We couldn't implicate Kuta in murder. No physical evidence. The place is clean."

I thought about this. Behavioral probability analysis is my forte. "Well, the body was dismembered," I said. "The likely place is a home or workshop, for privacy."

"No workshop," Brasse informed me.

My turn. "He skinned her. That can't have been a clean process."

"Nope. That's why we got a dog handler coming. She's from your way, North Carolina. I read about her dog in a police magazine. Mika's the name, I think. She finds traces of biological evidence. The dog's been qualified in courtrooms in over twenty states as a human remains specialist."

I'd never participated on a cadaver dog investigation. "I'd like to see this," I told him.

"Got it scheduled for end of the week. Come on over."

On the designated day, I gathered with Brasse, two other detectives, and two crime scene unit processors—all male. Natra arrived in a dented black Chevy Express van that had seen a lot of miles. So had her scuffed tan cowboy boots and faded jeans. I watched her bring the black-and-brown dog, Mika, through a sliding door on the right. Natra glanced at me and offered a quick nod. Rarely have I met a person whose presence radiates the warmth of a kitchen where cookies are baking, but that's how I'd describe it.

Natra let Mika sniff around before she tossed a chewed-up blue baseball cap with a Coyote team logo. The dog chased it with a delighted *yip*. I knew enough about cadaver dog training to realize that Mika worked for a few precious moments with the cap. This was her reward. And she *really* loved it.

Behind Natra, a chubby detective in an ill-fitting blue suit subtly nudged his red-haired partner, who looked about eighteen. I sensed they were up to something. When Brasse escorted Natra and Mika into the apartment building, Pudgy said to Red, "Double or nothing."

"You're on," came the response.

"What's the bet?" I asked. It was none of my business, but that never stopped me.

Pudgy shrugged and moved away, while Red looked embarrassed. Brasse had warned me that the guys under him weren't keen about using a psychologist—me. I was used to this. Our "voodoo" makes cops anxious. But I sensed these two disliked outsiders, period. Or maybe didn't like females invading their turf.

Alert to potential shenanigans, I watched them as I entered an apartment that smelled of cloves and bleach. Already in motion, Mika sniffed at several locations in the living room before she abruptly stopped at a wall near a dining table. I saw Pudgy smirk and wink at Red.

Natra focused on Mika. "What is it, girl? Find!" We all waited to see if the dog would indicate the presence of human blood, but she moved on. I noticed the subtle hand movement from Pudgy to Red that suggested an exchange of money. Pudgy looked peeved.

Mika trotted into a galley kitchen, where a pile of crusted plates sat in a stainless-steel sink. I pulled out my pocket notebook and wrote, *They're setting you up*. I tore it off and folded it into my hand. When I had a chance, I slipped it to Natra. She read it and nodded.

Again, Mika paused to sniff a spot. She went still. Pudgy's smirk told me he'd planted something to throw her off. Some cops think sniffer dogs are useless. Pudgy wanted to prove it. Maybe he hoped to embarrass Brasse for bringing Natra into the case.

But Mika didn't fully alert. She broke her pose and moved out of the room. Pudgy grimaced. I guessed he'd lost a few more bucks. I smiled as if I'd taken his money myself.

In contrast to the grimy kitchen, the first-floor bathroom looked like a *House & Garden* exhibit. The odor of bleach assailed us. Mika stopped, barked twice, and went down. She whined and looked at Natra. Despite how spotless the place looked, I believed they'd find blood in here—real blood, not a fake set-up.

"Show me, girl," Natra urged her. "Find." Mika got up and put her nose close to the flowered wallpaper. She barked again.

"Good girl!" Natra tossed the hat into the adjoining room, and Mika bounded after it.

Brasse leaned toward the indicated area on the wall and tapped with a glove-covered finger. "I can see it. Just a tiny spot that's out of place. Easy to miss." He pointed to two more in close alignment. "Looks like cast-off." He meant the spatter that comes from a bloody weapon being jerked from a wound. It seemed unlikely they'd have seen those reddish-brown spots on this busy pattern without an inch-by-inch grid search. Brasse called for the processing team. Sneering at Pudgy, I left. Outside, Natra played with Mika. I approached her.

"Thanks for the warning," she said. "They think they can drown frogs in water."

She must have seen my blank expression, so she added, "Ignorance. You see it in the eyes. They don't know how she's trained, so they dismiss her." She pointed at Mika. "I know my dog, what she can do. I saw where they put animal blood to distract her. I smelled it myself. Didn't matter. I knew she wouldn't go for it."

"I get the same treatment," I said. "Not that they put blood on me, I mean, but few cops respect the work psychologists do for criminal investigations." I introduced myself and asked where in North Carolina she lived.

"Asheville," she told me.

"Grew up there," I said. Although I'm a psychic brick when it comes to second sight, even I could predict that she'd be in my future.

Brasse came out. "Impressive," he said. "I figured she'd find somethin'. Sorry 'bout my guys. They can be assholes, but they'll tackle this case properly now. We'll take apart the pipes. Likely done in the tub, and human remains generally stick somewhere along the way. If yer dog's up to it, we got one more stop."

In a garage that housed twenty-five cars below the apartment building, it took Mika just ten minutes to alert on a maroon Honda Accord. "That's Kuta's," Brasse said. "We'll get another warrant. I figure he used it to transport the parts."

I always have mixed feelings when a case moves toward a positive resolution. It means we're getting justice for a victim but also that someone came to harm. Grief-tinged success is like a wedding in a cemetery. You can smile, but you can't party.

I saw Natra again at the grand jury hearing, which the DA hoped would pressure Kuta into a plea.

DNA had linked the body parts to the missing Imani, and the bathroom pipes had yielded bits of her tissue. The tiny blood spots were from her as well, although blood in a bathroom didn't necessarily spell murder. Kuta's former wife had agreed to testify about his abusive behavior and his butchering skill from his family's livestock business. I offered a report from research on the likelihood of a man with Kuta's background devising such a brutal act. Should the case go to trial, I'd do a full clinical work-up. With Leyla's testimony from my recording, backed up with Imani's medical records, the totality of evidence seemed certain to clinch a true bill of indictment. Yet Brasse knew there'd be questions about the cadaver dog. He'd asked Natra to offer a demo. For this, he'd hidden a tiny spot in the grand jury room.

When I entered the building to wait for my turn, I saw Natra with Mika. I went over and leaned down to make a fuss over the dog, who happily received it. When I stood, Natra offered me a small plastic baggie that held a crumbly greenish-gray substance. "I have a friend in Chattanooga," she said. "His name's Iron Braids. He sees part of you walking three feet behind. He sent this for you to make tea, but he thinks you should go to a doctor."

"What?" I asked. "How does he—?"

Brasse opened the door to the grand jury room and gestured for Natra. "Make tea," she repeated. "It will help." Then she took Mika inside.

The bag emitted a citrusy floral scent. Some kind of herb. I didn't see Natra after the hearing, which was successful, but that evening I made tea. It smelled potent, but with honey, it tasted okay. Then I made an appointment. My doctor discovered a health issue I wouldn't have noticed. We'd caught it early enough to successfully treat it with minimal downtime. *Three feet behind*, Iron Braids had said. I hoped I'd rejoined myself.

I traveled to Asheville to bring Natra a token of thanks I thought she'd appreciate: a bracelet made from shells picked up along my OBX beach. By this time, Kuta had crumbled and accepted a plea deal.

Natra welcomed me like an old friend. And she had a kitchen full of warm cookies. We fell into discussing another case I thought had been staged. Her intelligence and resources impressed me so much I invited her to come to my house and look through the file. She accepted, and she's been with me ever since.

Rodanthe Man: Psi Apps Podcast #10

"Dr. Hunter, I've heard things about this case you'd never guess."

Hi. It's Annie Hunter, back with another *Psi Apps* podcast. This time, I'll introduce another member of my team.

You already know I prefer coffee to tea, but only if it's suffused with sweet stuff. According to pseudo-science, this means I'm not a psychopath. *They* supposedly prefer black coffee, as well as dark chocolate, flat speech, and brash rap.

Back to *my* coffee, which led me to my team's PI. I went to the Treehouse Cafe in Duck on the Outer Banks to sit outside on a turquoise Adirondack chair with a hazelnut latte. Most customers on that breezy summer morning were tourists dressed for shopping or the nearby beach. Contact with the living takes my mind off the dead; it reminds me why I investigate crimes. Although I'm a clinical forensic psychologist, I also consult on death investigations. I'd just started my business. So far, I had a data miner-slash-dog handler and a part-time cyber guy. I also had a clinical report to proofread by noon if I could keep the pages from blowing away.

As the morning mob shrank, at a weathered picnic table near me, I noticed a blond guy in sandals, a black T-shirt, and shorts. His hair was barely on the groomed side of shaggy. Facing me, he leaned over a tablet screen and tapped his right thigh with a fidgety rhythm that suggested a delayed companion. I heard snippets from a weather report: "85 degrees" and "fifteen miles per hour."

I pegged him as a beach bum hoping for favorable surf report. Then I saw

"Rodanthe Man" lettered in yellow on his T-shirt. He'd know better places to surf than here. Those who rent or reside in that area to the south tend to avoid our more congested digs. So, yeah, he'd come to meet someone. His worn leather sandals suggested variable income. Early thirties, like me. The dark tan and toned hands said he spent time outside, probably on temp jobs in construction—lots of that here. Handsome enough in that outdoorsy way that attracts plenty of beach bunnies.

Rodanthe Man must have sensed me watching. He looked up. "Did you know that hurricanes can dump two and a half *trillion* gallons of rain in a single day?"

I took a sip and shrugged. "Little danger of that today." I returned to my report.

He took my reply as an invitation (it wasn't) and moved to the Adirondack chair next to mine. I flashed a "privacy wall" look, but he stayed in my space. He placed his tablet and a five-by-seven unlined scratchpad on the table between us. The pad showed the sketch of a woman's head.

"Girlfriend?" I asked. I hoped.

"Nope." He angled it toward me. "Murder victim."

I stared. Not just a murder victim. *My* murder victim, a young woman named Denise Loflin who'd been found dead in weeds near the Bodie Island lighthouse south of Nags Head. I'd just taken the case. A note in her pocket had convinced the cops she'd killed herself. Her mother had hired me, a suicidologist, to challenge this call. I'd said the note was a prop in a staged homicide and worked up the profile of a likely killer from the few scene photos in the file. This drawing was a striking likeness.

I narrowed my eyes. "What's your business with me?"

He leaned forward. "I'm Ayden Scott. I hear you hire freelance PIs."

I pressed against the back of my chair. "How did you find me?"

He tapped the 'R' on *Rodanthe*. "PI. A good one. You should hire me."

I raised an eyebrow. "Rodanthe Man?"

He leaned back to stretch the shirt, showing a dot after the word, 'Man.' "Rodanthe Management," he explained. "My business. Jack of all trades. Need your house fixed? I can do that, too."

"You look like a surfer bum."

He beamed. "I'm that, too, when I can. Gotta have some fun."

"Well, sorry, but I don't hire PIs. I leave that to the attorney."

"There isn't one on this case." He cocked his head. "The mother hired you. The cops won't bother. For them, the case is closed. And you need me. I have many talents. I do search and rescue. I volunteer for the turtle watch. I invent things. I—"

I shook my head. "This isn't a job interview."

"I'm good with people. They trust me. You could use that on your team."

I bristled. "You don't *listen* well. And I don't have a team."

"You have a dog handler and a digital guy. That makes three. You need a PI, at least for this case."

"I already know some."

"They don't know what I know." He leaned in, his blue eyes holding my attention. "Look, here's a deal you can't refuse. Let me work on it for a day. Just one. If you like what I find—and you will—then pay me. If not, you walk away. No loss to you."

"Except you'd have seen the file." I pulled my coffee mug closer. "I'm not about to hand it over."

Scott made a dismissive gesture. "Not necessary. I know enough to run down some leads." He opened a thin leather wallet and showed me his North Carolina Private Investigator card. "Dr. Hunter, I've heard things about this case you'd never guess."

He intrigued me; he also annoyed me. He'd entered my space through doors I hadn't thought to keep locked. "Mr. Scott—"

"Ayden. Hey, I get it. You don't know me, but I'll prove myself and you'll never look back." From within the pages of his drawing pad, he pulled an envelope. "I'm a local, born here. That's what this case needs. I can find people an' get 'em talking. Here's my references and contact info. Make your calls. By the time you're done, I'll have some intel. And here's a tickler. This woman was sold." He picked up his items and stood. "And sold out."

I didn't like this. Our conversation had been like training a golden retriever pup. You try to make them obey, and when they do, you think you're in control, but then they bound away, crushing your illusion. Still, if he worked up a good lead in a day, I'd happily pay. No commitment.

I finished my latte, ordered one to go, and glanced through his references. I shook my head. All females. Of course.

At home, I handed the latte and envelope to Natra Gawoni, my assistant. She's the cadaver dog handler that Scott had mentioned. "Can you call these people to confirm that this guy's legit?"

She glanced at his business card. "Yeah, I met 'im yesterday on the beach when I walked Mika. Said he was watching for baby sea turtles. He gave me the same card."

"Seems to know a lot about me."

"I liked him. So did Mika. He knew how to handle a SAR dog. I think he's involved in search and rescue."

I disliked being stalked, but I viewed Mika, her Doberdor, as our best reference. She approached strangers only when she sensed they were safe.

"I already looked 'im up," Natra added. "He's got a business, or at least a website. Thought we might use him one day. Not that you'd remember, but the last PI we worked with moved to Florida."

No doubt he knew this, I thought. "Check his references, then. But I'm not paying him unless he impresses me. His deal, not mine."

She glanced at the page I handed her and snorted. "All women."

"Yeah. No surprise, right?"

"One's a cop we know. I say he'll come through. Bet? Loser makes dinner."

"Nope. I never bet against the dog." I gave Mika a quick pat and left Natra to her work.

Ayden called three hours later. "Meet me at your digital lab."

Damn, this guy bugged me. For all his PI work, he didn't understand basic psychology, not mine, anyway. "You know where it is?" Of course he did.

"I told you. I'm good. I know who I work for."

"You don't work for me yet."

"You gotta see this. It's your kind of thing."

Hmm. Maybe he *did* understand basic psychology. That line always hooked me. Just like weather chats. Ah… now I knew why he'd tossed me that line about the hurricane. He'd studied me. He knew I'd respond.

I gave him a time, then planned to show up early so I could talk to Joe Lochren. He worked full-time as a forensic digital analyst, but he gave me free analytics in exchange for the use of my private lab for his moonlit contracts. I knew he'd be over there today.

But Scott had anticipated my move. Already there with Joe, he'd nicked my advantage. "Don't worry," he said. "I didn't ask him to show me anything."

"He seems to be the only one you didn't ask."

"Oh, you mean your dog handler? Guilty. But that's what a good PI does, right? She didn't say much."

"Come and look, Annie," Joe said. "This could be probative."

Joe looks like he just stepped off a *Law and Order* set as the lead detective. He had an image on the screen. "It's from a phone dump." He gestured toward Scott. "He got it."

"Legally?"

Surfer Bum shrugged. "Gray area."

That golden retriever thing again.

On the blurred video image, I saw two men in the room with a naked dark-haired woman who lay face-up on a bed. She looked limp, possibly unconscious. She resembled Denise Loflin.

"She's in the sweet condition, like you asked," one of them said. "Where's the money?"

I recognized his voice. Kyle something. Denise's mother had introduced him as Denise's boyfriend. In fact, his name had surfaced in her alleged suicide note. *I'm sorry, Kyle. It's not you. You were good to me. No one should blame you.* For me, that line was a red flag. Fake suicide notes often name the perpetrators in a positive light to divert investigations. This video confirmed my hunch. Kyle's description of Denise's recent depression—a surprise to her mother—had been a cover.

I'd already lined up a handwriting expert for the note. Superficially, it had resembled samples from Denise's script, but an expert's eye was needed.

The other man in the video poked the woman, but she didn't move.

"This looks like somnophilia," I said. "Getting aroused from sex with unconscious partners. It's not illegal if the partner agrees." I looked at Scott. "You said she was sold?"

He nodded at the screen. "Watch."

The man held up a white oval pill to the camera lens. To my surprise, he then went to the woman, reached between her legs, and seemed to insert it. Both men snickered before the clip ended.

"What did he show the camera?" I asked.

"You need to get her re-autopsied," Scott said, "with a more focused tox screen."

"Wait, wait. How did you get this clip?"

Scott hesitated before he replied. "I invented a device for cloning and surveillance. You can't use this in court, but with this intel, you can use *your* skill to encourage the mother to get a private autopsy. Once they have the tox report that shows this substance, the cops will investigate."

I held up my hands in exasperation. "Tell me what you know. Why did you clone this, and how did you get access to it?"

Joe watched him, too, apparently equally intrigued.

Scott shrugged. "I hear things. I hang out with friends, go to beach parties, listen to chats. I heard about this group, the Nappers, as in kidnappers, but they specialize in this sleep thing, somna…whatever you called it. Sex with unconscious women. They have a contest. These guys rack up points. They have to prove it with videos. The most competitive guys pay other guys to rent their girlfriends. For fifty bucks, all the boyfriend has to do is slip a downer in her drink and leave her for a couple hours. I know Kyle. When I heard Denise was dead, I remembered him at a Napper party. And you just heard him ask for money."

"A drug overdose and a date rape?" I asked. "Is that where we're going?"

"Yeah, but I don't think he thought she'd die."

Then I knew. They'd ensured her deep sleep with a vaginal administration of a fast-acting benzodiazepine, like Halcion. I'd heard of this, but I'd never seen it as a group activity. The drug triggered memory loss, which provided cover for the rapist. Yet in combination with some prescription drugs, Halcion posed dangers. I texted Natra to look for Denise's prescriptions in her medical records. At the very least, Kyle had participated in a homicide and its cover-up.

"Here's another tip I turned up," Scott said. "The cops arrested a Napper. He offered money to an undercover cop for her twelve-year-old daughter. They caught 'im with a tape of two other assaults, including his sister, and neither victim knew it happened. He's just cut a deal to help the cops invade a party. Go talk to them. I'll give you their names."

Natra texted back a list of three drugs. An anti-fungal medication stood out. In combination with a downer as strong as Halcion, it could be fatal. Their little game, it seemed, had killed her.

I lifted an eyebrow at Ayden Scott. "Okay, I agree. You're good. This is solid intel. I can get a tox report to show how they administered the drug and take it from there. Send me your bill, Rodanthe Man."

He held up a hand. "This one's on me, in exchange for hiring me for your other case." This time, he seemed to notice my frown because he added, "Full disclosure. I know the cop on that case. She told me. Said you do spooky stuff. That's all I needed to hear."

Now he *really* had my attention. "What do you mean?"

"Hey, I'll work any case with a ghost story. I wanna see one."

Joe winked at me. He'd done a couple of cases with me that had rumors of ghosts. Most PIs won't touch them, but I'm open. I regarded Ayden Scott carefully. Then I held out my hand. "Deal."

He pumped it with golden retriever fervor. "Dr. Hunter, you won't regret this."

"It's Annie. Welcome to my team, Ayden."

Missing Parts

rthur drank beer all day and smoked some dope. He formed a plan. He'd been a good man, but Lynn had loathed his habit of stabbing himself. She'd taken their girls to shack up with another man. She should be punished. Arthur's voices told him to act. He drank cough syrup and taped his mouth shut. Carrying three sharp knives in the pocket of his cargo pants, he strode over to Lynn's place and kicked in the door.

She ran to the kitchen. Arthur followed. He used the longest knife to stab her in the chest. She went down. He knelt to see the light leave her eyes before forcing his fingers into the wound to explore the dying heart. He gripped it, braced himself, and pulled it out. Satisfied, he offered it to God.

Then he entered the children's room. They struggled as he stabbed each with the knife meant for her. When they lay still, Arthur carved out their hearts. He placed all three slick organs into his pockets. Blood ran down his leg. Arthur felt God's approval. But murder, he knew, was wrong. Mathew 5:29 in the Bible fixed the price: If he stumbled, he should lose an eye. Arthur ripped the tape from his mouth and dug a finger into his right eye socket to gouge out the orb. He popped it into his mouth, chewed, and swallowed.

It's no surprise that people moved away as he walked three miles to a police station. At the intake desk, he announced, "I freed the hearts of my family!" Digging the crusted organs from his pockets, Arthur placed them before a startled clerk.

Attorneys debated Arthur's mental state at the time of the crime. Despite his delusions, he'd turned himself in, so he'd known his acts were wrong. This made him legally sane. The DA decided to take him to trial for the triple homicide. Arthur's attorney hoped to show he couldn't go. He gave me a call.

I'm Annie Hunter, a forensic psychologist. I consult on such cases, but Arthur's not the subject of this story. His case merely opened the door to the tale I'm about to tell and helped me to handle it. The mission mindset has many manifestations. Arthur was strange, to be sure, but his assault made sense as a drug-laced delusion. The other case proved more challenging.

Besides doing forensic evaluations, I run an agency, Nut Cracker Investigations. We accept "hard nuts to crack," meaning unique, complicated, and even spooky cases. The events I'm about to describe include all three.

My connection to the situation came through Natra, my half-Cherokee data miner. We'd met at a murder scene where she'd brought her cadaver dog, Mika. Several parts of a young woman had washed up on a riverbank. Her uncle, the chief suspect, had thoroughly purified his house. But Mika still detected blood in his tub. During court proceedings that landed the man in prison, Natra gave me a puzzling message from a Lakota shaman named Iron Braids. "He sees part of you walking three feet behind," she said. "He thinks you should go to a doctor." I caught a health issue just in time. Shortly afterward, I'd hired Natra as my investigative assistant, which expanded the kinds of cases I took on.

The weekend I went to evaluate Arthur coincided with a gathering of Native American tribes three hours west. Natra attended this pow-wow to reunite with friends. She soon called to say she'd offered our service for a murder case. "Just to give them ideas, pro bono."

We weren't in the best place to work for free. "I've got a complex report to write, Natra," I said. "Can't you handle it?"

She waited a beat, then said, "Iron Braids is coming. Involves his nephew. It's serious. He'd like to hear your assessment."

I owed him. "I'll wrap up here tomorrow and be there by late afternoon. What about Ayden?" The beach bum and all-around handyman worked part-time as my primary PI.

"Maybe. There's a ghost story attached."

"He'd never forgive us for leaving him out."

Via connected digital screens that evening, Natra offered what she'd learned. At the dances, she'd encountered Iron Braids' son, Red Feather. His cousin, Brock, had been arrested on suspicion of murder. Some fingers and an ear with a distinct earring had turned up on an abandoned farm next to Brock's father's property in West Virginia. Identification was traced to Celina King, missing for three days. She'd been dating Brock.

"At first, he denied being on the property," Natra said. "Then they found his fingerprints in the house, so he admitted he'd taken Celina inside before she went missing. The house has a reputation for being haunted, and he said she'd wanted to explore."

"Circumstantial," I said, "but he lied, so damning. Did they find the rest of her?"

"They searched the property, but I haven't seen any reports of a discovery. There was vomit in the house, but it turned out to be from a dog. I put the news articles on our team-source site."

"Good idea." My paranormal forensics podcast, *Psi-Apps*, has spawned a tight community of amateur sleuths. Unsolved crimes are bait. Our associates dig in and send ideas, and some even give us eyes and ears in the right places.

"Brock has been detained," Natra added. "No alibi. He said he was out hunting alone during the time Celina was missing."

"What's the ghost story?" Ayden asked.

"Murder-suicide in that house," Natra responded. "A while back, but it's an infamous local legend. A farmer's wife snapped and killed him. She cut him up, cooked him in a stew, and served it to his friends before hanging herself in the house. People say they hear shouting in the empty house and see weird lights moving in the yard at night. Rumors say the place is a demonic portal, so anyone who lives there will die. A series of bad storms one year washed topsoil off the garden, and someone found a skull—the husband's missing head."

Ayden snorted. "That's true?"

"That's the story."

"Perception is everything," I said. "True or false, the rumors can be a catalyst. Two murder tales involving body parts at the same place has potential significance, especially a place with the aura of an evil portal."

"Send me the address," Ayden said. "I have an associate in the area. She can do some digging for us."

"We're not investigating," I warned. "Just offering ideas to Brock's attorney."

"Copy, boss."

In the morning, I finished my business with Arthur's attorney. I warned him of an uphill battle. Arthur believed he deserved to be punished under the laws of man, despite acting on God's command. Yet, he'd also mixed drugs with booze. Even juries who accept crazy still think willing drug use makes them guilty. Without question, Arthur was psychotic, but on the day of the triple homicide, he'd been so high he'd ripped out his eye without feeling the pain.

"I can testify about the impact of schizophrenia on his biblical mission," I told the attorney, "but I can't change his BAC. His best defense is the deific decree."

"What's that?"

"The one that goes, 'I know murder is wrong, but God ordered me, so I had to.' Sometimes, it works." In truth, its success was akin to throwing darts at a target in the dark. "I'll add it to my report."

Eager to meet Iron Braids, I jumped into the car. Before I got there, Natra called. "We have a potential lead from the team-sourcing site. Closer59."

We'd heard from him before. An aspiring detective with a thing for haunted crime scenes. He wrote his posts with an imposing tone. No fun at a party, probably, but a good researcher.

Natra continued. "Here's what he wrote. About ten miles from where they found those remains, there's an old cowshed. Six months ago, some kids found a woman's purse outside in the mud. They went in the shed and saw a car with a tarp over it. The found a small room in a cellar that was nailed closed, and inside were traces of blood, like someone held there had tried to escape. Around back was a fifty-five-gallon barrel filled with charred wood. They sifted it and found bone fragments. The purse and car belong to a missing woman. Forensic tests confirmed her blood was in the closet."

"Does Ayden know?"

"He's already there, snooping around."

"I said we're not investigating."

"I know. He wants to."

"Remind him what *pro bono* means in case he doesn't know."

When I arrived at the spacious valley where Natra had directed me, I smelled roasting corn. I generally stood out at such gatherings, with my blond hair and pale skin. People stared but always welcomed me into the "all nations" dances. As I walked among teepees with flapping door covers, I breathed in the fragrance of fried flatbread and imagined it dripping with honey. Down to the smallest child, celebrants wore red, white, yellow, or blue tribal attire, decorated with fringe and colorful beads. Some had sewn small metal bells to their belts or ankle bands that jingled as they walked. A mother and daughter, in fringed white dresses with bodices beaded in light blue and red, practiced dance steps next to two men tapping on a single flat frame-drum. Chants and animated banter filled the air.

I found Natra watching a dance. She pointed out a young man in black and white leather who chanted and hopped in a tight circle. His leggings showed elaborate beading, and the abundance of colorful feathers in his back harness suggested a professional performer. Thin, with black hair cropped just short of his shoulders, he appeared to be in his late twenties. Natra waved him over and introduced me to Red Feather, Iron Braids' son. He invited me to call him Koda, the name he used in his ordinary life. He invited us over to his tent—a basic Coleman cabin six-sleeper.

"Borrowed this," he explained. "I wasn't going to stay till my father decided to come." He pointed in a southern direction. "He's on the drums right now. It's a storm dance." Koda pointed to five men gathered around three enormous kettle-type drums. They banged out an intense, infectious rhythm. "My father's wearing the hat."

True to his name, Iron Braids had gray-and-black braided hair, topped with a dark gray fedora that bore a single black feather. A stocky man, he wore a buckskin shirt and a carved-bone chest-plate decorated with black beads. He seemed to drum in a trance. Natra strode into the dance circle. Koda joined her.

I watched the clouds with a wary eye. They looked ready to spill. I felt a drop, then another. My leg muscles clenched. The drumming continued. After ten minutes, the dark purplish-gray color overhead diminished. I relaxed. It didn't rain. The drummers congratulated one another, laughing, as if they thought they'd held off the storm. Koda went over to his father and pointed in my direction. Iron Braids nodded.

Natra came up and handed me a chunk of warm flatbread that smelled of hot oil. "We'll meet Iron Braids in his tent, but just a warning: he won't answer your questions the way you're used to. He envisions; then he speaks. That's his gift to you. After that, we'll leave."

"We're not hanging out?"

"No. He's here for Koda."

At the tent, Koda invited us inside. The humid air, thick with the scent of smudged sweet grass, cloyed my skin. Iron Braids was seated on a red-and-black woven rug. Next to him were two long, feathered rods, a clay pipe, and a brown pottery jug. Dream catchers pinned to aluminum support poles twirled in gusts that came through the zippered screen door. Iron Braids greeted me, offered tea, and urged Koda to tell us the story before he closed his eyes and went still. Natra sat near Iron Braids. I took a seat across from him.

Koda told us what we already knew about Brock's plight but added some important items. "Brock had a rival. Jordan Metsker. He's connected. He's a financial advisor, and some of his clients are wealthy. The cops claim they investigated him and he's clean." He shrugged. "Who knows?"

I leaned toward him. "Do they have a time-since-death estimate for Celina, for when she was killed?"

"She was at an ATM on Tuesday night two weeks ago, around midnight, and was reported missing that Thursday. Without a body, they couldn't pinpoint a time."

"Did Metsker have an alibi?"

"His brother, Glen, vouched for him, and so did Glen's girlfriend. She calls herself Eve. I tried talking with her, but she looked scared and walked away."

"Any idea why?"

He shook his head.

"Does either brother have a violent history?"

"Not on record. They're active members of a local church. I think Metsker might even lead it. They recently purchased a pair of Rottweilers, if that means anything."

"Not much. What does Brock say about the victim?"

For us, victimology is a crucial first step; the more details we get, the better.

"Celina was an artist, but she was into some dicey occult stuff. She was engaged to Metsker for a few months but broke it off. She told Brock he'd hit her. She also said he had some odd ideas. He told her he was a spiritual potter. That's how he put it. He thought he could extract life energy from people to use to entice Jesus to return. Something like that. Celina called him crazy, but when she broke up with Brock, he saw her with Metsker again. Brock thinks he had something on her."

"Like what?"

"She'd opened several bank accounts and acted kind of weird about it. Said it was a favor for Metsker. That's all Brock knew."

"Why did Brock take her to the abandoned house?"

"Said it was her idea. When they were there, she seemed to be looking for something, like she knew the place already. He doesn't think she found anything. After that, she ended their relationship with no real explanation."

I asked more questions, but Koda had nothing else to offer. As for Iron Braids, Natra was right. Although he showed respectful hospitality, he watched me the whole time, as if evaluating whether I was worth his time. When we ended the meeting with a promise to brainstorm ideas, Iron Braids said one thing. "Look at the pointer, not where he points."

Natra gestured for us to leave. We got on the road.

Ayden met us for brunch the next day at a diner near the crime scene. Always in motion, his inner engine runs on coffee and urgency. Under the table, I felt vibrations from his restless legs.

"They were right," he said. "I went over last night and parked near the property. I saw the lights."

I looked at him sideways. "You saw ghost lights?"

"I saw *lights*. More like flashlights."

"Maybe just kids," Natra said.

"We should stake it out."

"We're *not* investigating," I reminded him.

"When it was light, I went over and looked around—"

"Ayden!"

He held up a hand. "I didn't cross any police tape. But I saw things. Someone's been camping out. Can't say when."

"See any cars?" Natra asked.

"Yeah, last night. A van, dark, but I couldn't tell the color or see the license plate. It wasn't there in the morning." He pulled out his phone. "Also, I found this." He showed us a photo. "Don't know what it is. It was visible but stuck in some dirt, easy for cops to miss. Didn't pick it up."

I leaned in. The image showed a square button or lapel pin. Against a black background, I made out a red logo that featured the outline of an open box, with the lines that formed the two sides terminating in claw-like hands. Inside, a circle enclosed a stylized A and G.

"No idea what that is." I looked at Natra. "You?"

She told Ayden to send it to her phone. "I'll do some research."

I turned to Ayden. "What about the other incident here. Did your associate know anything?"

Ayden chewed on a French fry before he said, "The missing girl is Faith Ridley. Her fiancé claims she was on her way home from work but didn't make it. Police told him she withdrew $10,000 from their joint account and disappeared. They wrote it off as a female scammer."

I nodded. "Money, again. Koda told us Celina might have had some kind of financial hassle from Metsker, and he's a money manager. I see a pattern." I watched out the window, pondering the potential connection.

"Metsker's part of some church around here," Natra offered. "Maybe one of us should go check him out."

A black van drove by. I squinted. I thought I'd seen a logo on the side that resembled the one in Ayden's photo, but it moved too fast to see it clearly. I looked at Ayden. "Did you see anyone following you?"

He raised an eyebrow. "I'm careful, boss."

"Okay," I said. "We'll stay another night."

By the time I'd booked hotel rooms, Natra had an idea about the red logo. "Part of it looks like the symbol for Ka, the Egyptian concept of a spirit double that contains a person's qualities. The symbol is two upraised arms, like a touchdown in football."

I checked it again. "The outer part does resemble that."

Natra continued. "And there's a potter metaphor: the gods make the *ka* from clay when they form the person. It becomes the source of their prosperity. Remember, Metsker calls himself a potter. And the *ka* survives after the host dies, moving on to other forms."

I snorted. "Reincarnation meets skin walkers. What about the A and G?"

She shrugged. "Couldn't find anything. But I asked Joe to look into public records on the two women."

Joe's our digital guy, a cybersecurity expert. In exchange for moonlighting in my digital lab, he does some work for me.

"Did he find anything?" I asked.

"A $4,000 check went into Celina's account the day she went missing, and $6,000 the day after."

"*After?* So, she was still alive."

"Or someone stole her identity."

"Hmmm. I wonder if the cops here spotted that connection. One missing woman takes out $10,000, the other deposits the same amount?"

My text alert chimed. "It's Ayden." *Got news. B rite over.*

I opened the door, and Ayden rushed in. "This Metsker guy has some kind of cult here. Listen to this." He raised his chin. "It's called Act of God."

Natra and I waited for the rest. Ayden's eyes widened as if it was obvious. Then Natra said, "Ah. The A and G."

I nodded. "So, someone associated with his group was on the haunted property. I have the impression Metsker took these portal rumors seriously."

Ayden held up his phone. "I got his client list, too."

I've learned not to ask how he finds things. "Is Celina on it?"

"Nope. But Faith is, and so is a couple, Karla and Roger Ellis, who went missing just before Faith did, but in Virginia. They just vanished from their house."

I crossed my arms. "Let's find out where this Act of God congregates."

"They don't," Ayden said, "or, at least, not in a building with a physical address. I checked. No website, either. Seems like a secret club. I wonder how they get members."

"Wait!" Natra said. "I think I know someone who knew about this cult. He lived here for a while. I'll try to reach him."

"You do that," I said, "and I'll visit Metsker. He's a financial advisor. I'll make an appointment."

Ayden shook his head. "He seems dangerous. If he senses you're posing, he could hurt you."

"Hey, Ayden, trust me. François Vidocq, the master of role-playing and disguises, is one of my forensic mentors. Grace Humiston as well. People called her Mrs. Sherlock Holmes, and she fooled a lot of people to get what she needed. Besides, you'll be there as back-up."

Ayden crossed his arms over his chest. But he knew I'd do whatever I decided. I was the boss, after all.

When I called the number listed for Metsker's practice, a young woman answered. I said I had a considerable sum of money to invest and asked for an appointment. I needed to leave town and wanted to get this taken care of ASAP.

"Mr. M-Metsker will be b-back around 3 p.m., so—"

"Perfect," I said. "I'm Anita King. What's the address?"

Once I had it, I hung up and told Ayden, "Let's go."

He cocked his head. "It's only 2:15."

"I have a new plan."

Metsker worked out of a two-story blue house hidden behind a tall wooden fence. The grass needed mowing, and I smelled evidence of dogs, but the house looked maintained. A sidewalk led to a side door. I rang the bell. A young woman opened it. The pink frames for her fashion glasses clashed with her dyed red hair. She introduced herself as Eve. This was the girlfriend who'd avoided Brock. Timid. Hesitant. A pushover. Just what I needed. I told her who I was.

"You're early!" she said. "He's not here."

"Yes, sorry," I said, "I must leave town earlier than I expected. Perhaps you can give me the forms and some literature about his services."

"Of course, of c-course. Come in." As I entered, I smelled the strong musk of her Patchouli—the most obnoxious perfume ever produced. Putting my hand to my nose, I closed the door.

As she talked, Eve pulled at her navy T-shirt, emblazoned with "Ready for Grace" across the front. "S-s-sorry. Please h-have a seat. One of our Rotties is s-sick. Just n-need to attend to him. Be right back."

Better than I'd hoped: I could look around unsupervised. I'd posted Ayden outside to alert me by text if he saw the guy pull up. Based on what I'd seen of Eve's insecurity, I figured she'd be a font of information. "Venting," as psychologists refer to shirt-pulling, can signal discomfort with lying or with one's body. In pudgy young women like Eve, more likely the latter. She also used lame chatter as a protective barrier. I just had to figure out which buttons to push.

The small office was furnished in the clean lines of Swedish style. The desk, chairs, and couch were expensive. On one wall, I noticed a framed slogan: "We are the potters; they are the pots. We pot for God."

So, there it was. His narcissism on full display in a pithy catchphrase. But this didn't make him a killer. Aware that a camera might be planted in here, I looked around as any potential client might. I hoped to see some brochures that would open the door to proselytizing when clients arrived for financial advice.

Eve's return interrupted me. "I called Mr. Metsker. He's on his way. He wants to meet you."

Whoops! Not in my plan. "Oh, that would be great," I lied. Desperate to learn something from Eve before he arrived, I noticed her necklace. I pointed. "What does that symbol mean?" It was the same one on the item Ayden had found.

Eve blushed and smiled. "Oh, that's f-for me. I'm engaged to Glen. Th-that's Jordan's…Mr. Metsker's b-brother."

"How wonderful. Is it a love symbol, then?"

"Well, i-it's not exactly. I mean, it's f-for our group. It means I'm a m-m-member. We receive b-blessings. We…." She glanced at the potter slogan and back at me. "I met him, Glen, at a m-murder mystery d-dinner. Isn't that amazing? And now I do important th-things, like… They t-trust me."

"So, you run this office?" I asked.

"Not that, but I m-make deposits. And feed the d-dogs."

"That sounds important. So, if I wrote a check, you'd take it to the bank?"

Eve shook her head and pulled at her shirt. "No, no. Not for clients. Besides, we c-can't use those accounts now."

My phone vibrated in my pocket. Ayden's warning. Metsker had arrived. I stepped toward Eve and looked more closely at her necklace. "You know, I've seen that design before. Maybe in a store?"

Even shook her head. "You c-couldn't have. Cel…we make them for us. Only m-members have them."

"I see. Well, thank you for your time. I'll come back when it's more convenient."

"Wait!" She looked at her phone. "He's coming."

"Then I'll greet him on the way out."

I left before she could stop me. I thought about slipping around the back but remembered the Rottweilers. As I rounded a corner, I ran into a tall man who looked exactly like what many white Christians think Christ had looked like but without the robe. Metsker's pale skin contrasted with his trimmed brown beard and shoulder-length hair. When he saw me, he smiled broadly. I knew at once why he succeeded; he made people feel singled out. This guy had charisma.

"You must be Ms. King," he said, his hand out.

"Yes, I am," I said, "but I'm afraid I can't stay. I'll make an appointment when I'm back in town. You come highly recommended."

His eyes narrowed. "By whom?"

I thought fast, then took a risky shot. "The Ellises. They said they'd invested with you. I haven't spoken to them in a while, but I remembered your name."

The mention of the missing couple elicited a micro-expression that only a trained observer would notice; it signaled fear before it disappeared. "Oh, yes," he said. "They're doing quite well. Satisfied customers."

I made a move to get past him. "Well, I'll be in touch."

I felt certain he didn't believe me. I couldn't let him probe. I knew nothing about the Ellises. But I did know he'd made a mistake not acknowledging their status. Relatives would have notified banks and money managers. Metsker's pretense confirmed my suspicions. I rushed out to Ayden's truck and jumped in. He took off at once.

"Geez, Annie! I thought he had you."

I looked back. I saw him at the gate, watching.

"It was close, I admit it." I took a deep breath.

"Get anything?" Ayden asked.

"Just ambiguous comments. Eve nearly mentioned Celina, I think, but caught herself. She did admit she makes deposits. And I'm afraid I might've blown our cover. I mentioned the Ellises."

Ayden looked at me in shock. He pumped the gas.

"I wanted to see his reaction. He's afraid."

"He should be."

I narrowed my eyes. "Do you know something?"

"I went around back and found a black van, unlocked. Inside were saws, some black duffel bags, and more dog vomit. And this." He handed over his phone. I expanded the photo. It was a driver's license. It belonged to Faith Ridley.

"My god!" I said. "This is evidence!"

"Yup. Sent the photos to my associate. She knows some cops."

"But you got them illegally. By trespassing."

"I told her about the pin they missed back at the portal house. If they get that, they might get a fingerprint."

"Actually, the jewelry is unique. Made by this cult, probably Celina. But it proves only that they were at the house at some point. Maybe that's what Celina was looking for. She knew she'd dropped it. I'll have Brock's defense attorney send his investigator. But that was risky, Ayden."

"If you say so."

"I think it's time we get out of here."

When we rejoined Natra, she added one more intriguing piece from her friend, Ahuli.

"Metsker claimed to be a prophet," Natra said. "He did refer to himself as a potter and proposed ten principles of magic for the chosen ones. He had a plan to adopt orphans from underdeveloped countries and train them as assassins to kill politicians and religious leaders. To raise the money for it, he blackmailed wealthy clients."

"Like the Ellises," I said, "and maybe Faith Ridley."

"Ahuli said Metsker's obsessed with clever killers like Ted Bundy and H. H. Holmes. He thinks they get their juice from their victims' souls."

"Aligns with the *ka* theme," I observed.

"He was especially intrigued with Michael Gargiulo."

"Why?"

"Gargiulo looked for attractive women in relationships so he could cover his tracks by throwing suspicion on the men."

I thought about what Iron Braids had said: Look at the pointer, not where he points. "That's like Celina with Brock. And Faith Ridley. So, the men in their lives were fall guys. But we still don't have solid evidence."

"I say we stake out that ghost place tonight," Ayden said. "They were probably there last night, searching for that pin. If they're suspicious of you, they might feel the heat and go back."

I sat back. "I think you're right. If Eve tells Metsker about my interest in the pin, he might act."

So, that evening, we went to the haunted property to watch for the "ghost lights." We found cover in some bushes. Around midnight, a dark van drove up to the abandoned house where a woman had once cut up and cooked her mate and hanged herself. A dim light flickered inside. Another flashlight beam caught the van's side door, open, and a dark figure shoving bags from inside.

"Metsker," I observed. "He's that tall."

Ayden stood. "I'm going closer."

But Natra held up a hand. "Wait! Watch."

A flashlight beam circled the house and came back around from the other side. I realized they aimed to burn it. "They're pouring fuel!"

No sooner had I said it than the first flames appeared. I called 9-1-1. I was pretty sure I knew what the bags held. The dog vomit gave it away. We couldn't let them burn. When the sirens sounded, the van fled. We stayed to explain that we'd been driving by when we saw the fire. By morning, we learned from news reports that six black duffel bags were found in the house. Most were saved. They contained the frozen body parts of three missing people. The Metsker brothers and Eve were arrested, the van confiscated. Brock was freed, and Iron Braids sent me a gift. We soon learned Celina's fate.

Eve quickly turned state's evidence against the brothers, the "pot" becoming the "potter." I got a copy of her confession. She told police the Metskers had required her to prove her loyalty by witnessing the murders, and she'd thought it was okay because Jordan was a prophet. He'd killed for God.

"He m-made me sit with the deadies in the van," she said. "I didn't like that."

The plan for Act of God had been to amass a million dollars to entice Jesus Christ to return to Earth and transport the chosen ones to Heaven. Eve had witnessed the Ellis double homicide after Jordan kidnapped them and brought them to his house. He'd forced them to write three checks that totaled $100,000. He and Glen had then bludgeoned them and cut them up. They'd purchased the Rottweilers to get rid of the body parts, but one dog had refused to eat human flesh, and the other had gotten sick on it, so they'd stored the remains in a freezer. They'd repeated this with Faith Ridley, blackmailing her and burning her remains.

"At one p-point," Eve revealed, "I had to pick up a h-head so Glen could knock out the teeth. He said it was an act of God. I believed him."

Jordan had wooed Celina to get her to open bank accounts to deposit the checks, which were written to her. She'd suspected something and left, but he'd reeled her back in and bludgeoned her to death with a hammer. They'd taken her dismembered remains to the abandoned farm, which Jordan believed held enhanced spiritual energy. That's where one of them dropped the pin Ayden found. They were interrupted, so they'd kept her remains frozen until they could try it again.

Awaiting trial, the brothers claimed schizophrenia ran in their family. Their lawyer heard about my clinical evaluation of Arthur, the eyeball eater who'd answered God's command to kill his wife and daughters. She'd invited me to join her team. I declined. The Metskers had answered no deific decree in some psychotic state. Their missing parts were not their minds but their souls.

Acknowledgments

I'm grateful to my first readers, Susan Lysek and Sally Keglovits, as well as my OBX hosts Mark and Lisa Safarik, who offered helpful ideas and a place to immerse. Nothing replaces being on site for inspiration and authenticity. Special thanks to my enthusiastic LBB editor, Verena Main Rose, and my long-time agent and friend, John Silbersack.

About the Author

With her Nut Cracker Investigations series, Katherine Ramsland injects her expertise in forensic psychology into her fiction. She consults for coroners, trains homicide investigators, and has appeared as an expert on more than 250 crime documentaries. She was an executive producer on *Murder House Flip,* A&E's *Confession of a Serial Killer: BTK,* and ID's *The Serial Killer's Apprentice.* The author of more than 2,000 articles and 74 books, including *I Scream Man* and *How to Catch a Killer,* she also has a Substack and pens a blog for *Psychology Today.*

AUTHOR WEBSITE: http://www.katherineramsland.net

SOCIAL MEDIA HANDLES:
    Facebook: https://www.facebook.com/katherine.ramsland
    Blue Sky: https://bsky.app/profile/katherineramsland.bsky.social
    Blog: **http://www.psychologytoday.com/blog/shadow-boxing**
    Instagram: https://www.instagram.com/katherineramsland/
    Substack: https://katherineramsland.substack.com/publish/home

Also by Katherine Ramsland

Dead-Handed, Level Best Books

In the Damage Path, Level Best Books

I Scream Man, Level Best Books

The Serial Killer's Apprentice, Crime Ink/Penzler

How to Catch a Killer, Sterling

Track the Ripper, Riverdale Avenue Books

The Ripper Letter, Riverdale Avenue Books

Heartless: Iowa's Bloody Murders, Notorious USA

Murder Alley: Nebraska Fiends and Felons, Notorious USA

Cold-blooded: Kansas Murders, Notorious USA

Confession of a Serial Killer: The Untold Story of Dennis Rader, the BTK Killer, University Press of New England

Haunted Crime Scenes, with Mark Nesbitt, Second Chance Books

Blood and Ghosts: Paranormal Forensic Investigators, with Mark Nesbitt, Second Chance Books

The Mind of a Murderer: Privileged Access to the Demons that Drive Extreme Violence, Praeger

The Forensic Psychology of Criminal Minds, Berkley

The Criminal Mind: A Writer's Guide to Forensic Psychology, Writer's Digest